BY SAMUEL HAWLEY

NONFICTION

I Just Ran:
Percy Williams, World's Fastest Human

Speed Duel:
The Inside Story of the Land Speed Record in the Sixties

The Imjin War:
Japan's Sixteenth-Century Invasion of Korea and
Attempt to Conquer China

America's Man in Korea:
The Private Letters of George C. Foulk, 1884-1887

Inside the Hermit Kingdom:
The 1884 Korea Travel Diary of George Clayton Foulk

FICTION

Bad Elephant Far Stream

BAD ELEPHANT
FAR STREAM

❧ ❧

SAMUEL HAWLEY

CONQUISTADOR

BAD ELEPHANT FAR STREAM
Published by Conquistador Press, 2013

Library and Archives Canada Cataloguing in Publication

Hawley, Samuel Jay, 1960-, author
    Bad elephant Far Stream / Samuel Hawley.

ISBN 978-0-9920786-0-7 (pbk.)

    1. Topsy (Elephant)--Fiction. I. Title.

PS8615.A8217B33 2013   C813'.6   C2013-905661-0

www.conquistadorpress.com
info@conquistadorpress.com

Visit the author's website:
www.samuelhawley.com

This novel was inspired by the life of a real elephant that performed for many years in the Adam Forepaugh Circus and the Forepaugh-Sells Circus. She was known variously as Topsy, Forepaugh Topsy, Crooked-Tail Topsy, and Tops.

PROLOGUE

LUNA PARK ON CONEY ISLAND was to be the premier amusement park in New York. Visitors would enter along a promenade called the Court of Honor, leading to a Venetian canal with gondolas. There would be rides: the Helter Skelter, A Trip to the Moon, the Shoot the Chutes plunging passengers down into a great splash of water. There would be fairy castles and incubators with premature babies and a building in the shape of a battleship and other fantastic structures. There would be manicured grounds for strolling, a Japanese garden, a monkey theater, a Dutch windmill, model villages from around the world, elephant rides and a two-ring circus with acrobats and performing animals and riders and clowns. And best of all, there would be illumination: 120,000 electric lights to dazzle visitors like nothing before.

On Sunday, January 4, 1903 these many wonders were still under construction; Luna Park's official opening was not scheduled until May. A crowd of people had nevertheless walked across the bridge from Brooklyn or taken the train from points beyond to be on hand that afternoon, for the New York papers had promised amusement. A female Asian elephant named Topsy, recently acquired by Luna Park, was to be killed.

The initial plan was to hang Topsy. A stout scaffold had been built for the purpose out over the lagoon at the foot of the Shoot the Chutes ride. Facilities for electrocution were then added in the final forty-eight hours, the Edison Light Company providing the power from its Coney Island generating station and sending out a man to string up the wires. Luna Park's owners welcomed the alteration, for it turned the execution of their elephant into a spectacle of the first order, something to which they could sell a projected two thousand tickets. Officials from the Society for the Prevention of Cruelty to Animals quashed this idea at the last minute. No ticket sales, they said; it would make the euthanizing unseemly.

There was nevertheless a sizable crowd on hand at the appointed hour that Sunday. Invited officials, city councilmen, SPCA representatives and other dignitaries were seated in the first row. Behind them on bleachers and standing were several hundred others who had finagled their way through the gate or climbed over the fence. Others looked on from the roofs of neighboring buildings. A camera operator had his Kinetograph camera set up, ready to start filming. It wasn't every day that one had the opportunity to witness 6,600 volts of electricity coursing through four and a half tons of living animal flesh. That was something viewers would pay a nickel to see.

The elephant made her appearance at one o'clock in the afternoon, a gaunt older man at her side carrying a hooked goad called a bull hook. A leather martingale harness encompassed the creature's chest, forehead and trunk. It was connected by a chain to her forelegs to restrict her head movements so she couldn't lash out. She shuffled along slowly, not appearing to notice the crowd. She seemed to be drowsy, oblivious, in a world of her own.

"It doesn't look dangerous," observed a young boy who had come out to Luna Park with his father. "It looks old."

"Well, looks can be deceiving," replied the father. He had slipped fifty cents to the man at the gate to get in. "Because that's a man killer. It's been in the papers."

"But it doesn't look dangerous. What are they giving it?"

"Looks like carrots."

"Those carrots are poisoned," said a man seated beside them, hunkered in a worn overcoat, chewing on a toothpick. "They're going to get her three ways."

"Why are they going to do that?" the boy asked.

"They want to make sure they kill it, I guess," said his father.

"That's exactly right, son," said Toothpick. "See those wires over there? First they fill her with poison, then the electricity, then they draw that rope tight around her neck. It's a triple deal."

"But it doesn't look dangerous. It just looks old."

"Listen," continued Toothpick, leaning over. "An elephant's the cunningest creature you'll ever meet in your life. Smart and cunning. It'll be nice to you and quiet for years. It'll fool you into thinking it likes you. Then one day it'll go and try to kill you. The only thing that holds 'em back is fear. And when that goes . . . well, you don't want to see what they can do to a man."

"You worked around elephants, have you?" asked the father.

"I worked around a circus, yeah. Anyway, you can't never trust an elephant, son. Never. And when they go bad like that one"—he jerked a horny thumb at Topsy—"why, there's nothing you can do but chain 'em up or kill 'em. They just aren't safe to have around anymore."

"Why did that one go bad?" asked the boy.

"Don't bother the man, Eddy."

"Oh, that's all right, friend. I don't mind. Like I said, son, it's in an elephant's nature. There's a wickedness in them."

"Is that one wicked?" asked the boy.

"Well, she's killed five men. I'd call that wicked. Like your dad said, looks can . . . Ah, here we go, here we go."

The gaunt man with the bull hook had prompted Topsy to raise her foreleg for the Edison electrician to attach a dinner plate-sized copper disk. Another was placed on her hind foot.

She seemed to mind the imposition and kicked one off, then the other. The men tried again.

"What's that they're putting on its feet?" asked the boy.

"It's for the electricity," said his father.

A murmur ran through the crowd of exchanged information. Toothpick leaned over with, "It's called an e-lec-trode."

"I wish they didn't have to kill it," said the boy, anxious.

"Pipe down now," said his father. "Let's just watch the show."

CHAPTER 1

SHE WAS BORN IN THE YEAR Grandmother led them to the place beyond the far stream. She spent the dawn of her life on her side, quivering, bewildered and staring, a delicate grey creature with touches of pink in the soft tender places. Then she was nudged to her feet. After a struggle with her new-found legs and the thing in front of her face that would in time become useful, she located the breasts between her mother's forelegs and seized a nipple and started to drink. The thick milk slowed her heartbeat and sent contentment washing over her little two hundred pound body. It was then that she became aware of the huge shifting shapes all around her and the comforting odors and the sounds of shrill trumpeting and deep rumbles and humorous chirping. It was her family expressing joy at her arrival. She was their baby Far Stream. She made them eleven.

Far Stream's place at first was beneath or beside her mother, of whom she was in proportion a perfect miniature copy. Mother's looming form was her sky, the caressing trunk reaching down her chief source of comfort. Very soon, however, she began to notice interesting things occurring around her, things that needed exploring. She started venturing out.

She was four months old when she discovered that she did not like her brother, Fear Wind, four years her elder. His play was too rough. It frightened her when he acted wild and lunged about and lashed from side to side with his trunk. When he became like that she stayed close to her mother or to her aunts Seven Were Taken and Man's World and Into the Mountains, or to her favorite, her elder sister Red Moon. Red Moon was the oldest female of the family's third generation and the first to become a mother herself, giving birth the year before to baby Darkness at Day. Far Stream liked to play with Darkness at Day. His fun was gentle.

She learned to use her trunk when she was seven months old. Until then it had been little more than a nuisance, something that got in the way when she wasn't sucking on the end. As her dexterity improved she began using it to turn things over and pick things up, leaves and rocks and sticks, clods of dirt, a bone, a withdrawn turtle. Then she started throwing. That continued until one of her missiles hit Darkness at Day in the eye and he started bawling. After examining the eye to ensure that there was no damage, Red Moon gave Far Stream a swat on the rump. So did her mother and each of her aunts. After that she confined herself to throwing dirt on her back to keep down the insects.

She was in her second year when Sinkhole appeared and took up residence at the edge of the family. He was ancient and wasting, eating on his last used-up molars, uncommunicative but wanting company as he neared the end. Grandmother let him stay.

Sinkhole made them twelve, but only for a short while. After the rains ended it was time for Into the Mountains' firstborn to go off on his own. He was grown now and knew he had to leave, but he still needed the encouragement of head butts from his aunts, pushing him on his way. He stayed nearby for several days, making plaintive sounds that filled Far Stream with sadness. Then he wandered off. They would not see him again.

The gloom cast by the necessary departure still hung over them when Lightning, Man's World's son, departed. He was blind and unable to fend for himself and therefore had stayed with the family despite it being long past his time. When Far Stream heard his groans in the night she knew it meant pain. Lightning lay on his side at dawn, taking shallow gasps, his sightless eyes filmy and staring. The others gave him water and tried to feed him grass from the river. It did no good. At noon he gave a final groan and went rigid. Then he was still. They stayed by him for three days, touching him, caressing him, trying to raise him, ignoring the flies that settled in clouds. Finally Grandmother led them away.

She led them upriver to a meadow of flowers where the air was fragrant. And as night follows day they returned to happiness and contentment, with Seven Were Taken at last giving birth. The new addition was Flowers for Lightning, fat and healthy and with a thick covering of brown hair on his head. He made the family eleven again. They welcomed the stunned little creature loudly and joyously. This time Far Stream joined in.

It was at the fragrant place that Far Stream discovered the new way of hearing. Grandmother was the first to come into her head. Far Stream had wandered some distance from the others, following her sister Red Moon along a patch of sweet grass, lost in a reverie, when something told her: *Come back.* She turned and there was Grandmother looking straight at her, surprisingly far off. Soon Far Stream was hearing the others. Then she found that she could answer.

Look at me.
What is this?
What is that?
Where are you?

She began to babble—learning, imitating, absorbing. Her mother and Red Moon and her aunts patiently bore it. Grandmother was more apt to grow weary if the plaguing continued too long. She would heave a loud sigh to signal that she was growing impatient. And if that didn't bring peace and quiet, she would say, sometimes quite sharply, *Be quiet.*

With the growing of her understanding, Far Stream began to share more deeply in the inner world of her family. She learned that they liked to tease and to joke and that her mother and her aunts in particular often squabbled. *You are weightless* was one of their favorite insults when caused irritation. *You are weightless* or *You are floating away* followed by an annoyed toss of the head. When her brother Fear Wind, rapidly growing, would start shoving and displaying, Red Moon would taunt him with *Your penis has gotten too big.* When they were at the bathing place, lolling in the water and spouting, they enjoyed pushing each other under. *Look, there is something down there,* the perpetrator would say. Or: *There was a snake on your back.* Or: *You needed a drink.*

And then came the stories. They were told in the darkness, under the moon and stars slowly revolving in the heavens, Sinkhole close by but never part of the group. Grandmother, as matriarch, took the lead in the telling, the sharing, the learning. This was their collective history being passed down.

Far Stream sensed the importance of these moments, the family standing together in the blue moonlight. Grandmother would always begin with, *I can only sing this story to those who can understand it.* Far Stream knew this meant Darkness at Day, Flowers for Lightning and herself, the family's newest members. She struggled just the same to grasp the complex sounds and hazy images that came next, a fast-flowing river of strange sensations. But she could not. She was still too young. She would become hopelessly lost in the torrent and eventually grow sleepy and lie down and drift off to sleep.

It was the next season, when Far Stream was in her third year and no longer a baby, that the line of fire appeared through the forest and Grandmother said, *Follow me.*

CHAPTER 2

THE FIRE WAS HELD BY MEN approaching from the south. The family roused at Grandmother's warning and hurried after her down the path by the river, Far Stream staying between her mother and Red Moon, wide awake now, sharing the collective alarm. Then a second line of fire appeared to the east, and a third ahead to the north.

West was the only open direction. When they reached the waterfall Grandmother led them off the path and into the dense forest, branches scraping against their skin, the undergrowth crunching loud underfoot. The crescent moon was just disappearing when they emerged onto the path leading to the Shining Sun Cliffs.

Flowers for Lightning was struggling. He was too young for such heavy exertion. Far Stream could hear him whining and Grandmother and the aunts urging, *Hurry, Hurry.* As they continued, Seven Were Taken and her baby fell to the back, trailed only by arthritic old Sinkhole, now badly limping.

Then, like the shock from a bolt of lightning, a cacophony of man-noise struck them from either side and closed in behind them. Clanging cymbals. Howling trumpets. Clapping. Shouting.

"Dah! Dah! Dah!"

Grandmother broke into a run, the family behind her, trumpeting now, screaming in panic. They did not notice that the foliage on either side had become impenetrable and was closing in. All they saw was the path ahead. They followed. They followed into the darkness until they passed through the opening and crossed the space beyond and came to a barrier that had not been there when they had come this way before.

It was a barricade of timbers lashed together with vines. A man-made structure. Grandmother turned left and shuffled urgently along it, searching for an opening. Finding none, she threw herself against the wall. She would smash a way through. The structure quivered but held.

"Dah! Dah! Dah!"

There were men on the timbers, shouting and waving fire that formed a ring all around them. Grandmother continued on along the barricade, the family following in confusion. She stopped again where there was a gap in the fires and placed her forehead against the wood and started pushing, straining, digging her feet into the ground. Men rushed toward her with fire, something flashed through the timbers, a sharp stick piercing her cheek. She roared and stepped back.

"Dah! Dah! Dah!"

They continued on, turning with the fence lined with fire until they were back where they had started, back at the gap they had entered. It was now barred with a double row of rough-hewn logs. Grandmother lowered her head again and tried them, closing her eyes tight against the wounding sticks and the fire waved in her face. The timbers held. Man's World rushed against them next. They held. Mother tried, a ferocious onslaught. They held.

They were in an enclosure. The family was trapped.

They rushed from one side of their prison to the other for more than an hour, the group becoming ragged as the weaker ones tired and slowed. Old Sinkhole was the first to give up and stop. When the rest were all thoroughly exhausted, they huddled together, Far Stream and Darkness at

Day and Flowers for Lightning protectively kept in the center. They were all too frightened to sleep.

The fires had gone out by the next morning—all but a few, around which the men squatted, talking and eating. Far Stream could clearly see now the palisade all around them, the barred gate where they had entered, the blocked path leading to the Shining Sun Cliffs. And for the first time she noticed that there were others like her beyond the enclosure, a family of adults standing in a straight line. Why did they stay there so close to the men, dozing and calmly eating grass and plantains? Why did they allow the men to touch them? Why did they let the men climb up on their backs?

The gate was opened two hours after sunrise. One of the tame elephants entered, a big male with long tusks. He carried two men on his back: one in front on his shoulders, the other just behind, carrying a looped vine. A second elephant followed with two other riders. They slowly meandered toward Far Stream and her family, stopping often to sample the grass or probe for a root as if they didn't see them. It was only when they were quite near that the lead elephant seemed to notice them and stepped forward in a purposeful way, his trunk extended in friendly greeting. Grandmother led the family a few wary paces to meet him and touched his trunk with hers. The second tame elephant, a female, advanced with her own greeting, crowding in.

There was movement beneath. Grandmother roared with fury and threw her head to one side.

A man, hidden beneath the tusked male, had tried to slip a noose around her leg. Her violent reaction shook it off before he could secure it and sent him sprawling. Grandmother lowered her head to finish him but the two tame elephants together stepped in her way. The injured man retreated to the palisade, limping and clutching his chest, there was a flurry of shouting and another man came forward. This one climbed up onto one of the tame elephants, who had retreated a few paces. Far Stream and her family returned to their huddle.

When the tame elephants advanced for the second time they pushed their way into the midst of the family, the male using his tusks to gently open a space. They worked their way in until they were on either side of Grandmother. Their calm boldness seemed to confuse her. She did not try to move as they pressed up against her. She did not notice when one of the men dropped to the ground and prompted her to raise her hind leg with a soft touch and slipped on the noose.

She pulled away as soon as she felt it tighten and found she was tethered to the tame male tusker. He dug in and, with the second tame elephant pushing with her head, began moving Grandmother away from the family. Grandmother tried to resist, roaring and thrashing, but together the two elephants were too strong. They forced her to a stout tree at the side of the enclosure and the tether confining her leg was quickly wound round. She tried to pull free but the buffalo hide was strong and only dug into her flesh. Then there were men around her. Her second hind leg was noosed with buffalo hide and bound to the other, hobbling her, impeding her struggles. Then they had one of her forelegs, noosed by a small darting man and, with the help of the tame elephants, pulled tight and bound to a second tree, spreading her out.

Grandmother continued to fight but it was now hopeless. She pulled back and strained with her whole body until the buffalo hide dug deep, deep into her foreleg. She pressed her head into the ground and arched her back and heaved forward at the bonds on her feet. She tried to raise the cords to her mouth to grind through them with her molars. Every time she did so one of the tame elephants stepped on the cord and pressed it down to the ground.

Grandmother's plight so upset Far Stream and the rest of the family that they began racing about the enclosure in straggling disorder. They roared and screamed every time

12

they passed her, sometimes pausing and thrashing but not approaching too close. Their courage had entirely left them. Eventually they sought comfort by again huddling together.

As soon as they did so the tame elephants with their riders repeated their casual advance. This time they worked their way into the group to flank Red Moon. One of her hind legs was noosed in an identical fashion and she was dragged, tugging and squealing, to a tree near Grandmother. Her young son Darkness at Day followed at first, bawling, then turned and retreated to the huddle to find comfort with his aunts and his cousins. Within a few minutes Red Moon was hobbled and secured by all four legs and left to wrench and writhe herself to exhaustion.

Far Stream's mother was next selected. Her leg was noosed and she was in turn dragged to a tree on the other side of Grandmother. She went resisting but silent. Far Stream stayed at her side the whole way, leaving the group's safety and her brother Fear Wind. She was quiet at first, only whimpering softly. Then she started to lash out when the men closed in with their cords and their hobbles, amusing them with her childish attempts to protect her mother. When she persisted, they shouted at her and thrust sticks in her face. Still she continued, determined to free her mother. She kept throwing her little head about and lunging until she felt something pull against her hind leg. In a moment she was dragged away and tethered to a tree where she would not get in the way. The men did not bother to hobble her. She was too small to break free from the single hide cord.

It was now Far Stream's turn to begin her futile struggle, tugging against the cord, feeling it bite into her leg as the men returned to her mother. They were trying to slip a noose onto Mother's other hind leg, a tricky business for she was giving them trouble, standing rigid and refusing to raise a foot for the restraint.

A piercing roar. The men stopped and looked across the

enclosure. Then they were running forward, shouting, waving their arms.

It was old Sinkhole. He was no longer standing off to the side, placidly watching. With a terrible scream he came running at the two tame elephants securing Mother and threw his full weight against the tusker, toppling him over and freeing the cord that was wound once round the tree. He then wheeled about and charged headlong at the timber barricade that blocked the path leading onward. Men outside the enclosure sprinted toward the spot to head him off with spears but it was too late. With a mighty crack Sinkhole's lowered head smashed into the palisade with such force that the deeply buried logs were splintered and uprooted and his own skull was broken. His momentum carried him on through the breach he had made, on for several more faltering steps until he collapsed.

For a moment elephants and men alike stared in amazement at the wreckage up the now-open path. Bird song, monkey calls, the buzzing of insects—all forest noise ceased. Then the moment passed. The men were going to prevent the family from escaping.

Man's World was the first to see the opportunity and run for the opening. Into the Mountains set off after her, followed by Seven Were Taken and little Flowers for Lightning, his hairy head bobbing as he worked hard to keep up, and then the rest of the family, Darkness at Day swept along in the flight, carried away from his captured mother Red Moon. They stampeded through the opening and past Sinkhole's body and disappeared through the forest to the safety of the Shining Sun Cliffs.

Fear Wind was the only one to hang back, frantically running in circles, toward the opening in the barricade and then back to his mother and his sisters Far Stream and Red Moon and his Grandmother tied to their trees. He could not bring himself to leave them. They cried out to him and pulled at their restraints and redoubled their efforts.

14

Then Mother was free. With the big tusker down and injured, the strain on the cord had been released enough for her to get it between her teeth and grind through. She raced across the enclosure and led Fear Wind through the breach after the others, knocking aside the tame elephant that the men had prodded into the gap. So great was her agitation that she continued on down the path with Fear Wind a considerable distance before recovering her senses enough to remember those left behind.

When the realization hit, she cautiously doubled back through the trees. She did not re-enter the enclosure. She remained on the far side of the opening, close enough to see Grandmother and Far Stream and Red Moon but beyond the reach of the men with their spears and their nooses. She called to them, *Come with us. Come with us.*

Grandmother and Red Moon struggled until blood flowed down their legs from the cords that restrained them, the air filled with the smell of iron and crushed foliage. Far Stream tugged as well, less strongly, then stopped and bitterly wept. She wanted to go with them, to go with her family. But she couldn't.

Mother and Fear Wind stayed nearby until sundown. By then Grandmother had exhausted herself and collapsed onto her side, her body so contorted that her forelegs and hind legs pointed in opposite directions. Only the end of her trunk continued to move, beating slowly on the ground in despair. Red Moon was in a similar condition, collapsed, exhausted, contorted, defeated. Far Stream stood behind them at the end of her tether, softly moaning, unable to reach them, unable to follow the others. *Come with us*, her mother's voice continued to plead in her head. *Come with us ... Come with us ... Come with us.*

She heard it on into the night. Then there was silence.

≪∘≫

The breach smashed open by Sinkhole had been repaired. A second family of elephants was driven inside the enclosure

15

and methodically separated and tied down and left to struggle to exhaustion. None escaped. A third family followed, a small one. When the men were finished there were twenty-five elephants scattered throughout the enclosure, each of them hobbled and tied between trees.

Far Stream continued to intermittently struggle. She would cry and tug at her tether for a few minutes, then settle down to poke about in the grass and eat the plantains the men set before her, then she would recall her confinement and start crying and struggling again. Red Moon, after reviving from her exertions, did not protest. She heaved herself upright and stood beneath her tree in morose silence, mourning the loss of her baby, of her family, brushing aside all offers of food. She threw dirt onto her back and sprayed herself with water drawn from her stomach. As she settled further she occasionally reached out with her trunk to spray Far Stream as well.

Grandmother took longer to recover. Her resistance had been so extreme, so intense, so tearing, that she was still on her side at dawn of the second day. Finally, toward noon, she struggled to her feet. She stood unmoving until sunset, flapping her ears and spraying to cool her great body. Like Red Moon, she ignored the food set before her.

On the fourth day a tame elephant was tethered to a nearby tree and presented with a heap of grass, which it began eating. It did not communicate with them but kept up a reassuring hum of complaisance. Food was then offered again to Grandmother and Red Moon. This time, after only slight hesitation, they ate. This continued through the fifth day, eating and drinking and growing resignation.

And sleep. For the first time since the capture Far Stream slipped away from the present and dreamed deeply, dreams that caused her to twitch and whimper until she awoke with a start and forgot. Red Moon eventually lay down as well and drifted off for a troubled hour. Grandmother was content to lean against her tree and doze.

16

On the sixth day the tame elephant tethered nearby was moved directly beside Grandmother while a second elephant flanked her on the opposite side. Men rode on the backs of both. Grandmother shifted uneasily but did not try to resist as the two creatures leaned in against her. It was an easy matter for the men to then detach her restraining cords from the tree and affix them to the harnesses around the tame ones. When they were finished and the riders ordered the tame elephants forward, Grandmother offered little resistance and went. Red Moon, similarly pinioned, followed. Far Stream tagged along behind, loosely tethered. She reached out with her trunk as she went to take mangoes from one of the men walking alongside. The smell of wood smoke on his outstretched hand no longer alarmed her.

They were led out the gate of the enclosure and back down the path to the pool by the small falls. Far Stream yearned to enter the water. She was instead tied with Red Moon to a tree. As they looked on, a dozen men surrounded Grandmother, men in front pointing spears in her face, men behind stepping close to lay their hands on her haunches. "Ho, my mother," they murmured, their voices soft and soothing.

The unwelcome caresses brought Grandmother roaring to life. She lashed out with her trunk, the only part of her body she could move with the two elephants on either side pressing against her. She lashed out only to meet the sharp iron points of the spears. Another touch, again she lashed out, again she succeeded only in causing herself pain. It continued until her trunk was so sore that she was forced to curl it in toward her head to protect it. But even then the touching continued. The process was halted only when Grandmother ceased her lashing, then her uneasy shifting, and accepted. When the men were satisfied that she had submitted, they led her into the pool beneath the waterfall and allowed her to bathe with Far Stream. As the two luxuriated in the coolness, spouting and rolling, the men turned their attention to Red Moon.

By the end of the second week Far Stream and her older sister Red Moon had given themselves up to the men and did as much of their bidding as they understood. They were particularly compliant with the one named Muni who fed them and took them every day to the river. At first Far Stream did not like his orders, but gradually resentful resignation gave way to something like contentment. Muni provided her and Red Moon with grass and fruit in abundance and delicious morsels they had never tasted before. And down at the river he scrubbed them all over, a wonderful feeling that left their skin all aglow.

Grandmother had become similarly obedient and content by the end of the third week. She even allowed the man who fed her to attend to the wounds on her legs where the cords had dug in, a painful procedure. He extracted the bloody strips of buffalo hide, cleaned out the corruption and trimmed away the dead flesh and applied an ointment that made her groan with relief. By the seventh week her legs were healing and she was regaining lost weight and even allowing her keeper to climb up onto her shoulders.

Then she was gone.

She went quietly and Far Stream and Red Moon at first did not miss her. When the realization struck, first Red Moon and then Far Stream, they became agitated and started tugging at the double restraints that had been casually slipped over their hind legs that morning. Muni was immediately there to calm them. "Ho, my children," he said in the voice that they had come to find soothing. "Ho, my children. There is nothing to fear. She is working. She will come back."

They accepted his comfort and the sweet things he offered. And sure enough, several days later, Grandmother returned, snorting from a bath after learning to move logs in the forest. When she disappeared the next time, there was less fretting.

❧

It was three months after their capture when the journey began that took Far Side and Red Moon out of their native hills and away from their forest. They traveled along the path past the waterfall pool in a line with six others, five adults and one other young one, Muni close by their side. This time they did not stop for a leisurely bath but kept on all day, then a second. They kept on going, west and down away from all that was familiar, west and down until they were among fields of bright green and villages under tendrils of smoke. With Muni beside them, Far Stream and Red Moon plodded resignedly onward, taking comfort from each others' presence. As long as they had each other, they had family. They had something left.

The journey ended on the fifth day in a noisy, man-filled place that Muni called Colombo. The pathways here were as wide as a river and hard packed and lined with men's houses, the air filled with a cacophony of strange scents and jarring noises, worst of all the shriek of the huge dark beast that breathed out smoke as it huffed by on two shiny rails. They passed through a gate and stopped at a place beside a body of water, water so immense that the far bank was out of sight. There were more smells here: men's sweat, horses, pungent piles of sacks and boxes, an overlay of sulfur, salt and decay wafting in the breeze. Men hurried by carrying heavy loads, grunting their way up ramps onto lighters and barges moored alongside the quay. "Ho, my children," Muni soothed when Far Stream and Red Moon became fretful at so much that was different. "Ho, my children. There is nothing to fear."

They spent the night in a stable with horses, the other elephants that had accompanied them out of the hills audible in neighboring buildings. On the following morning they were led out together and formed up in a line with a number of others, an impressive array that attracted a crowd. Soon a tall man appeared, different from the others.

He wore a black suit and had imposing whiskers on either side of his red face. He examined each elephant in turn as he passed down the line, speaking a strange language to a well-fed Sinhalese dealer clutching a ledger.

"And here is a baby," said the dealer when they stopped in front of Far Stream. "A baby elephant, as you request. Very small baby."

"Yes, I can see that," replied the bewhiskered man. "I want small, but I also want healthy. It's no good if it dies and I have to drop it over the side."

"Oh no, Captain Sahib," said the dealer, feigning horror. And then brusquely in Sinhalese to Muni: "Tell the Captain Sahib that this elephant is healthy."

"This elephant is healthy," repeated Muni with a respectful bow of his head.

"Say that it is the finest specimen you have ever encountered so young."

"It is the finest specimen I have ever encountered so young."

"Oh, Captain Sahib," continued the dealer in English with great satisfaction. "This man say that this is the most healthy baby elephant he has seen. He say it is fed the most fine foodstuffs and is in most prime condition."

"Good," replied the tall buyer, prodding and poking Far Stream in an uninformed manner that the dealer observed with a straight face. He then passed on to Red Moon—a sacred elephant from the Temple of the Tooth in Kandy, the dealer informed him, Muni confirming.

"It is royalty, Captain Sahib. A very fine creature. One of the best."

Far Stream and Red Moon were selected by the tall man for purchase from the first batch of elephants lined up that day. Later in the afternoon they were led to a cargo boat tied alongside the quay. Far Stream, being the smallest and most manageable, was the first to be loaded. Muni backed her up until her hind legs dropped off the edge of the quay and found the blocks forming a step onto the deck of the vessel. She hung in this perilous position, half on land, half on water, resisting and bawling, then was muscled the rest of the way on board and secured.

When it was Red Moon's turn she backed herself onto the cargo boat very cautiously but without hesitation, Muni giving her the time she needed to feel her way with each step. "Ho, my child," he kept repeating to soothe her. She stepped fully on board, her nearly two tons of weight setting the boat swaying. A third elephant followed, another young female somewhat smaller than Red Moon. With her in position the vessel sat very low in the water. With much shouting and running about it was cast off and sculled out into the harbor, the men watching anxiously as the three elephants shifted their weight to brace themselves against the swell.

They made for a three-masted ship anchored off shore. When the cargo boat was tied up alongside it, a crane was swung over the side from the high deck and a canvas sling lowered. Far Stream remained still while Muni positioned it about her body, her fear of upsetting the boat greater for the moment than the alarm caused by the sling. Then, with a shout on deck of "Heave away!" she was rising into the air, bawling and flailing in terror, rising until she was above the deck of the ship and being swung over and lowered down through a square hole, Muni scrambling aboard and below to receive her. "Ho, my child," he cooed as her feet touched the lower deck. "You are safe. You are here." He released her from the sling and led her to one of the stalls that had been built in the low space and chained her to a pair of ring bolts buried deep in the ship's timbers. "Ho, my child," he murmured as he caressed her. "You are safe now. There is nothing to fear."

When the loading was complete Red Moon was chained in the stall beside Far Stream and the third creature on the side facing and down at the end. Muni served them water and fresh-cut grass he had carried across in the boat, all the while cooing gently, calming them with his soft voice. Far Stream began to settle. She trusted Muni. He was her keeper. He would care for her and keep her safe even in this strange place.

The tall man with the bewhiskered red face came down to see them. "A very fine start," he said, pleased. He offered Far Stream a hard ship's biscuit. She ate it and reached out for another. Then other men were there, similarly bewhiskered and smelling of unwashed clothes and tobacco. More biscuits were held out, followed by petting and poking that Far Stream allowed as she ate.

But where was Muni? He had disappeared. The light coming through the open hatch faded and still he did not return. When food was again served to them in the evening one of the new men brought it, a stranger whose words carried no comfort. He fed them the next day as well, and the next, and the next, as more elephants were lowered through the hatch and the other stalls filled.

Muni never returned. Far Stream did not know where he was or why he had left them. She did not know what had become of Grandmother and Mother, her brother Fear Wind and her aunts and her cousins. She did not know what was happening to her now, where the light had gone, why she had been abandoned, why the ground was moving, why she felt sick.

She started to cry.

Red Moon reached across the wall between them. They stood with their trunks entwined as the ship in which they were chained sailed southwest.

CHAPTER 3

"If you want to buy elephants cheap in Ceylon," said Captain Anthony Smalley of the bark *Nehemiah Gibson*, "you must go to your hotel, throw yourselves back in a chair, stick your thumbs in your vest and say, 'I want to buy some elephants.' The native dealers will seek you out eagerly and tell you yarns about the fine beasts they have on hand for your consideration. Stroke your chin musingly and tell them to fetch along the elephants for inspection, and they will do it. If you want one, you will be shown a hundred."

Captain Smalley did just that upon stepping ashore at Colombo in early 1871. Within the space of a week he had acquired a dozen fine beasts and had them safely stowed between-decks. "Everybody said, 'Smalley, you'll never get those elephants safe to New York, carrying them between-decks like that. They haven't got enough head room. They'll die certain.' You see, it had been customary, heretofore, to carry them in the hold. I said to them all, 'You just let me alone. I know what I am about.' And here they are today, all but the one who had died on the passage.

"I made good preparation for the elephants, you see. I had stalls built of teak wood, strong enough on all sides to resist a pressure of 2,000 pounds, and so constructed as to keep each animal in his place, and securely separated from the others in the roughest weather.

"We sailed from Colombo on the 20th of March, bound for the Cape of Good Hope . . . ."

୧୨

There were twelve of them crowded into the dark space inside the ship, the air thick with the smell of tar and cordage and stink from the bilges. The deck above was so low that Red Moon had to bow her head slightly; her chains were so short that she could move only a half step forward and back. Most of the others were of comparable size and similarly constricted. Far Stream, being smaller, had more freedom, but for the most part she stood in one spot like Red Moon and swayed. It came naturally, a response to the ship's motion and the sickly feeling that kept her from food and water. When that passed she continued for the numbing peace that it gave her. She closed her eyes to the present and swayed her head from one side to the other, back and forth, back and forth, hours and then days of hypnotic swaying that took her out of herself and transported her away from the ship.

During the day, in the dim light that filtered down the steps at the far end of the deck, she could make out Red Moon in the stall beside her and the three others, strangers, in the similar booths facing. The rest were hidden from view, off to the sides in the gloom. They stood in sullen silence for a long time, sharing nothing more than a monotone buzz of upset and fatigue. When they finally began to emerge from their collective stupor, Far Stream found their language confusing, an elusive whisper just past the edge of her comprehension. And when she tried to join in the shared communication, her childish efforts were not understood.

Red Moon by this time had lapsed into silence. She was despondent. It came with the start of the voyage and the resulting sickness and remained after the stomach heaving subsided. It sank her head low, made her incapable of offering comfort, unwilling even to take the food set before her.

Soon she started to lose weight.

It was the shifting of the sun and the moon, unseen above the deck planking but still strongly sensed, that so disturbed her. She could feel their altered position above in the heavens, feel her home receding far into the distance, the ship drawing away to the southwest. And with the feeling came a wilting of her spirit, for she realized she would never see her family again.

Far Stream was aware of her feelings. They drifted into her mind like dark clouds. She reached up in an effort to touch the larger form of her sister, seeking and offering reassurance, but she could not extend her trunk far enough over the barrier between them. She only encountered rough boards. As the days passed she felt herself sinking too, no longer wanting, no longer caring, ignoring the biscuits the sailors brought her on their visits below. Eventually Captain Smalley himself came down to investigate and squint at her in the lamp light. "Get that mash into her," he said to the man holding a bucket. With much coaxing she ate some of the contents. But not much.

It was four weeks before Red Moon struggled back out of the blackness. The change came quickly, as if she had awakened from a deep sleep. One moment she was not there, the next she had returned, draping her trunk over the partition in response to a whimper Far Stream was unaware she was making.

The caress was electric. Far Stream grasped the tip tightly with her small trunk. The renewed connection, the warmth, the shared life swept aside her own blackness. They stood again with their trunks entwined, making sounds of sorrowful acceptance, until Far Stream grew so sleepy that she had to lie down.

As she drifted away she heard her sister at last begin to communicate with the others. *I am Red Moon*, she was saying in the general way of the family but not quite the same. *I am from the Shining Sun Cliffs country.*

I am Three Times Falling, said the big male facing with the double lines around his eyes. *I am from the low country that leads to the ocean.*

I am Earth Moves, said the withered-looking female beside him, *also from the low country.*

I am Lone Tree Mountain, said a third, unseen off to the side in the darkness. *I too am from the Shining Sun Cliffs country. Are you of Found the Salt's family?*

Found the Salt is our Grandmother, said Red Moon.

Far Stream, sinking fast, felt her own mind open, curiously open without effort. *Found the Salt is my Grandmother*, she said. *Long Way Down is my Mother. I am Far . . .*

Before she could finish she was back in the forest with her family. She stayed with them for hours. It was her most vivid dream yet.

The second month of the voyage was brighter. Far Stream's appetite returned and she ate what the men brought her, especially the balls of cooked rice and lentils and the hard biscuits they fed her by hand. When she became lonely or frightened, usually at night in the darkness when rats rustled underfoot in the straw, there was always a touch from Red Moon to soothe her. Red Moon became more than Far Stream's older sister. She became her mother, the other beings her family. With her new comprehension she entered into their shared life and at times became playful, taking pleasure in their thoughts, their memories, their rumbles, their snorts and their whistles—even their evacuations. When Three Times Falling's bowels moved after a week of profound constipation, the thunderous results and the accompanying groans of relief started the whole group chuffing with amusement. They started again when Three Times Falling tripped the man with the shovel and sent him stumbling into the vast raked-up pile.

There was no mirth when the ship turned west and then north and the sea grew violent. Men came below and secured each of them more tightly to the posts and the ring bolts, a chain on each leg. In the hours that followed, the ship began to lean alarmingly from side to side and Far Stream had to wrap her trunk around the bar at the front of her stall to stay on her feet. It was an exhausting struggle in continual darkness, hatchways battened down against the seas that washed over the vessel. Water was soon trickling down onto her back through the seams that opened in the strained deck. It was cold. Far Stream started to cry.

Then the gale reached a crescendo and the terror set in. The ship was pitching so violently now that the elephants were thrown upward, nearly off their feet, the backs of the taller ones thumping hollow against the deck above. The first horrific lurch squeezed a strangled roar from several, then it was the whole group, a panicked wave of trumpeting that drowned out Far Stream's weak bleats. Men came down with lanterns to investigate, legs braced against the swell, hanging on. They took in the strange scene, eyes wide in the lamp glow, and quickly retreated. There was nothing they could do.

The storm continued for nearly a week, reducing Far Stream to staggering numbness long before it had expended its fury, her whole body aching from the repeated smashing against the unyielding sides of the stall. Her stupor became so intense that she was able to stare without feeling at the rats that invaded up from the bilges to overrun the compartment, her fear stuck down deep inside her like a mass too viscous to flow. Red Moon was undergoing similar trials of her own. Her greater bulk added to the force of the sideways blows that she was absorbing. The upward lurches put tremendous strain on her legs and hurt her when she came crashing down at awkward angles. The food set before her, before them all, was ignored.

It was several days after the storm abated before Far Stream and Red Moon returned to themselves and were able to eat. The crackling fear abated, the rat infestation subsided and life in the between-decks returned for most of them to what it had been.

Earth Moves, from the low country, was the exception. She did not recover. There had been indications of distress from her for some time before the storm. Afterward, the signs became acute—acute enough that even the men noticed, and they could not hear. They shone a lantern on Earth Moves, peered at her and murmured together, agitated by her moaning. They tried to coax her to rise when she crumpled gasping onto her side. She responded with a few brief struggles, then gave up and lay still.

Earth Moves left them during the night, in the darkness. They were all awake, watching, as her spark flared to fill the compartment. When the men came below the next morning, she was gone. They prodded her for a time, then opened a hatch and began the hard work of hoisting her up onto the deck. Those chained in the nearest stalls reached out and caught hold of her body as it was dragged toward the square of light above, blinding after weeks of dimness. "Let go there," the men barked, swatting at the trunks as they labored. When the body was in position, the ropes were rearranged and there was a *click, click, click* and it rose into the air and disappeared through the square in the ceiling. Shouting on deck followed—"Swing it over . . . Free that cable"—and there was a splash.

The eleven left behind were subdued after that. Far Stream sought Red Moon's caresses but there was no pleasure in them, only consolation. They glided along in their chains through the third month, heading northwest now, the air growing warmer. A stop was made at a place unseen from the between-decks. There was thumping against the side of the ship and above and the hatches were opened and there was light again and green fodder was served them and they ate it with relish. Then they were moving again, timbers creaking, the song of the wind in the rigging, northward and westward, northward and westward, sailing on, sailing into the fourth month.

꧁꧂

It was summer and hot when the hatches were again opened and the scents wafted down indicating that they were near land. As they drew closer, the smells became stranger and were joined by the sounds of a big harbor. Then the men above were running and shouting, cables were being run out and set, winches were turning, then a gentle shudder as the ship touched the side of a pier.

The work of unloading was commenced early the next morning. Three Times Falling was the first to be unchained and led to the square of light on the deck under the hatch. He was compliant at first, moving slowly and stiffly on legs unfamiliar after so long a confinement. It was only when he saw the canvas sling being lowered that he became alarmed and began to resist. Earth Moves had gone this way, up through the hatch and into the sea after her spark had burned out. Three Times Falling did not want to follow. The men bellowed at him, prodded and jabbed, but they could not force him into the sling. Finally one of them said, "Let's try the young one."

They allowed Three Times Falling to retreat a few paces, two men holding him in place with pitchforks extended. Far Stream was then unchained and brought forward. She was also fearful and bleated and tried to resist. But she was small and the men could control her. After some rough handling she was lashed into the sling and hoisted up off her feet through the opening. She thrashed her legs wildly as she cleared the deck and rose into the sunlight. Then she stopped, paralyzed by fear of falling out of the sling. She hung stiffly as she was swung over the side and lowered onto the dockside, the ground oddly motionless after the months aboard ship. As she calmed and returned to her senses, she noticed the multitude of people gathered nearby, leaning out windows, standing in wagons. They were staring at her, pointing and laughing, grinning, bared teeth.

The rest of the unloading proceeded almost without incident. Reassured that Far Stream was safe outside on dry land, the others allowed themselves to be hoisted up and out of the ship, doing little more than flapping their ears as they hung suspended. Only Three Times Falling caused a commotion, heaving and roaring in midair until he was swinging, the men on the ropes straining to arrest the motion. When they were all landed the men chained them in a line, Far Stream beside Red Moon, and led them into a nearby building. They walked awkwardly and stiffly, grunting with the effort of making their legs work. The way was lined with hooting spectators, some extending canes and sticks to poke them, others throwing bits of debris.

They spent the night in a big musty structure near a wide ocean-river, agitated by the unfamiliar sounds and smells and the periodic rumbles that rose up from the ground. *What is this place?* Far Stream asked Red Moon and the others. No one knew. They had traveled so far that the magnetic pulls that oriented them had lost all meaning. They had no way of knowing that they were on the far side of the world, in a warehouse on the Thirteenth Street pier in Hoboken, New Jersey, across the North River from New York City.

The next morning, preparations were begun to move them again. Again they were chained together to be led off single file, men with sticks walking alongside. Again there was a large excited crowd waiting outside to see them, others rushing forward when the cry rose, "Here they come!"

But there was something wrong. Far Stream had not been chained behind Red Moon. When the line started moving she tried to follow but couldn't. Her distress caused Red Moon to pause and reach out with her trunk.

"Not you," said one of the men, prodding Far Stream back. "You're for Forepaugh. These ones are for Howes." He turned on Red Moon and applied his stick with vigor, forcing her to advance with the others, forcing her to leave Far Stream behind, whimpering at the end of her chain.

Come with us, Red Moon urged her, not understanding. The others, feeling Far Stream's agitation, joined in. They said, *Come with us, come with us*. Far Stream tugged and strained and pleaded to follow but no man would unchain her and lead her along.

The others were gone now. The warehouse door was closed. She was alone. *Are you there?* she asked, hoping that Red Moon was waiting for her somewhere nearby. There was no answer. *Are you there?* she repeated. There was no answer. *Are you there?* she tried a third time. But the connection was broken.

She had retreated inside her mind, swaying, when the tall bewhiskered man from the ship appeared, the red-faced one that the others feared and respected. There was another man with him, a well-dressed stranger, and a third man, quite young, who deferentially hung back.

"There she be," said Captain Smalley, giving Far Stream a pat on the head. "As plump and frisky as the day she came aboard at Colombo."

The stranger appraised her for a time, head cocked, then began to examine her closely. He felt the end of her trunk. "Cold," he murmured. He roughly pried her mouth open and looked at her first set of molars, which had grown in to replace her milk teeth after her first year. He prodded the muscles in her neck and her shoulders, kneaded her hams, raised each of her feet and pressed his thumb into the pads, soft from long confinement.

"She stinks," he said at last. "And I'd say she's a bit wasted."

"If it's freshness you want, Mr. Forepaugh," snapped Smalley, "you should acquire your elephants closer to home. I'm sure you have fine herds of them in Pennsylvania."

"Just observing," said the man named George Forepaugh. He motioned to his young assistant standing close by. "Eph, see that she's cleaned up and fed and on the train in plenty of time, down there where I showed you. Now Captain, if you will accompany me to the bank, we can settle our business."

The two men departed, leaving Far Stream alone with the young man. She had never seen a man like him before, one with black skin. He led her outside for a drink and a wash from a trough smelling of horses, then served her a meal of bran mash and greens. She ate without appetite and found no comfort in the sound of his voice, stern but soft underneath. "I don't want no trouble from you," he told her. "You just mind me, youngster. You mind Eph. You mind Eph good and we'll get along fine."

It was only when he started to scratch her behind the ear that she came to life and began to explore him, running the tip of her trunk all over and probing inside his pockets. Like many men, Eph smelled of tobacco.

"Well," he said when she had finished, "we have a few hours. Let's get started and give Mr. Forepaugh a surprise."

He produced a bag of spotty apples and cut them into pieces. When he was finished he held a bite above Far Stream's head. "Salute," he said as she reached up with her trunk to take it. "Salute," he repeated, using his free hand to make an upward gesture, then manually straightening her raised proboscis before he gave her the treat. A second bite of apple was offered, the command and gesture were given, the trunk straightened, and the bruised morsel delivered. "Salute," he commanded again and again, until all the pieces were gone and the lesson was done.

The sun had passed its zenith when Eph led Far Stream out of the warehouse and down a street leading away from the harbor. For the first time she had a clear view of the great city growing up on either side of the river. She brightened as they went along and picked up the scent and then the visible marks of the others. They had come this way. Perhaps this new man was taking her to join them. *Are you there?* she said hopefully, but there was no answer. Then the scent veered off to the right. Far Stream tried to follow. Eph wouldn't let her.

"What did I tell you about minding me?" he said.

He prodded her along until the comforting wisps of odor disappeared altogether, overwhelmed by violent man-smells, none of them fresh, some of them frightening. And jarring noises, clangs and screams and whistles. They overwhelmed her, assaulted her, forced her to close her mind as she shuffled down the filth-blackened street through the crowd that was gathering.

Eph walked beside her with a protective hand on her back, occasionally making sounds she did not comprehend. People pressed in close and touched her as they moved briskly along. Some offered her treats. She accepted them and mindlessly put them in her mouth and swallowed. A bit of wilted green. A crust of bread. The tang of a penny. Then the petting became rougher, jeering boys making grabs at her tail, her ears, her trunk, slapping her sides and her bottom. Eph yelled at them and brandished his stick, driving them off. They returned like settling flies.

She continued on in a fog until they entered a rail yard and came to a train. The half mile they had covered would have been nothing for her back in the forest. Now, after the months of no exercise aboard ship, she was flagging. "Almost there, youngster," said Eph, seeing that she was tired. He led her on a little farther, to a boxcar with a ramp, and coaxed her up and inside. There were horses at one end, a pile of sacks at the other. Far Stream was secured on a bed of straw in between.

Eph stayed with her in the boxcar when the door was closed and the train jerked forward, talking to her and stroking her and scratching her behind the ear in a way she found soothing. As they jolted westward, the inside of the car illuminated by shafts of sunlight seeping in through cracks, she felt trust for this new man kindling inside her. And with the trust came a willingness to please him. When he set to work again with more pieces of apple and the command to "salute," she quickly grasped the lesson. Soon she was raising her trunk at the sound of the word and the sight of the gesture.

"Well done, youngster," said Eph when he let up in the dwindling twilight. "You're going to do just fine for Mr. Forepaugh. You're going to make a fine Baby Annie."

CHAPTER 4

"ON THE *SIXTH...DAY...OF CREATION...*"

The master of the circle paused and gazed about the arena, waiting for his words to quiet the audience arrayed on the tiers of benches. They were nearing the finale of the evening performance. Lanterns affixed to crossed planks hung suspended overhead like crude chandeliers, casting an orange glow upon the great circus tent.

"On the *SIXTH...DAY OF...CREATION,* after God had fashioned His many four-legged wonders. The dromedary of the scorching desert. The camelopard with its long neck. The blood-sweating hippopotamus of Holy Writ. He took up His la-a-a-rgest brush..."

Voice and arm-shaking as the ring master hoisted the imaginary great weight.

"...He took up His hea-a-a-viest mallet. He took up His gra-a-a-ndest measure. And He created..."

A pause.

"...He created the awe-inspiring, the magnificent..."

A flourish of the arm to a parting curtain.

"...*ELEPHANT!*"

The great creature was led into the arena, bobbing his head as he went to acknowledge the cheering. George Forepaugh, the show's chief elephant handler, walked alongside in a high-collar military tunic and matching cap with gold braid. The ring master increased the flow of his words.

35

"Ladies and gentlemen, Adam Forepaugh's unabridged and unapproachable Zoological Aggregation, Museum and Circus presents for your edification and amusement the *greatest* elephant to visit these United States since the untimely demise of Hannibal on the Pawtucket Road. The most *sagacious* elephant to perform inside the sawdust circle. The *grandest* of God's many wonders. The *largest* of all earthly dwellers. Behold, oh citizens of Cincinnati, Adam Forepaugh's unparalleled behemoth, ten feet high and weighing ten thousand pounds, a mountain of living flesh, instructed by the only man who can control him, the renowned elephant hunter and trainer George Forepaugh. Behold the mighty...*ROMEO!*"

Thunderous applause and the stamping of feet. Many of the spectators had already seen Romeo in the street parade earlier that day. Here, in the soft glow of the evening performance, properly introduced, he seemed even bigger.

"And as a counterpoint," continued the announcer, "as an exclamation mark to Romeo's Olympian vastness, we present a suckling calf of the same species, the most interesting natural curiosity in the whole world, recently plucked from the deepest, darkest forest of the exotic East and brought to this country at untold expense to the Forepaugh concern. We present, ladies and gentlemen and children, the tiny..."

A pause.

"...the diminutive..."

A pause.

"...the Lilliputian..."

Another sweep of the arm.

"...*BABY ANNIE!*"

Far Stream entered the arena at the side of George Forepaugh's teenaged assistant, Ephraim Parker, known about the show as Eph. It was her first time in the ring and the excitement caused her to forget her lessons. "Slow down," hissed Eph, restraining her before she broke away altogether. When he had her nicely promenading around the raised edge of the ring, he gave the order, "Salute." Far Stream, frightened by the noise, bewildered by the thousand pairs of eyes upon her, did not respond. "Salute," Eph repeated, giving her a tap under the chin. The touch focused her mind on what it was that he wanted. She raised her trunk. The audience cheered.

After another turn she took her position on the side to watch Romeo's act. It was the strangest series of movements that she had ever witnessed. Romeo began with a lumbering waltz in time to the band's music, steps forward and back and from side to side, bobbing and swaying, dog-like compliant as George waved him about and called out commands and at one point joined in the sashaying. When the memorized steps were completed, Eph gave Far Stream a tug on the ear and commanded, "Shake." A more urgent repetition and she shook her head up and down as George had taught her, conveying to the audience that she was pleased with her giant companion's performance. Romeo responded by lowering his head to the ground in a bow.

In the rest of the ten-minute act, as Far Stream looked on and at intervals shook her head and saluted, Romeo sat on his haunches and raised his forelegs in the air and tooted; he picked George up and placed him on his back; he set him back down and stepped over his prone body; he lay down himself at George's loud prompt, "You are dead, sir." And then, when it appeared that his sagacity and agility and docility had been pushed to the limit, he clambered onto a massive cask and stood on his head.

That was the capper. With the audience on its feet now, George led Romeo triumphantly toward the exit, head bobbing to acknowledge the applause as he went. Far Stream tagged behind, Eph hissing at her, "Salute. Salute."

It was night outside, the canvas all around glowing orange from the lanterns and candles within. The smaller sideshow tents, quiet when they entered, were opening again in anticipation of the exiting crowd that would soon follow. The candy butchers, soap salesmen and miscellaneous hucksters were assembling for their final assault of the evening, confidence men and pickpockets and worse hanging back in the shadows.

"Evening, Mr. Forepaugh," said a grizzled veteran from behind a tray of twenty-cent fancies.

"Fair turnout, Mr. Forepaugh," observed another, concealing a flask.

"Pretty fair, Frankie," said George, passing with Romeo and Far Stream into the menagerie tent. He chained Romeo in the center to stakes driven into the soil. Eph did the same to Far Stream, beyond Romeo's reach.

This was her new home, an immense oval tent supported by three rows of poles and held in place with cables. It was two hundred ten feet long and one hundred twenty-five feet wide, forty feet high in the center, eight at the edges. Her place was in the center with the rest of the led stock. Romeo stood on her right, then a llama; a giraffe was on her left, a reindeer and a pair of camels and a musk ox further down. Lining the periphery was a ring of wagons carrying odorous cages confining all the other animals in the show: a variety of bears and lions, a collection of monkeys and birds, two baboons, a jackal, a Japanese pig, an African porcupine and much more. Beyond them was canvas. It was Far Stream's new sky, her new horizon. It was a myriad of brownish-orange shades in daytime when sunlight filtered through it, a different hue for every sag, fold and billow. At night it was a more uniform grey. As in the main tent, light came from a collection of lanterns suspended from hanging crossed planks. They provided uneven illumination that left many dark corners and set shadows swaying when there was a breeze.

A final roar from the main tent, the band launching into "Good Night, Ladies" signaling the end of the two-hour performance. A hum outside of movement and laughter and chatter, snatches of patter from the sideshow barkers and hawkers. "Only ten cents, ma'am... An exotic wonder from Asia... Friend, do you suffer from itching in the nether regions?... Just five cents more for the extra fancy... This way for the two-headed baby." Then people drifting back in for a final inspection of the menagerie to round out the evening before heading home to bed, sated.

George Forepaugh was gone, back to the hotel for that rarest of luxuries with a touring circus, a good night's sleep. Eph, seventeen years old but six feet tall and looking older, was left in charge of Romeo and Far Stream, answering questions, watching that patrons didn't do anything foolish.

"My child wants to pet the small one," demanded an imperious mother, handkerchief pressed to her nose.

"She surely can, ma'am," replied Eph. And to the little girl: "Just pet her soft."

A little hand reached out for Far Stream and started to stroke her. Then there were others, people all around, touching, probing, petting, poking. They marveled at the texture of her skin, the softness of the tip of her trunk as they held out peanuts and candy, the coarseness of the sparse hair on the top of her head and down her spine. "Just like pig bristles," pronounced another child, yanking. Far Stream shifted uneasily, nervous of the touching and crowding, glad of the treats.

"Hey boy, how old's Romeo there?"

"He's over a hundred, sir," replied Eph. Then, because he liked his fun: "See all them wrinkles down the front of his trunk? You count 'em up and that'll give you his age pretty close." It was a line he had picked up from George Forepaugh.

Another man pushed his way forward. "I saw Baby Annie last year, when you all were in Sandusky. This is not the same creature. The other was bigger. It came up to here." He touched the middle of his chest. "And its ears were bigger."

39

"You are absolutely right, sir. That *was* a different Baby Annie. Got too big, weren't a baby no more, so Mr. Forepaugh sold it. It was the Africa kind. The Africa kind's got the big ears."

"How old's this one?"

"Practically new born, ma'am."

"What do they eat?"

"Hay mostly. Some bran mash. Sometimes a big feed of potatoes and gravy."

"Does the biggun like plug tobacco?"

"No sir, he don't."

"How 'bout we try giving him some?"

"Steady there, Ned," said the man's more sober companion. "That beast's a killer."

"That true?"

Eph nodded emphatically. "It's true, sir. And he don't like to be teased."

"Say boy, what are those marks all over Romeo?"

"Those are scars, sir."

"That's a terrible lot of scars. How'd he get them?"

Far Stream squealed and stepped back, bowling over a young boy hanging onto her tail. Her throat was on fire. The man with the plug tobacco had fed her a piece. The boy, unhurt but scared, was bawling. His incensed mother struck Far Stream with her fan and bellowed at Eph, "Maintain control of your beast!"

"I apologize, ma'am. Annie's still a bit skittish." And with a sharp look at the man with the tobacco: "And she surely don't like to be teased."

❧

One o'clock in the morning. The menagerie tent was dark. Eph was curled up under a blanket on a bed of straw nearby, softly snoring. Like all good circus men, he had developed the knack of sleeping rough in all sorts of conditions. Far Stream, although desperately tired, could not do the same. The strange sounds of the other animals confined under the

40

canvas upset her, their snorts and snuffles, their occasional growling and squealing, their shifting and flapping and grunting and cackling. Every time she was able to relax enough to slip into a doze, something would jolt her awake and set her heart racing.

Romeo was still on his feet, a swaying shadow blocking the light from the dimmed lantern over the tent's entrance, now closed. He was silent. Far Stream had tried to communicate with him upon her arrival but there had been no coherent answer. The giant had gazed at her with his one good eye and responded to her greeting with something jagged, disordered, disturbing. She knew he was to be feared. Romeo confirmed this by taking a swipe at her when Eph had led her too close, his trunk just grazing her side. For reasons she could not understand, Romeo wanted to hurt her.

George Forepaugh returned the next morning for what would be for Far Stream an almost daily session of training. He required her to perform what he had already taught her, the salute and the head shake, countless repetitions, standing still at first, then parading about, more stick now, harsher words, no pieces of apple.

Then he introduced another command: "Lie down." Jabs from George and shoves from Eph prompted Far Stream to get down and roll onto her side.

"Up." Pulling her ear now, jabbing her back.

"Lie down."

"Up."

"Lie down."

"Up."

"Lie down."

"Up."

This continued for an hour. When it was over Eph served Far Stream her food. Then the entrance was opened and people were once again milling, asking questions, petting, peering, poking. In the middle of the afternoon she again followed Romeo into the main tent to repeat her little performance, this time a bit sharper. Then it was back to the menagerie tent for more public viewing, a brief lull, then the evening performance, a long day of excitement and anxiety that left Far Stream so exhausted that the unsettling sounds of the other animals could no longer touch her. She lay down and slept, dreaming of the forest.

On the following morning the lesson was conducted outside in the sunshine as roustabouts took down the tents and with military efficiency loaded the circus onto a long line of wagons. The luxury of the four-day stop in Cincinnati was over. Adam Forepaugh's Zoological Aggregation, Museum and Circus was again on the move. For the animals in cages the journey to the next town meant a bumpy four-hour ride on the back of a wagon. For Far Stream and Romeo it meant a fifteen-mile walk, George Forepaugh and Eph riding alongside on horseback.

They proceeded slowly, lagging behind the wagons to give Far Stream the time she needed. She was still out of shape from the long confinement aboard ship and was whining with fatigue and sore feet long before they were finished, too tired to notice the prime fields of corn and wheat they were passing, the wealth of smells, the gaping onlookers gathered at crossroads—even the moving form of Romeo before her, his chains ringing, his eyes scarcely open. More than once she nearly walked into him when he halted.

The next stop was Hamilton, Ohio, the venue an open field transformed in the space of three hours into a city of canvas. Far Stream numbly submitted to another pawing by strangers in the menagerie tent and stumbled through an afternoon and an evening performance. Then the pace quickened. From now on there would be no time for resting. The tents came down as soon as the evening performance was finished and the show was again on the move. This time Far Stream walked through most of the night, eighteen long miles to give two performances in the town of Lebanon the next day. When she arrived in the morning she and Romeo were paraded through the streets with the other animals, the performers and wagons, Adam Forepaugh leading the way in his open carriage, stirring the place up before heading out to the show grounds, what the circus people called the "lot." The tents were erected, people poured in, two shows were given, two o'clock and seven, the tents came down, the wagons were packed and set out, another night of travel along dark roads to another town and another, Wilmington, Xenia, Dayton, Piqua, Troy and Springfield and Urbana, on and on to a different town every day, plodding on and on as if to the end of the world until Far Stream's muscles firmed and her cracked feet hardened and her mind became inured to the continual upset until like Romeo she could doze on the move.

October. Lashing rain at three o'clock in the morning on a deserted road in eastern Pennsylvania, Romeo's feet rhythmically moving three yards ahead of her, squelching in the mud with each step. Far Stream was stronger now after eight hundred miles of night marching but the fatigue still enveloped her and was made worse by a cold. Eph had been treating her each day with a pail of hot vinegar in a bag placed over her head. The sharp vapors gave some relief but it was fleeting and the cold lingered. Her breathing now, out on the road, was labored, a steady stream of mucous dripping out of her trunk.

A commotion ahead, George and Eph straightening up in their saddles, Romeo coming to a halt at the barked command, "Tut!" Behind him Far Stream stopped and stared glassily into the mud.

"We've been waiting on you," said a dimly seen circus hand in a streaming slicker, walking back from a line of stalled wagons. "Can't get 'em up that damn hill. The road's too slick for the horses."

With a grunt George dismounted and directed Romeo forward with a perfunctory "Go on." The big form shuffled along the line of wagons to the first at the base of the hill, a tarpaulin-draped cage wagon with menacing growls emanating from beasts unseen underneath. With scarcely any direction from George—shunting wagons was Romeo's most frequent chore after performing—he placed his head against the back of the frame and effortlessly pushed the wagon forward, a steady plod to the top of the hill, the horses in front scarcely needing to pull. A snort, a turn and a plod back down for the next, up and down a dozen times with seemingly no effort until all the wagons were again on the move toward the next town.

"I hope you was watching," said Eph when he came back to rouse Far Stream and set her moving again. "That's how it's done."

The wagons were already swallowed up ahead in the darkness when they joined Romeo and George at the top of the hill to begin the gentle descent down into the next valley, willows on either side of the road, a bridge up ahead. Far Stream walked on in Romeo's now more purposeful footsteps, scarcely aware that the rain was easing, her stuffy head throbbing with her heartbeat, her trunk drip-drip-dripping onto the ground.

A pause at the bridge, a ten-yard span over a minor stream now swollen with runoff. Romeo with his usual caution tested the boards with his forefoot before committing his full weight.

"Go on," said George, tapping him on the shoulder, impatient to get the miserable night over. "We were over this bridge last year. Go on." Romeo ignored him and continued with his careful pressing, one foot, then two feet, the timbers creaking over the rushing water below.

He was just past the middle when the splintering came and the left side of the bridge collapsed and toppled him into the stream, his stabbing squeal cut short by the immense splash. Far Stream, waiting behind, fearfully backed away, tail high, back until she was off the road and under the trees. Eph sat frozen in his saddle, frozen as George's horse ran away past him, frozen as he stared at Romeo thrashing in the water. Then he was running forward to George sprawled where he had been thrown.

"You all right, boss? You all right?"

George rose stiffly with a stream of curses, his clothes muddy from pant cuff to collar. He looked back down the road at his horse trotting away in the opposite direction, forward at Romeo on his feet in the stream.

"He's going to be crotchety now," he said. "Get on back there and round up my horse. Where's Annie?"

Far Stream had not moved. She was still standing under the willows, watching Romeo, a huge glowering black boulder with tusks, the water rushing by just under his chin. His mind was crackling. She did not want to get any closer. In the darkness it was some minutes before Eph found her and secured her in place to a tree.

Romeo stood in the stream for a quarter of an hour before emerging on his own to clamber up the bank and onto the road. He was cold and limping—one of his hind legs had been wrenched—and a nasty scrape ran down his side. When George tried to approach him he was warned away with the trunk. "Go on," he roared, threatening with the bull hook that he carried, trying to get Romeo again on the march. Again the trunk lashed out, accompanied this time by a loud, fearsome trumpet.

"He don't look like he's going anywhere soon," Eph suggested, returning with the horse.

George sighed wearily. "I guess I'll be waiting here until this big bastard gets a mind to move. You may as well go on with Annie."

"The bridge is wrecked, boss."

"Well, go along that field until you come to a place that's shallow."

Far Stream followed Eph in skirting the field, corn plants on one side, the swollen stream on the other, patches of sky overhead clearing, stars emerging to twinkle. Behind them, George leaned against his horse, sharing its warmth.

❦

December. The incessant traveling had ended. Far Stream and Romeo were in Philadelphia, the Adam Forepaugh show's winter quarters, in a large barn on Ridge Avenue between the railway tracks and the Schuylkill River. The giraffe, the hippopotamus, the monkeys, the birds and many of the more tropical creatures were housed in the same building. The place was heated by a pair of large coal stoves. The slate tiles covering the roof rattled every time a train passed.

The wearying travel and excitement of the touring season now gave way to boredom. It was winter. Apart from infrequent walks outside on mild days with Eph, Far Stream remained in the warmth of the barn, standing, dozing, eating, swaying, taking perhaps fifty steps about her stall between sunrise and evening, her road-hardened muscles and feet gradually again turning soft. Bathing, even a scrub at the trough, became a distant memory. It wasn't done in the winter. Her hide became brown and rough and itchy with the accumulation of dirt and dead skin that was no longer sloughed off. Some relief came when Eph and George appeared with buckets of linseed oil, a large brush and a ladder. After finishing with Romeo—Eph did the actual work, painting the creature like a house while George kept guard with a pitchfork—the remaining oil was slathered on Far Stream, leaving her a dark grey bordering on black. The treatment softened her hide and gave her relief from the itching. It also increased the trust she felt for these men, her trainer and keeper. When they resumed her lessons at the start of the New Year, she was eager to please them. She wanted to learn.

George had been satisfied with Far Stream's performance during the months she spent with the show on the road. Although not quite four years old, she had quickly picked up her first simple tricks and was evidently capable of things more ambitious. A bit of humor, George thought, would be just the thing to enliven Romeo's act.

Far Stream was first taught to sit down on her haunches. This was accomplished by force. She was pushed down in the rear by Eph applying his weight to her back while George pushed against the back of her knees to buckle them and commanded her, "Sit." The manhandling at first confused her and she resisted, shifting nervously as the two men pushed, sweated and pounded. But eventually she gave in and lowered her bottom to the straw. On the second day, after countless repetitions, she was performing the action with George only having to press down on her rump with one hand. On the third day even this light pressure was no longer required; she responded to his spoken command.

From this newly acquired seated position she was next taught to lie down on her side at the same command given to Romeo, "You are dead, sir!" This, like the sitting, was accomplished with pushing and prodding. It came fairly quickly.

The next movement, to sit up with her forefeet in the air like a dog begging, did not. Ropes were fastened around her forefeet and run through block and tackle affixed overhead to the timber frame of the barn. The opposite ends were secured to a harness around Romeo's chest. After getting her seated, George commanded, "Head up, Annie!" and Eph led Romeo forward, pulling on the ropes and in turn pulling up on her legs. The treatment frightened her. She whined and struggled and wobbled about on her bottom and did not try to balance herself and relieve the strain of the ropes. Eph backed Romeo up and they tried again, and again, and again, and again, the lesson remaining unlearned after a very long session.

"It's all right," said Eph, applying ointment afterward to where the sharper jabs had broken her skin, stroking her tenderly to quiet her whimpering. "It's all right now. You settle down."

"I told you before," snapped George, calling over. "Don't treat her like a pet. In a few years she'll be big enough to kill you with a swat."

"Yes, boss." Eph removed his warm hand from her head.

It took a week of repeated sessions before Far Stream's fear abated enough for her to grasp what they wanted. That, George had explained to Eph, was the biggest hurdle. Once she understood, she began to struggle with learning to balance on her bottom with her front feet in the air. It was uncomfortable and difficult, straining new muscles, but she was eventually able to do it. When she accomplished it for the first time on her own, raising herself up for a teetering moment in response only to the spoken command, George and Eph laughed with pleasure and fed her handfuls of treats. She was glad she had pleased them.

By the middle of January of the new year, 1872, Far Stream had learned her lessons and George scaled back his time with her to a half hour each day. He would drop by in the morning and work first with Romeo, running through the act to keep him sharp for the upcoming season, then he would put Far Stream through her paces. She was an eager pupil, responding to commands promptly and with increasing assurance, even the most difficult move, the sitting-up, becoming easier as the muscles that the alien position required grew stronger.

And then, one morning, George found her seemingly stupid. He had just finished with Romeo, a resentful, glowering session, and had returned him to his place and Eph was bringing him water.

"Annie!" George barked, annoyed at Far Stream's lack of attention. "Sit down! Sit down!"

Far Stream still did not obey him. Her attention was on

Romeo. Why was Eph so close to him? Did he not feel what was bubbling inside Romeo's head?

"Sit down, Annie." George gave her a whack on the hip with the flat of his bull hook. She shifted about and finally responded. *Come away*, she said to Eph, not wanting him to be hurt. *Come away.*

"Lie down!"

And then she was rearing away and screaming for Romeo was attacking, the great trunk lashing out at Eph, a strangled yelp, the keeper thrown ten feet. He landed heavily in a heap and rolled onto his back and lay stunned for a moment, staring up at the rafters as the whole menagerie in its cages came to life with shrieks, cackles and roars.

Without the slightest hesitation George ran at Romeo and brought his bull hook crashing down between his eyes. It did not have the intended intimidating effect. Instead of backing up and submitting, Romeo lashed out again and strained against his chains trying to break free. George only just avoided being caught before scrambling out of the way. "Frenchie! Joe!" he roared, seizing a pitchfork. Two men came running, both old hands with the show.

"Double those chains," George ordered, holding Romeo at bay with the pitchfork, his eyes never leaving the animal. "Careful, Frenchie, watch the head." And to Romeo, with a vicious stab that pierced flesh: "Stay still!"

Behind them Eph was slowly getting to his feet, looking sheepish. "Damn brute nearly got me," he joked when Romeo was immobile and the others were able to attend him. Eph was young and wanted them to know he was tough but he couldn't help clutching his side for the pain.

"Let me see," said George. "Take off your coat."

"No harm done, boss. No harm done."

"Get that coat off. Let me have a look."

George began examining his chest, gently probing. When he reached the cracked ribs, Eph drew a sharp breath and hissed, "Sweet Lord Jesus..."

Adam Forepaugh, George's younger brother and the circus's owner, visited the barn later that day. Far Stream knew him well now, the high forehead and mutton chop whiskers, the heavy eyebrows, the hard gaze. His only child, Adam Jr., "Addie," was with him, a sharp-featured boy, only eleven years old but already doing an equestrian act in the show.

"By God you're a troublesome one," said Adam, eying Romeo coolly. It was not the first time his prize possession of the past six years had become vicious. Romeo glared back, tugging at his chains.

"He's a caution, pa," said young Addie. "What are we going to do?"

"We're going to leave him right there stewing is what we're going to do. A month in the chains should settle him down."

"A month in the chains," Addie repeated. "That'll settle him down. Won't it, Uncle Georgie?"

CHAPTER 5

ADAM FOREPAUGH HAD ALWAYS made his living with animals. He started in his early teens in a butcher's shop, cutting them up. From this he went on to working with a whip as a drover, herding cattle to market. Then he became a horse trader. He was reputedly adept at buying worn-out nags from companies, sprucing them up and selling them back as fresh stock. By 1861 the rough-hewn Philadelphian had transformed himself into a man of substance. Four years later he invested in a business that he believed would pay even better: the circus.

It came about when John "Pogey" O'Brien offered Adam a share in his touring show as collateral for a consignment of horses. After letting the debt ride for a time, Adam paid Pogey a visit to settle the matter—with his fists if need be. But it didn't come to that. Instead he bought Pogey out.

To enliven the struggling attraction, Adam added a collection of exotic animals purchased from Jerry Mabie's bankrupt menagerie and hired a number of top acts. The resulting show, fifty cents for adults, twenty-five cents for children, was called Forepaugh's Mammoth Menagerie and Circus—"4-Paws" for short. It featured Shetland ponies with monkey jockeys; performing leopards; a band playing popular airs; a variety of birds and snakes and four-legged creatures; acrobats and contortionists and equestrian riders;

wax figurines and grotesqueries pickled in bottles; a river hog and a rat kangaroo and an Abyssinian ibex—and a giant male elephant named Romeo that was covered with scars.

Romeo was not a hundred years old as Adam Forepaugh liked to claim. He was perhaps thirty. He had been brought to America from Ceylon in 1851 as part of a shipment of nine elephants to P.T. Barnum and Seth Howes, who were putting together a circus. His original name, Canda, was changed to Canada upon his arrival. He passed into Jerry Mabie's hands four years later—auction lot 13, purchase price $1,500. Mabie rechristened him Romeo, a venerable circus elephant name used multiple times going back half a century. The first Romeo had toured the country in the 1820s and '30s before dying "from an overdose of pitchfork," the *New York Tribune* reported, "chained to a tree."

The Romeo that Adam Forepaugh acquired from Mabie was prone to outbursts of violence. Much of this was likely due to musth, the periodic spiking of testosterone levels that can drive mature male elephants to extreme behavior they cannot control. In Romeo's day there was little understanding of this condition and even less patience. An elephant that was unmanageable was simply of no use and had to be broken. The process by which this was accomplished was typically referred to in newspaper accounts as "conquering" or "subduing." Circus folk used a more obscure term, one derived from the necessity of forcing a recalcitrant beast to accept the authority of a new keeper. They called it "taking" an elephant.

There is no record of how many times Romeo was "taken" during his four years with Barnum and Howes and his ten years with Mabie. In his final seven years with Forepaugh, judging from reports that made their way into newspapers, the process was repeated five times at least. The first occurred in November 1865, following a rampage in which Romeo attacked his keeper and demolished a building. Romeo was chained down and left for a week

52

without food and water. Then the hard work started. When it was over he had more scars and was missing an eye.

The treatment was repeated in April 1866, then again in December 1867, after Romeo killed another of his keepers, Bill Williams. Bill was administering a punishment for some infraction when Romeo seized him and smashed him to the ground and drove a broken tusk through his stomach. He immediately calmed down after the outburst, standing placidly as the chains were applied and Bill screamed out his last. The session that followed left Romeo good for two years. Then he erupted again, throwing George Forepaugh against a wall in December 1869 and turning a dog that had befriended him into red pulp. George, bruised but otherwise uninjured, presided over the taking. "A child could drive him now with a rye straw," he pronounced when it was done.

There had been tension in the barn all morning. Far Stream could feel it radiating off the men as they prepared the block and tackle and laid out the ropes, as they paused for a smoke and to warm themselves by the coal stove, as they shot glances at Romeo chained.

She was facing the giant from the opposite side of the barn where they had moved her to keep her out of the way. She did not look at him. She kept her head down, eyes averted, but the energy pulsing off him penetrated her head just the same. It was the same incoherent rage that had turned him bad earlier that winter, the same glowering menace—and this morning, something that was new for Far Stream and even more upsetting. For the first time in her eight months with the circus, she felt dread percolating somewhere in Romeo's mind. Whatever was coming, a part of him feared it.

"All right," said George Forepaugh shortly after noon. "Let's get to it. Addie, you stay back now." This last was directed at Adam Forepaugh Jr., Adam Sr.'s indulged son. He had insisted on watching.

It began with the ropes being attached to the chains securing Romeo's legs. George aimed a shotgun into his face while this was done. "No!" he roared every time Romeo lashed out, punctuating the command by firing a load of rock salt into his trunk. The shattering blasts caused Romeo to bellow in rage and pain and kept him reasonably still. When everything was ready, the men who had been called in to help took up the ropes and started hauling, pulling Romeo's legs out from under him until he toppled onto his side and the whole building shuddered. Far Stream, already upset from the shotgun, backed further away.

Then the men started beating. They used pick handles and iron rods, striking on every part of Romeo's body. It was real labor and necessitated working in relays to make the punishment unceasing—an essential part of the process, George believed, giving the animal no respite in which to muster his strength and his courage. Pitchforks were also employed, thrust into Romeo's side, his legs and his haunches. Eph, unable to wield a club on account of his cracked ribs, took his turn one-handed with a fork. He had heard about how elephants were broken but had never witnessed the treatment. It was upsetting.

The punishment continued for an hour, then two hours, then three. Young Addie was taken home to his father and mother, deeply impressed by the spectacle but as hard as nails throughout. Four hours, then five, the smell of the men's sweat mingling with the pungency of the giant's struggle. Still Romeo resisted. He strained at the ropes and the chains and roared and lashed out, trying to strike them, to tear them, to gore them, to crush them. The men knew their business and kept out of his reach. There was no particular satisfaction in it. It settled into just another job after the nervous excitement of the start, a monotonous chore, like hauling water or chopping wood for the fire. They were methodically breaking Romeo down.

Far Stream did not watch. She had long since turned

away to face the wall. But she heard every grunt of effort, every roar of anger, every shriek of pain. There was no escaping the noise. It swept over her. It soaked into her like the winter coating of oil. It trampled down the vegetation that had grown on the trails of her mind, the growth masking what she had left in the forest. Hearing Romeo's struggle, she found herself back in the clearing, back in the enclosure on the day of her capture, back watching Grandmother and Red Moon struggle themselves to exhaustion. The returning memory made her whimper. Then she heard Mother urge her with crystal clarity, *Come with us*, and she started to bawl.

That attracted the attention of the men. "Put a stopper in it, Annie," they called over, amused. "We ain't touching you."

Romeo's ordeal continued on through suppertime, the beating unceasing, the blood steadily seeping, shadows playing across the walls as it grew dark and lanterns were lighted. Sandwiches were brought in and wolfed down by the men who were resting. When they were done eating they took up their clubs and set into the huge body again while the others fell back for a bite.

It was nearing midnight when Romeo finally surrendered. He gave up with a distinctive noise often described as a squeal, a high-pitched sigh that an elephant makes when it has had enough of disciplining and is ready to submit. When George Forepaugh heard it he raised a weary arm to stop the treatment. "Leave off," he said. "We got him."

"You sure, boss?" asked Eph, wary as George began to loosen the bonds.

"We got him. When he squeals like that you know you got him. Joe, go fetch him a pail of water."

Romeo was so exhausted that he was unable to rise and was clumsy with his trunk when he sought out the pail for drink. He lay in the same position the next morning, a square of light falling on him from one of the barn's small dirty windows. The ropes and pulleys that had been used to drop him were now repositioned to help him onto his feet. When he was up he stood with muscles trembling, looking miserable, his whole body aching, his spirit quite broken. He did not meet the eyes of the men as they dug the rock salt out of his trunk, washed off the blood and applied ointment to his many wounds. He did not resist when they examined the gouges the chains had dug in his forefeet. He remained still and silent, his head bowed low, a five-ton picture of subjugation.

Adam Forepaugh's Celebrated Museum, Caravan and Zoological and Equestrian Aggregation began its 1872 tour under four mammoth tents on April 1 in Washington, DC. In addition to the wonders of the previous season the show now featured a rhinoceros, an orangutan, crocodile and gorilla; a automaton group of Swiss bell ringers, the "far-famed Electrical Algerian Drummer" and other mechanized marvels; a representation of the Last Supper in which Jesus appeared to be breathing; wax representations of Charles Dickens, Otto von Bismarck and other luminaries in the Museum Department; and, for a limited time only, the renowned Siamese twins Chang and Eng, coaxed out of retirement for display with the conjoined Ohio pair billed as the Two-Headed Baby.

Far Stream was transported with Romeo the one hundred and forty miles from Philadelphia to Washington in a railway boxcar. When the six-day engagement was finished, she started walking. The next stop was Baltimore, forty miles. It was fortunately another six-day engagement so she was able to recover from the unaccustomed exertion before the circus packed up and moved on.

The schedule now became grueling, the show meandering west into Pennsylvania and then on to Indiana, a new town almost every day. For Far Stream, like the human employees, it was a return to a permanent state of fatigue bordering on exhaustion. After half a night's rest following the evening performance, George Forepaugh and Eph Parker would sleepily lead her and Romeo down dark roads for several hours of plodding to some new town. Another short rest, then the parade at mid-morning, Romeo carrying on his back something new for this season, a beautiful woman dressed as the Goddess of Liberty riding in a canopied howdah. Then is was back to the menagerie tent for public exhibition, a performance at two o'clock, the menagerie tent again for more noise and petting, a performance at seven o'clock, another short rest amidst the hustle and bustle, then back on the road for another walk through the night.

Far Stream kept walking. She put up with the pawing. And she remembered her lessons. When George now ordered her to "Sit up," she would assume the position beside Romeo and the crowd would clap louder. When he barked, seemingly just for Romeo, "You are dead, sir," Far Stream standing off to the side would crumple onto her side, eliciting roars of laughter as Eph did some wide-eyed mugging and George turned in feigned surprise and said, "Not you, Annie." But of course it was just what he had trained her to do. The hard-learned lesson had left a permanent mark.

As for Romeo, he remained satisfactorily subdued. But there was something wrong. The problem centered on his forefeet, the deep lesions caused by his repeated tugging at the chains he had worn for so many years. The wounds had turned putrid despite daily applications of salve and were visibly, audibly causing Romeo pain. He groaned his way through his act and he moved about stiffly. He groaned through the night marches and was exhausted when he arrived in each town. He was gradually wearing down, losing weight, growing sicker and sicker from the rot in his feet and the poison entering his system. By the time the show reached Illinois in the last week of May, it was clear that action had to be taken or he would soon die.

Chicago was the obvious place to perform an operation. The show would be appearing there for ten days, the longest stop of the season. With luck it would be enough time to get Romeo cut clean and back on his feet.

❧

Far Stream caught the first hints of devastation when they were still some miles from the city, a smoky tang wafting on a northeast breeze, the impression of a large body of water behind it. An hour further on and they were among the actual ruins, blackened timbers, crumbled buildings, fields of scorched collapse extending block after block.

"Ain't that something," breathed Eph beside her. And to George: "Hey boss, you ever seen something like that?"

Romeo did not seem to notice the ravages of the calamitous fire. He was laboring heavily along the soot-begrimed streets, on his last legs by the time they reached the lot overlooking the great lake. The tents were up but he and Far Stream were not led there, nor were they included in the parade. With Romeo unable to perform, they had both been temporarily removed from the program. They were instead taken to a small warehouse in a nearby freight yard, Romeo to be chained in the open space in the center, Far Stream tethered off to the side. Trains chugged and shrieked and clattered outside on into the evening and continued all through the night.

Veterinary surgeon R.J. Withers arrived the next morning. There would be no general anesthesia for Romeo, only a gargantuan dose of laudanum fed to him in some mash. With a knot of railway workers looking on, he was brought down onto his side and thoroughly chained, an easier task now that he was so weak. To keep him still, George Forepaugh held a pitchfork in his face. Eph guarded his trunk.

After a careful examination, Withers selected a large knife from his tool chest, freshly honed on an oiled stone, and proceeded to cut into the giant right foot. He quickly had several pounds of rotten flesh excised and was at the

58

seat of the corruption. After repeated jabs in the face, Romeo groggily settled and bore the pain with a low groaning, his great body quivering with each incision. Everyone was sweating now, for a furnace had been lit to heat up the irons.

The next step was to sear the flesh with hot irons to staunch the bleeding and hopefully destroy any putrefaction remaining. With the wounds so extensive, twenty irons were needed, repulsing Far Stream with one of the few smells she couldn't endure. She waved her head about but couldn't escape it. The men covered their noses.

Romeo was scarcely conscious when the ordeal was over. Ointment was applied and his wounds were bound up and his restraints removed so that he could stand back up when he recovered. But he didn't recover and he never stood up. He lay on his side for the next three days, his breathing shallow and increasingly labored, George and Eph hovering about him looking increasingly grim.

Romeo took his last shuddering breath in the middle of the night, Far Stream the only witness. It came after he raised his head for a moment and peered at something in the darkness and said, coherent for the first time, *What is this place?*

❧

The body was hauled to the show grounds and placed in a funerary pavilion decorated with evergreen boughs and flowers and draped with a velvety shroud. A solemn procession was made from the main tent after each performance for the rest of the Chicago engagement, a bit of Forepaugh theater, the cast of the show leading the audience in filing past the great form while the band played Handel's "Dead March."

Far Stream was included in the proceedings, the only animal present. She stood beside Romeo playing the part of the fallen hero's distraught young companion, a black sash about her chest to match the arm bands worn by the assemblage. "Let her go," Adam Forepaugh hissed when she began to move from her place during the first performance, reaching out with her trunk. She felt a need to touch the cold flesh. It was the way.

The show set out again for four months of mostly one-day engagements through Illinois, Wisconsin and Indiana. A new elephant, an African billed as Romeo Jr., was hastily acquired but proved a mediocre replacement, being neither as large nor as skilled a performer as its namesake. Far Stream felt little inclination to know him. He was a strange creature, low-slung head, gangly legs and grossly oversized ears, communing in a lilting inner language of complete incomprehension. He made no sense at all.

Her Baby Annie act in the meantime worked its way off the program, her modest repertoire of tricks not so impressive when presented on their own or paired with a trained pony which was tried for a week. Without Romeo's imposing presence the crowd's response was unsatisfactory. By the time the season ended and the show returned to Philadelphia for the winter, Adam Forepaugh had decided that the elephant act would have to be drastically reworked. He needed more of the animals, six or eight, a whole matching set. And they had to do something special.

Far Stream did not fit into his plans, at least not for the moment. To make something off her he decided to lease her out for the off-season, then perhaps work her back into the show in the spring.

It began with a visit by two men from New York, one short, rotund and balding, the other younger, tall and weedy, legs grown out of his pants. They followed Adam Forepaugh into the winter quarters barn and stopped in front of Far Stream and began to appraise her. Eph wasn't there.

"Bring her out, Matt," said the short one. The tall young man untethered Far Stream and led her from the stall for a closer examination.

"Your man knows elephants, does he?" asked Forepaugh. "This is a prime beast here. She needs to be properly cared for."

"Just come off Coles, sir," replied Matthew Stoddard without looking up from his probing.

When he was finished he fixed Far Stream with a stern gaze and told her to sit. The order confused her. She was accustomed to directions only from George Forepaugh or Eph. Where was Eph?

Stoddard tried again, then jammed his cane hard under her chin and roared, "Sit!"

She sat.

"I suppose it looks well enough," said the short man, named Mr. Freleigh. "What terms do you offer?"

"Eighty dollars a week, paid monthly," said Adam.

"Oh come now, Forepaugh, you can't be serious. Let us make it twenty and speak no more about it."

"Twenty ain't even in it, Freleigh. But I do like a stage show so I'll settle for sixty. Sixty dollars a week, promptly paid every month."

"Sixty? By God, not in this life or the next. Come, let us say thirty."

Adam, lips pursed, left the offer hanging and slowly began to pull on his gloves. Finally Freleigh relented and said, "All right, let us say thirty-five."

"Fifty."

"Forty."

"Forty-five."

"Done."

CHAPTER 6

PHINEAS FOGG STRODE ACROSS THE STAGE of New York's Bowery Theater, his French valet close on his heels. "Quickly, Passepartout," he cried. "We must get this train moving. We must reach Calcutta in time for the steamer or all will be lost."

It was the second act of Connelly and Pillet's stage adaptation of Jules Verne's wildly popular novel *Around the World in Eighty Days*. The scene was India, vividly realized in a backdrop painted in pastel shades giving the impression of depth. The audience, as usual for the Bowery, was boisterous.

"Why is this train stopped?" Fogg demanded of the conductor entering the scene from stage left.

"The railway's not finished." The matter-of-fact reply produced a wave of laughter.

"What! Not finished? But the papers announced the opening of the line all the way through."

"All the way but for the fifty miles from here to Allahabad. The line begins again there."

"You're stuck now," a voice sounded from somewhere near the back of the house.

There was nothing for it. Fogg and Passepartout would have to find another way onward, and quickly, if they were to reach Calcutta in time for the next sailing to Borneo Isle.

"We will continue on foot," Fogg pronounced after a

moment's reflection, drawing himself together for what would be a difficult march.

That was Far Stream's cue. She stepped into the light at the back of the stage, dwarfing the old mahout beside her and looking to the audience to be at least seven feet tall. She could not see past the footlights but she could hear and feel and smell all the people out there in the blackness, beyond the orchestra in the tiers that rose to the roof.

"Right there, Jimmy," whispered Matthew Stoddard from his hiding place behind the wooden bush nailed beside her. The five-year-old boy dressed as the mahout stopped and assumed the tableau position while Stoddard drew Far Stream close with the lead he held in his hand. When he had her in position he reached up with a thin rod, the end whittled sharp. Far Stream squealed before the point touched the wound he kept open behind her right ear. She had learned in the first week of the play that Stoddard wanted a noise and she loudly delivered. But still he kept jabbing, night after night, causing her pain. It made her angry. She squealed again and threw her head about, aggressive.

"That's it," murmured Stoddard.

"Monsieur," said Passepartout, apprehending Far Stream's squeal with an expansive gesture signifying a brilliant idea. "I think I have found another means of conveyance."

Far Stream was called upon to deliver two more squeals before the curtain was brought down eight minutes later. Stoddard then rose from his crouch behind the bush and led her off stage as hands rushed out to set up the next scene. She would spend the following hour waiting out of the way in the shadows, the child-mahout growing sleepy beside her, Stoddard seated on the floor, smoking his pipe. They would wait through Borneo, San Francisco, aboard ship in mid-Atlantic, then back to the Eccentric Club in London for Fogg's entry with "Here I am, gentleman," just as the hour was chiming. The curtain would then come down to applause, the cast would assemble on stage to take their bows and Far Stream and the child-mahout would make their final appearance. "Why, it's a *little* elephant," people in the audience would say in amazement. "It looked so much bigger. And that old Indian is only a boy."

After the show it was out the back door of the theater and into the stable down the alley where the sun never reached. It was nearly spring but Far Stream still minded the night chill. There was the usual shying from the horses, still unnerved by her presence. They were stupid creatures, no source of companionship at all. Stoddard threw down some hay and gave her some water, then went away, taking the light. He would be back in the morning with her sole comfort, a pail of mash.

Three weeks had passed and still she felt no bond with her new keeper. Stoddard did not seem to want it. He was a young man but hard, his mind a resentful, brooding affliction. His only words to her were barked orders, his only touch blows from his cane, his only method of training to force her into position before she had a chance to respond on her own. He did not seem to realize that she comprehended more than a fifty of his words and could follow most of his orders without physical prompting. He did not seem to understand that she could be clumsy and stiff in the morning, or that unnatural movements like rearing up on her hind legs were difficult to perform. If he would just give her time to work things out. But he wouldn't.

Saturday came. It was the busiest day of the week with two performances, a one-thirty matinee and the usual eight o'clock show in the evening, followed by a private appearance at eleven. There were gentlemen in New York who liked the idea of having an elephant at a party and William Freleigh, manager of the Bowery Theater, was willing to oblige for a price. When they returned to the stable behind the theater in the wee hours of the morning, Far Stream's head was spinning from the liquor that had been fed her and Stoddard was staggering, three dollars in tips in his pocket.

Around the World in Eighty Days was a hit at the Bowery, a grand spectacle of almost unprecedented proportions that filled the house nightly. It therefore came as a shock to Stoddard when manager Freleigh strode into the stables early the next week with the bad news.

"That's it. We're closing down. Take the beast back to Forepaugh."

"But Mr. Freleigh, we've been doing so well..."

"Of course we've been doing well," snapped Freleigh. "That's what's so God-damned aggravating about it. No, it's this legal nonsense, the Kiralfy Brothers with that prancing version they're putting on in Paris. They say copyright infringement and now they've got an injunction. So that's that. We're closing it down."

"But sir, you promised at least three months steady work."

"Oh come now, Matthew, you've been with the circus, you know this business, you know how it is. Now look." Freliegh reached into his pocket and withdrew five dollars. "Here. This should get you and the beast back to Philadelphia. You can keep whatever's left over. And leave an address with Henrietta. I'll send for you if we start up again."

Matthew Stoddard really had intended to proceed directly to Philadelphia with Far Stream as Freleigh instructed. He was going to do it the very next day, in the afternoon. But an opportunity turned up before he was able to lead her to the train, a chance to earn twenty dollars with one last private performance, twenty dollars that would go into his own pocket and not into Freleigh's, plus tips. Since it would delay his departure by only one day, he seized it. It seemed only just, considering that he had just been put out of his job.

But then another opportunity arose, and after that another, until a week had passed and there was no turning back.

❧

At Rolfe's Opera House on Sunday evening, Madame Birch-Pfeiffer's version of "Jane Eyre" was presented to a full house. We are sorry to say that Mrs. Jenny Kuester, who assumed the leading role, does not improve with acquaintance. Her artificial manner and awkward gesticulations were even more painfully apparent than on her first appearance. Owing to these defects the concluding scene provoked laughter from the audience instead of touching a deeper emotion. The performance was on the whole an unintended comedic prelude to next week's change, Belmont & Hathaway's Variety Congress. We are informed that the program will include illusionist and ventriloquist Signor Blitz, juggler and barrel performer Monsieur Gororx, singing clown Master Johnny and his clog dancing minstrels, and Professor Simpson and his elephant Zazu.

Far Stream arrived by train in Cleveland at noon on the first day of the week-long engagement. It was her twenty-seventh stop on the Belmont and Hathaway tour through the Midwest, the twenty-seventh venue where Matthew Stoddard would lead her onto a stage with a gaudy fringe constricting her neck and white rings around her eyes and introduce her as Zazu and make the most of her simple tricks with light banter.

Stoddard was a different man since their flight from New York. He had been nervous at first, leading Far Stream through the streets at night to the train. As they jolted west into Pennsylvania, however, he began to relax. Their first stop had been Pittsburgh. When Stoddard returned to the stable to claim her, his heavy growth of beard was gone, replaced by a clipped mustache. Then came a new suit, new hat, new cane, a pair of spectacles—and a new name, Professor Matthew Simpson, engaged by Belmont and Hathaway's touring outfit at sixty dollars a week.

The first performance had been a disaster, Stoddard so tense that he vomited before entering the theater, Far Stream tentative and awkward under his quavering hand. With repetition, however, they found their footing and the shouts of derision from audiences turned into appreciative laughter. By the end of the third week, as the Belmont and Hathaway troupe passed into Ohio, Professor Simpson and the sagacious Zazu were skipping through their act with assurance.

"It is said, ladies and gentlemen, that the elephant is fond of hard liquor," Stoddard would begin his lecture, his arm draped over Far Stream's back. "But this is not true. The fact of the matter is...." A secret poke behind Far Stream's ear and she would start shaking her head. "I said, Zazu, that this is not true." Another poke, another vigorous shaking of the head. "What's that, Zazu? You say it *is* true?" And so on.

The third evening of the Cleveland engagement began for Far Stream at seven-thirty with Stoddard coming into the stable and ordering her up on her hind legs. It was the most difficult trick he had taught her. The unnatural upright position applied pressure to her innards and prompted a bowel movement on the stable floor, a precaution before going on stage. She would perform the movement again at the close of the act.

Stoddard ordered her up with the same roughness he had used in New York, jabbing her hard with his cane. In other ways, however, he was gentler, less angry, less brooding. He now brought her occasional treats and even absently stroked her as he talked to himself about the farm he was going to buy once he had saved up the money, about how his parents would be proud, about how Irene would regret it. Then it was another walk down a dank alley and through a back door and across a floor that creaked under her weight;

another wait in the shadows, listening to the syncopated clatter of the clog dancing minstrels, Stoddard silent beside her; another booming introduction, "a sensation in Boston, Philadelphia, New York," another stage entrance to clapping and cheering; another disorienting experience of performing in front of people unseen beyond the glare of the footlights.

When it was over they proceeded to a downtown hotel to give a private performance. Stoddard rounded up one or two of these engagements every week, adding significantly to his earnings. The assembled guests when they arrived were already primed for enjoyment, the four tables in the dining room littered with bottles. They poured Stoddard a tumbler and settled back for the show, roaring with glee during the part about liquor. "Give 'er a drink!" they cried, bringing the act to a halt while Far Stream was served a huge tot. She downed it readily, the burning in her throat now a familiar and welcome sensation. When they saw how she really did seem to like it they called for a bottle of cheap whisky, doubling over with mirth when she upended it and drank the whole thing. A second bottle was produced, then a third, and she began to feel boisterous.

"Professor, I believe your elephant is drunk. Sit it up again. One more time. Sit it up."

Stoddard, by now tipsy himself and forgetting his stage accent, issued the order and poked Far Stream back onto her rump. She sat down heavily and tried to heave up her forelegs but her balance was gone. At the third attempt she toppled over, causing so much red-faced laughter that one of the men slid off his chair. Far Stream, lurching back to her feet, found it all very amusing. She staggered around and bumped into tables. She stuck her trunk in the punch bowl and filled somebody's hat.

By one o'clock in the morning the men had tired themselves out and the party had backed to a simmer, everyone sprawled comfortably in their chairs, talking and dozing,

Far Stream moving between them like a great pet. She slowly and unsteadily circled the table, stopping here and there to accept the offer of another drink, another roll, another crushed walnut, another affectionate stroke. "I would take you home," cooed the one who had fallen in love with her most, planting a kiss on the wet end of her trunk, "but my wife wouldn't have it. Oh, she's mean to me, Zazu, she's terrible mean. Made me a miserable man. Hey Harry, isn't Zazu the sweetest thing? Sweeter than any horse I ever had."

"Clumsy-looking brutes, though," observed the British gentleman the others called Alfie. "The way they shuffle about. Can't touch a horse for grace."

"Clumsy?" said Stoddard, slumped low in his chair. "You wouldn't say that if you seen as much of them as I have. When I was with Cole's I seen... I saw this one elephant trying to reach for a peanut on the floor. It was just out of its reach. D'you know what it did? It blew that peanut against the wall—it *blew* it—so that it bounced back and it could reach it. What do you say to that?"

"I don't doubt their intelligence for a moment," said Alfie. "But you have to admit that they're clumsy in their movements. Just look at Zazu there. Clumsy and slow."

"Slow! I guess you've not seen an elephant on a tear, friend. They'd run you right over. They can be fast when they want to."

Alfie fixed Stoddard with a wavering eye and an unsteady raised finger. "That may be, sir. But can your beast out-pace a man? I think not. I think not. It may have the advantage over the shorter distance, the wild onrush, the tear as you call it. But extend the distance, sir, extend it, and man will prevail." He glared defiantly for a moment before settling back in his chair, mumbling into his glass as he did so, "A man in a reasonable state of fitness, of course."

"Done some racing yourself?"

"A bit of heel and toe work," replied Alfie. "Years ago, of course."

Far Stream returned to Stoddard and with a feeling of infinite benevolence nuzzled him with her trunk. He absently fed her a biscuit as he mulled something over, taking note of Alfie English's middle-aged paunch and heavy gold watch chain. When the wheels were done turning, slowly done turning, he waved her away.

"Would you say that you're in a reasonable state of fitness, Mr. English?" he ventured.

Alfie replied without raising his chin off his chest. "I would, sir. Out riding every morning."

"What would you say then to a race?"

The head swiveled over. "A race?"

"A race. My beast's legs against yours. A go-as-you-please."

A long moment of dawning comprehension, then another of gathering firmness. Then Alfie leaned forward and gave the table a slap. "A race! Yes, by God, a race. Man against beast. The distance?"

"Five miles."

"Make it . . . make it three. The wager?"

"Fifty dollars."

"Make it a hundred."

❧

Far Stream's head was aching the next morning when Stoddard roused her from her stall and led her into the thin winter sunlight. The horse blanket thrown over her did not keep out much of the cold as they hurried down the street between mounds of grey snow, ice in the gutters, Stoddard impatiently waving the curious off.

There was a small crowd awaiting them in Monumental Park by the silent fountain in front of the courthouse. Most of the men from the previous evening were on hand, joined by friends who had caught wind of the unique contest and passersby who had stumbled on the scene, everyone buzzing excitedly, some arranging side bets. The challenger, Alfred English, was pacing around the dry fountain. He was hunched in an overcoat and looked nervous now that he was sober.

"Get a move on," he said testily upon the arrival of Far Stream with Stoddard. "Let's make a start of it before we all drop with the cold."

There was a huddle, Stoddard and English and some of the principal others, to confirm the parameters of the race. They would circle the promenade around the perimeter of the park, which measured one-fifth of a mile, for a total of fifteen rotations. That would make their three-mile distance. It would be go-as-you-please for both parties, meaning that English and Far Stream could run, walk, crawl or shuffle, whatever they found most convenient.

"You understand, of course," said Stoddard, "that I'll need to go alongside my animal to keep it moving." English frowned at this, noting the bull hook, but consented. It was the only practical way.

The crowd had swelled to nearly a thousand when the appointed starter bellowed out to everyone's delight, "All right then. Let us begin this unprecedented contest. Toe the line. Man and beast, toe the line."

Stoddard removed Far Stream's blanket and prodded her forward. English shrugged off his coat and moved alongside to assume an intense stance, head down.

"Ready... Hold your elephant there, Professor...

"Go!"

English was away and in the lead at a rolling gallop before Far Stream had taken a step. "Go on," Stoddard commanded, giving her a jab in the tender place behind her ear. She squealed and broke into a shuffle, Stoddard jogging along beside her. English was by now fifty feet in the lead. "Faster," barked Stoddard, giving Far Stream another hard poke. She squealed again and quickened her pace, her breath steaming from her open mouth.

They completed the first lap with English one hundred yards in the lead, Far Stream holding even, red starting to show on the side of her neck. They remained similarly positioned through the first mile and on into the second. Then the distance was closing. "Alfie's laboring!" Stoddard's backers shouted at him as he passed. "He's shot his bolt! He lit out too quick!"

Far Stream was laboring herself, breathing in ragged gasps. It had been a year since she had been on the road with Forepaugh, a year in which her body had grown unaccustomed to doing much walking. Stoddard's tormenting was the only thing driving her forward. His sharp jabs had opened the old wound behind her ear and the blood was now flowing. It stained the side of her neck, then it reached her leg, then it was leaving marks on the snow. A few concerned spectators called out, "Stop torturing that creature." The rest were too caught up in the excitement to care.

They were entering the penultimate lap, rounding the corner near the fountain where the crowd was thickest, when a man stepped into the middle of the promenade and raised his hand and commanded them, "Stop!" There were two policemen with him. Stoddard, who was himself straining hard now, ceased his prodding and allowed Far Stream to halt, her wheezing turning to bawling as she recovered her breath. English, who had just been passed, stopped as well and bent double, hands on his knees, coughing and spitting.

"Sergeant," said the man who had stopped them, addressing one of the policemen. "Do your duty."

⋘⋙

It was the first time that an elephant had been brought forward as evidence in the Cleveland courthouse. The case was unusual and thus newsworthy, which accounted for the theatrics.

A policeman led Far Stream up the stone steps and into the courtroom. She saw Matthew Stoddard sitting there, head down, hands clasped on his lap. As she was held in place, the judge called the veterinary surgeon forward to conduct an impromptu examination. "The animal is in no immediate danger," he concluded. "But it is unmistakable that it has been cruelly treated. There are puncture wounds behind its ear. And I note marks on its stomach that appear to be burns."

The judge thanked him and began to question the witnesses: the policemen who had made the arrest three days before, a concerned citizen who had witnessed the spectacle and now cast Stoddard black looks. Then it was Alfred English's turn to give the particulars of the bet and the contest. He did so in an advanced state of nerves and promptly fled the courtroom. He was not charged.

The judge turned to Stoddard, whom he still believed to be Matthew Simpson. "Professor Simpson," he said, "do you dispute any of the testimony that you have heard here this morning?"

"No, sir," said Stoddard, having been privately assured that he should expect only a fine.

"Any extenuating circumstances that you would like to relate?"

"Well, sir, I would just say that elephants must be handled in ways that would shock most people, but it's how it must be done. It's how it has to be done because..." He stopped, noting the judge's sour expression. "But I guess I shouldn't of driven her so hard."

"No, you shouldn't have. Anything else?"

"No, sir."

"Well, then. I hereby find you in violation of Section One of the Act to Prevent Cruelty to Animals, enacted by the General Assembly of the State of Ohio: 'That if any person shall overdrive, overload, torture, torment, deprive of necessary sustenance, or unnecessarily or cruelly beat, etcetera, etcetera, every such offender shall, etcetera, etcetera, be deemed guilty of a misdemeanor.'" The judge looked up from the law book. "Now, I believe it goes without saying that you overdrove this animal; indeed, that you . . . Yes?"

The last word was sharply directed at an older man who had entered the courtroom and was now standing in front of the bench, holding up a sheaf of papers. Far Stream knew him. It was the young black attendant hovering just behind him, however, that attracted her full attention. She ran toward him with a cry of delight, dragging the policeman holding her lead.

Eph Parker, smiling broadly, stepped forward to greet her and settle her down. "You're all right now, youngster," he whispered as she explored him with her trunk. "You're all right. You're all right."

"My apologies, your honor," said Adam Forepaugh, "but I have information here about the ownership of this elephant and"—a withering look at Stoddard—"about that low article sitting right there."

The judge beckoned him forward for a hushed consultation. "Let me see those," he said after a moment, beginning an irritated perusal of the papers. When he was finished he fixed his eye again upon the accused.

"Is your name in truth Matthew Stoddard?"

Stoddard hung his head and did not reply. He knew what was coming.

"I ask you again, sir. Is your name in truth Matthew Stoddard?"

An almost imperceptible nod.

"Speak up, sir."

"Yes."

"And were you in the employ in March of last year of a Mr. William Freleigh of New York City, manager of the Bowery Theater?"

"Yes."

"Speak up, sir."

"Yes, I was."

"You were charged with tending the elephant that was part of a theatrical production presented by Mr. Freleigh?"

Stoddard's shoulders sank even lower, so low that resignation set in and with it relief. "Yes, I was," he replied, looking up.

"And when you were instructed to return said elephant to Philadelphia, this elephant here, you made off with it instead?"

"Yes, I did."

The judge nodded gravely and made a notation, then removed his pince-nez. "Well, then, it would appear that this animal is the rightful property of Mr. Adam Forepaugh of Philadelphia. I therefore order it released into the hands of same.

"Now, as for you, sir." The judge returned to Stoddard. "With regard to the matter of cruelty already before us, I sentence you to a fine of one hundred dollars. With regard to this *new* matter, you are hereby charged with the theft of an elephant. Bailiff, remove him to the cells."

CHAPTER 7

SHE KNEW THAT SOMETHING was different even before she entered the winter quarters menagerie building. It was in the air, mixed with the smell of hay, dung and coal smoke. It was coming from somewhere inside.

"Come on, Topsy," said Eph Parker, urging her forward. It was a cold morning and he wanted to get into the warmth of the barn.

Topsy. That was Far Stream's new name, given to her by Adam Forepaugh after seeing how she had grown during her year-long disappearance. It was a reference to the hugely popular novel *Uncle Tom's Cabin* and the expression "to grow like Topsy" that it had spawned, meaning to shoot up quickly and without intention, much like a weed. "Have you ever heard of God, Topsy?" asks Miss Ophelia in the well-known scene. "Do you know who made you?" The unschooled slave girl gives a laugh and answers, "Nobody, as I knows on. I spect I grow'd."

They were inside the immense barn now, passing cages of sleeping bears, sluggish lions and panthers, tethered camels, some loud shrieking birds. And then Far Stream caught sight of them and stopped, unsure of her welcome.

"You got company now," said Eph. He allowed her a moment to gaze.

There were four of them, all larger than her. They were the first elephants she had seen since Romeo and his short-lived African replacement Romeo Jr., neither of whom had been a companion.

"This here's Betsy," continued Eph, leading her forward to the largest. "Betsy, say hello to Topsy."

The big female left off dusting and extended her trunk, a long patch of pink down the front, her wide head upright and commanding. She was eight feet high, more than three feet taller than Far Stream, and of a mature age. They touched—a profound gentleness from Betsy—and Far Stream felt a strong surge, so overwhelming that she was unable to answer.

"And this is Basil. I don't know why she's called Basil, because she's a lady. And this here's Duncan. And here's Dick. Say hello, Dick."

Basil was slightly smaller than Betsy, and older, some-what hunched at the shoulders. She had a long pendulous lip, one ear that flopped over and a fringe of brown hair on each of the two knobs on her skull. Duncan was a tuskless male, a half foot taller than Far Stream and two years older. They each reached out to touch her. She found them as communicative and as friendly as Betsy. Dick, a tusked male about twelve years old, was less so. When Far Stream brushed his trunk, aggressively thrust forward, she picked up a hint of danger behind the pushing playfulness that danced in his eyes.

Over the next few days she settled into place in the group. They were her new family; being among them made her happy. They could not replace what she had lost in the forest but they provided companionship and that was better than being alone.

Betsy, beside whom she was chained, was her new Grandmother, the one Far Stream considered the leader, the one to whom she directed her memories after overcoming her shyness—memories of family; of the terror of capture; of the journey across the ocean; of the sacrifice Sinkhole had made. The images that Betsy conveyed in turn of where she had come from seemed to contain flashes that Far Stream felt she recognized from her Mother, the flavor of places the family had visited in earlier times. Basil and Duncan, she decided, were also somehow distantly related to her home forest, the descendants of families that had once trod the same paths.

"Stop that, girl."

Betsy was at it again. She and Basil liked to play tricks. Eph—he was fully grown now, twenty years old and six feet four inches tall—was their favorite target. They would try to trip him with their trunks as he walked past or nudge him off balance as he worked around them or hide a pail or a shovel when he wasn't looking. He was wise to their ways and usually caught them before they could do any mischief. "Stop that, girl," he would say, annoyed but not really angry, and they would chuff with amusement. Far Stream enjoyed these sessions and was soon joining in.

George Forepaugh began working with Far Stream in the ring barn beside the menagerie building when her allotted three days to settle in were over. She pleased him with her ready responses, performing the tricks she knew, the saluting, sitting, kneeling and lying down. When George turned his attention to the others, however, it became evident that he was expecting much more. As Far Stream watched from the side, her four new companions embarked on the most astonishing series of revolutions, dancing together as George called out instructions, "Head couple. Right and left. Half promenade. Ladies change." Betsy and Duncan had mastered the movements and glided about the ring on their own. Basil, slightly less sure, required the occasional poke from an assistant. Dick, the most recent arrival before Far Stream, had to be physically—and not always happily—led through the steps.

After being allowed to watch the first session, Far Stream was incorporated into the performance. She was led about by Adam Forepaugh Jr., "Addie," now fourteen years, being groomed by his Uncle George to be the show's elephant boss, the boy-trainer sensation. His commands were to Far Stream a whirl of confusion, a series of steps and turns and circles that she could make no sense of, could not put together. "Turn left," Addie would order her fiercely, pushing her shoulder, kicking her leg. "I said turn left. Turn left. Turn left! Now straight. Keep going. Circle. Damn it, circle. Circle!" It was frustrating not understanding what it was that he wanted. It made her want to stop and not move at all. When she tried that, Addie jabbed her. When she became upset and even more resisting, it only got worse.

The lesson was repeated again that afternoon, another three hours for Far Stream of bewilderment and frustration, and punishments from Addie for being stupid. Then again the next morning and again the next afternoon and still no understanding, only mounting pressure and strain and then desperation, worse than anything she had felt under Stoddard learning his few simple tricks.

Finally, like something breaking inside, she could stand it no longer. At another touch from Addie's bull hook, only a light one, she lay down in the ring and her body started to heave as she blubbered.

"She's crying," said Eph, stopping with Dick and looking on in amazement.

"Elephants can't cry," said Addie.

George came over and knelt beside her, dumbfounded. He laid a hand on her side, felt the convulsive heaving, touched the tears that were streaming from her eyes down her cheeks. "That's all right, now," he said softly. "You just rest now and we'll try again tomorrow."

"You ever seen that before, boss?" Eph whispered, reverential.

"Nope," said George.

"Elephants can't cry," said Addie.

They were gentler with her when they resumed the next morning. It was the day that she began to comprehend what was expected and how she could learn it, watching Betsy and Duncan, mirroring their movements, responding at last to their urgings, *Follow me, follow me.* With this hurdle cleared, the routine began to stick in her mind over the course of the next weeks—so much so that she obsessively repeated some of the movements in the menagerie building at night. After a month and a half she had nearly mastered the dance and was well along with her role in the band act, contributing to the elephantine cacophony by banging on a drum. By the time George Forepaugh departed at the beginning of March to join another circus, Addie had everything in hand, a bigger and better elephant act for the coming season with himself as the world's youngest elephant trainer. All that remained to work on was the pyramid that would serve as the closing tableau.

There was also the baby elephant, which didn't yet require any training. Addie personally accepted delivery of it in New York City and brought it home in a crate.

"Oh, Add, you got it," gushed Eph, squatting before the small creature after they had it safely inside the barn and the doors bolted. "Lordy, it sure is small."

They led the little one over to meet her new family. Far Stream was delighted but had only a moment to greet it, a little boy, before it was pushed on to Basil and Betsy. Both were curious and friendly. Neither expressed particular motherly instincts.

"Maybe Basil's the more likely," suggested Addie after observing for a few minutes.

"I suppose," said Eph. He wasn't sure.

✍

A small crowd of newsmen assembled in the barn the next afternoon, summoned by Adam Forepaugh to bear witness to his latest marvel. "Other showmen," he began, hands on lapels in speechifying fashion, "may claim to own an elephant baby. But today, gents, today I've got a fair piece more. I present the first elephant ever born in these United

States. A suckling infant, come into this world just three days since, in this very building."

The waist-high creature was brought forward and the crowd closed in to pet him. No one noted the significance of how well he controlled his little trunk as he reached out and probed in their pockets, looking for treats.

"Born three days ago did you say, Mr. Forepaugh?"

"On Saturday, sir, in the middle of the night. He was standing there when my man come in the next morning. It surprised the hell... it surprised the life out of him. Didn't it, Eph?"

Eph nodded emphatically. "Yes, it did, Governor. Yes, it did."

"What's its name?"

"Haven't named him yet. Any ideas?"

"How about Young America?"

"Young America. Remember that, Addie. Young America. I like that."

"Which one's the mother, Mr. Forepaugh?"

"That big one on the end there. Basil. Never gave us the least indication."

"And which one's the father?"

"Well now, I suppose Dick would be the most likely. The one there with the tusks."

"It had to be Dick," said Addie, smirking.

"Mr. Forepaugh, can we see the little one take the tit?"

"He doesn't spend much time with his mother, and we can't push him. But he does suck several times in a day. Doesn't he, Eph?"

"Oh yes, Governor. Several times a day."

"How much would you say he's worth?"

"Why, I wouldn't take twenty thousand dollars for him—or *fifty thousand* if it was coming from Barnum. I reckon that makes him well nigh on to priceless."

The new arrival and the treats from the newsmen left Far Stream and the others feeling playful after the monotonous confinement of the long winter. It was Basil who started the fun after the visitors left, catching Eph's foot and sending him sprawling. His cursing as he picked himself up added to their good humor. Duncan next snatched the hat off the head of one of the menagerie workers, a man named Skunky, and flung it to Betsy who flung it again.

Then Far Stream noted the cap and the jacket that Addie had left on a chair before stepping out. She was the nearest to it. Inwardly chuckling, she picked up the cap. It was Addie's pride and joy, part of his new ring outfit, a gold braid-adorned copy of the cap worn by his Uncle George.

Stop.

It was Betsy, eying her sharply. Far Stream, caught up in the moment, kept on destroying the cap, then picked up the jacket.

Stop.

She held the jacket under her foot and, using the finger on the end of her trunk, began to pluck off the buttons.

Stop.

She had all the buttons off. She could hear Addie now. He was returning. She quickly replaced the jacket on the chair and set the smashed cap on top and returned to her place.

"Eph," cried Addie. "Come on in here. Let's get..."

He caught sight of his ruined cap, wet with elephant spit. He picked it up, turned it over. Then he examined his violated, buttonless jacket. Far Stream, seeing his consternation, started expressing her mirth.

"Why you god-damned whore," roared Addie, snatching up the blacksnake whip he favored and coming at her with the weighted handle, full force. The attack stunned her for a moment. Then she instinctively protected herself, lashing out with her trunk and knocking him off his feet. Eph saw it happen. He came racing over, pitchfork in hand.

"Watch her," Addie commanded, rising from the barn floor and brushing himself off. He advanced again on Far

82

Stream, this time slowly, radiating menace.

"Keep that fork on her. Let her feel it."

He started beating.

"That's probably enough, Add," said Eph after the first dozen blows.

Addie didn't stop.

"That should do, Add. She's learned her lesson."

Addie stopped, his chest heaving. He began walking around Far Stream, hands on hips, still simmering with anger. And then he had her by the tail, twisting it in a loop, drawing it tight.

He yanked hard. There was a crack.

The pain was so intense that Far Stream lurched forward, the points of the fork piercing her trunk as Eph was forced to step back. Then she was running wild about the practice arena, around and around, squealing and thrashing and bawling. When she finally slowed and then stopped, she continued to whine.

"You'll remember that now, won't you," said Addie, approaching. Far Stream cowered before him. When he held out his hand she presented her trunk. When he moved in close she allowed herself to be petted.

"You broke her tail," said Eph, sullen.

"She'll be good now," said Addie.

≈୧୨∽

The training intensified for it was now March, the new season scheduled to start in just a few weeks. For the horses it meant long hours of ring practice, trotting in endless circles as their riders balanced, leaped, posed and occasionally took bruising falls. For the lions there were visits from Adam Forepaugh's younger brother Andrew, billed as Professor A.J. Forepaugh, wild beast tamer. They did not attack him when he entered their cage because they feared the iron bar that he carried, thrust in the stove and heated to just short of red-hot. "Stay back!" the Professor would command, cracking his whip in their faces. They knew what a hot iron bar felt like. They stayed back.

For Far Stream, work continued with the dancing, music and tricks, twice-daily sessions until she had the act fully memorized and could perform it without guidance. It was salute to the left, salute to the right, walk with the others in a line like soldiers, ten steps, turn right, ten steps, turn left, face Duncan, bow, step to the left, pirouette, three steps forward, circle around Duncan, three steps back and so on through the dance, then pick up the drumstick, watch Addie for the signal, bang, bang, bang, bang, sit up, lie down, onto her knees, one step following another until the twelve-minute act was complete.

Or almost complete. She was slow to master the closing tableau. So were the others. It was a five-elephant pyramid, Betsy standing in the center to serve as the base. When she was in position, Far Stream and Duncan were to climb up onto high pedestals, one on either side, and place their fore-feet on Betsy's back. Basil and Dick were then to climb onto lower pedestals farther out and place their forefeet on the higher pedestals to complete the effect.

Duncan was the first to master the climb up onto the pedestal to form half of the pyramid's apex, forefeet on Betsy. Far Stream refused to do the same on the opposite side. The upper pedestal was five feet off the ground and it scared her. After several failed attempts, stalled between the lower and upper pedestals, she broke away and re-treated to the far side of the ring. She was forced to return. "Up," Addie commanded, tapping her feet. Far Stream stepped onto the lower pedestal. That was not hard. "Up," Addie repeated, this time indicating the higher perch. "Up. Up." Some sharp jabs. "Up. Get up there. Get up. Get up."

Whining with fear, she finally heaved herself onto the top pedestal and managed to maintain her balance, all four feet crowded together on the small platform. Now came the worst part, Addie indicating Betsy's back, tapping Far Stream's forefeet and ordering her again, "Up."

84

They kept at it for a week, Eph cautioning Addie to be patient. "She'll learn it," he said. "She just needs to get her mind set right to being up there." And she did. After a great deal of fearful hesitation, Far Stream at last stepped across the void and got her feet positioned on Betsy. Duncan was then brought forward and positioned on the opposite side and the pyramid was half built.

Attention then turned to Dick and Basil. Their pedestals were lower but there was still fear. More repetitions of "Up, up, up," flashes of resistance met with sharp blows, and they learned. They learned to perform the mid-air straddle between the two pedestals without hesitation, trunk raised at the order from Addie.

"That's worth a hundred thousand dollars," Adam Forepaugh the elder pronounced after watching the complete performance once through. "But get on top there, Addie. Climb up on Betsy's head. Show your domination."

Addie saw the perfection of it even before his father was done speaking. He was in position in a moment, head back, arms spread wide.

"Now there's magnificence," said Adam Sr. with satisfaction. "Look at that, boys. That right there is *splendor*."

CHAPTER 8

THE HORSE-DRAWN WAGON DAYS for Adam Forepaugh were over. His show when it embarked from Philadelphia in April 1877 did so for the first time by train, carried in custom-built, extra-long rail cars. Forepaugh had ordered them the previous summer, enough to form two trains pulled by thirty-ton steam locomotives. It amounted to a huge investment, particularly with the show coming off two years of slim profits. Forepaugh was confident that it was money well spent. Moving his aggregation by rail would increase the distance he could travel between engagements, allowing him to concentrate on bigger towns while tightening up his schedule at the same time, a new place every day, six days a week. It would also save on the horses that would otherwise drop dead hauling his wagons, as many as five a day in the hot weather. And it would eliminate the expense and inconvenience of putting the company up in hotels. Everyone would now bunk in the train.

The first of Forepaugh's two trains, the one that preceded, was composed of twenty open-topped gondola cars, painted white with "Forepaugh's Menagerie and Circus" in red letters. These were used for hauling the Golden Chariot and the other show wagons, the poles and ropes and stakes and canvas, the cook tent and accoutrements and miscellaneous baggage. The second train included passenger cars with upholstered seats for the performers and workers, two

Pullman "palace" cars with tiers of bunks for sleeping, more gondola cars for the canvas-draped animal cages, and freight cars for carrying the rest of the show.

Far Stream jostled along in one of the freight cars—the "Elephant Palace Car," the show called it. She and her dancing companions and the baby elephant entirely filled it, with just enough room left for a too-short bunk at one end for Eph. Powerful odors whipped back from the camels and the rhinoceros and hippopotamus in the car forward, occasional murmurs from the cages of lions and leopards behind. She was used to it now after two months, nine states and twenty-five stops; used to the swaying and jolting, the clackety-clack of iron wheels on iron, the shriek of the whistle, the acrid smoke from the engine, the hours of waiting in rail yards listening to banging, bumping and shouting as the train was unloaded and loaded, unloaded and loaded, unloaded and loaded again and again.

Used to it—but that did not help her sleep. She was like Dick, kept on edge by the motion and noise of the train.

Occasionally, to help pass the time in the darkness, Betsy or Basil would share stories of great beings; stories of creation, endurance, sacrifice, caring. Far Stream was old enough now to flow with the river of their images and thoughts, the river that was the history that they could remember. She learned of a courageous matriarch named Burned who had come generations before Betsy—Betsy who was known to her own as Hunger Valley. She learned of a great aunt in Basil's long-ago family who saved her baby from tigers and subsequently died of her wounds. It was her death that was commemorated in Basil's name, Strong One Passes. Far Stream absorbed these and other stories as if her own, filling the vacant rooms in her mind where her own history would have resided had she lived with her family long enough to learn it. As it was she could not remember the many things her grandmother Found the Salt had conveyed, or the significance of her mother's

87

name, Long Way Down, or the stories behind why her aunts were named Into the Mountains, Man's World and Seven Were Taken.

She was like Dick, also captured at a young age. She remembered only the names.

✍✎

Next stop, the twenty-sixth of the season, was Wichita, Kansas. The show was further west now than ever before. Eph got up from his bunk and stretched as the train screeched to a halt and then a final jolt in the depot. "Lordy," he mumbled, opening the door and surveying the raw town, "the Governor's picked a dodgy one this time." He walked back to the horse car, past the crowd of locals gathering to watch, and returned in a few minutes on horseback.

"Okay, Betsy," he called. "Step out, girl."

Betsy rode nearest the door and exited first. She moved stiffly to the opening and lowered a cautious foot to the block step that Eph had positioned, then another, then her whole body was out, the car swaying as it was relieved of her weight. Shouts outside now, "An elephant, an elephant," people running to see.

Dick went next. After chaining him to Betsy, Eph called for the others in turn. When Far Stream heard her command she stepped down and out and took her place beside Duncan and began her usual probing. It was like any other railway siding going back through Missouri, Indiana, Ohio, Pennsylvania and Virginia, tarry ties and rusty rails, sooty stones, cinders, bits of debris.

Young Addie, co-manager of the show now in addition to being head elephant trainer, cantered over from where he was overseeing the horses.

"Where to, boss?"

Addie pointed to a dirt road veering away from the rail yard. "Right down there. We got a nice flat lot down by the river."

"Mile up," Eph commanded, getting Betsy and Dick moving forward, Far Stream and Duncan falling in behind. There were spectators on both sides now, open-mouthed gawking, as they made their way down the road, boys running alongside and occasionally getting too close.

"Best stay back there," Eph cautioned, careful to keep it friendly. There had been an incident the week before, an eight-year-old with a broken arm courtesy Basil. It had been the boy's own fault, getting in the way of an animal outweighing him by three and a half tons, but it still cost Adam Forepaugh seventy-five dollars to placate the parents.

The tents were up, the lot nearly ready, the smell of steaks, potatoes and coffee strong in the air. After chaining the elephants in the menagerie tent and laying out food, Eph hurried off for his own breakfast at the cook tent where the red flag was flying. As Far Stream ate, workmen wheeled the thirty-six traveling cages of animals in and positioned them in an oval around the periphery of the tent. Only the lion cage was left out, ready to be hitched to a team of four horses.

Eph was back at eight-thirty. He draped Far Stream and each of the others with purple blankets, then jogged over to the property man when his number was called to collect the Biblical robe and headgear that was his parade outfit. When everyone and everything was ready, A.J. Forepaugh climbed in with the lions and the assembly set out on a meandering tour along Wichita's principle streets, Adam Forepaugh leading the way in his carriage.

Thousands lined the route to watch. Some, clad in their best clothes, had traveled by train from nearby towns for the day. Others had come on wagons or horseback from outlying farms, pitching camp outside town and planning to stay a few days. For many it was the first time to see a big circus. They said things like, "Look at them painted donkeys." And, "Those aren't donkeys. Those are zebers." And when the elephants passed: "Just think what one of those feet would do to your head."

Far Stream ignored them, favoring the mildly interesting odors, the clop of Eph's horse close on her left. She preferred it when Eph stayed close and protected her from the people. What came from him soothed her. When they rounded a corner and Eph lagged back and Addie drew close, she veered away slightly. "Come in," Addie commanded, drawing her back in line.

They were back on the lot at ten o'clock in the morning. Two hours of relative peace and quiet followed, sounds outside continuous but the public not yet admitted inside the tent. Far Stream ate for a while, watching as Betsy and Basil took turns distracting Dick while the other filched mouthfuls of his hay. They took pleasure in the stealing. One of the performers, a lady rider named Molly, stopped by with her daily treat, today a soft biscuit slathered with butter. Far Stream savored the morsel and reached out for another. When Molly was gone she lay down and slept.

One o'clock, the entrance open, a rush of people and no more dozing. Talking, pointing, hands extended with offerings, most taken, some rejected. She knew she should not put anything casually in her mouth when it came from a stranger but the hubbub around her could be numbing. Sometimes she made a mistake.

Not today. Today is was Duncan who ate a potato packed full of red pepper. He thrashed his head about to rid himself of the burning, bumping into Far Stream and making her stagger while a young man and his companion laughed at the joke. Eph fetched a pail of water for Duncan while Addie restored order.

"I'll ask you not to do that again," he said coldly.

"I'll do what I like," taunted the prankster, fifty pounds heavier and three-quarters drunk. Addie took note of his face.

Two o'clock and the afternoon performance, then back to the menagerie tent. The show ended and the sound of people filtering away, excited chatter, bursts of laughter, snatches of song. Voices behind the tent now, men passing around a bottle, muffled talking, rising agitation, a scuffle, the indentation of a back against the canvas, the owner leaning over, gasping and spitting.

It's approaching eight o'clock now, getting dark. The second surge of visitors to the elephants is thinning. Then, with a final rush, they are gone, hurrying off to the big top for the start of the evening performance.

Here is Addie. He's wiping off the weighted handle of his whip. He says to Eph, "I found that mouthy bastard. He's not grinning now." He dons the jacket and gold braid-adorned cap he wears in the show. Eph puts on a black and scarlet outfit, cap matching Addie's minus the gold braid. They get Far Stream, the four others and the baby elephant—they've taken to calling him "Chicago"—lined up in order of size and lead them outside for the opening procession. Soft murmurs of conversation, animal snorts and snuffles as they wait in the twilight, the sky in the west an orange glow fading to violet. Off to the side there are no more smells from the cook tent. The workmen are taking it down. They work with speed and precision, the only sound the occasional curt order.

The band strikes up and the procession moves forward. Far Stream passes through the entrance and into the light, following Duncan around the arena, baby Chicago tagging behind. The announcer is holding forth, laying out for the audience the unparalleled sights they will witness in the coming two hours. Far Stream plods on, mindful of Eph at her side and Addie in front. She doesn't look around at the audience, a blur in her peripheral vision. Then she is passing out through the exit, out into the twilight and back to the menagerie tent. She waits here as it grows dark, swaying, idling picking at the last of the hay, throwing it onto her back. The baby, on a long tether, wanders close by. She extends her trunk to caress him.

91

The workmen have finished with the cook tent and side-show. They appear now with wagons, hitches and canvas to get the animal cages ready for hauling back to the train. Overhead, the flickering chandeliers are lowered, extinguished and packed. Then the quarter poles come down, the canvas sagging, supported by only the center pole and the ones at the side. It is dim inside now, light coming from a half dozen lanterns.

Nine o'clock. Eph gives Far Stream her second quick brushing of the day and moves on to the others. Basil especially likes to heap hay on her head. Then it is time to return to the main tent for the evening performance.

Her entrance with the others is greeted with enthusiastic applause. Circus audiences like elephants, even more so when they perform. At Addie's command she launches into the preliminary tricks, the kneeling down and sitting up, the playing lame and lying on her side on command. Then the band begins the waltz. She raises her feet high and starts prancing. An excited response from the tiers of onlookers, for she and her four companions appear to be actually dancing in time to the music. The effect is achieved by musical director Tony Frank subtly adjusting the tempo of the piece to match their movements. Betsy and Basil as usual are not as sharp as in rehearsal. They know that Addie cannot punish them in front of the crowd. Far Stream, much younger, is less wily. She raises her feet high and gives the performance her best.

Next comes the band act, Far Stream banging on the drum, Duncan tinkling a triangle, Dick shaking a bell, Betsy grinding away on a hand organ, Basil tooting a horn. And then the finale, the five-elephant pyramid, equally pleasing. Far Stream is now used to the procedure, assuming her position with caution but no overt hesitation. She stands facing Duncan, forefeet on Betsy, she waits while Dick takes his position behind her and Addie climbs up on top in the center, she waits through the applause and the cheering, then she carefully steps back down and resumes her place in line with the others. "The Forepaugh performing elephant herd, ladies and gentlemen!" are the announcer's last words as she passes back into the night.

The menagerie tent is down when they exit, the poles loaded, the canvas being rolled up. Eph, back in his work clothes, takes them straight to the rail yard. Far Stream shuffles up the incline from the river toward the lights of the town, the road bathed a soft grey by a half moon. Behind, a collective shout of alarm from the main tent, then cheering. Conwell and Stowe are engaged in their death-defying leaps. The music from the band is fading now in the distance. It stops, there is a hush, then scattered oohs and aahs, then another crescendo of cheering.

They stop at a trough and Eph allows them to drink. For a moment the only sound is of sloshing, blowing and sputtering. When they are done Eph leads them on to the rail car, lights the soot-blackened lantern at the end and orders them inside, the car swaying and creaking with each heavy step. Far Stream resumes her place between Dick and Duncan and Eph attaches her leg chain to the ring affixed to the car's frame. When they are all secured, he lights his pipe and sits on the edge of his bunk for a smoke before heading off to the rest of his chores.

Eph is gone, the car door shut, Far Stream and her four companions standing alone in the darkness. Outside, wagons rumble by, hauling the show back to the train for reloading. It will take three hours to finish the job, until two o'clock in the morning. The train will leave at three. It will arrive at the next stop at six. The process will then begin all over again.

৵৶৽

"It's Dick, boss. He's acting up."

Addie, summoned from the lot where the tents were coming down in another town in another part of the country, surveyed the situation from horseback. It was close to midnight. A dozen men were looking on from a safe distance, some holding lanterns, the soft orange light illuminating Dick planted in front of the elephant car, blocking the door.

Far Stream was standing with Betsy and the others off to the side. She was wide awake and watching, alarmed by the musth aggression that had burst forth from Dick after three days of build-up. He was coming into that time of life.

"I think he's got a spell coming on," said Eph. "Damn fool won't get in. And he won't get out of the way."

Addie, still astride his horse, rode up to Dick— recklessly up to Dick. "Step in," he ordered. Dick shifted slightly but held his ground, his feet splayed, indicating that he wasn't moving one step. He feared Addie most but to-night other feelings were stronger.

"Step in," Addie repeated in his menacing voice, mov-ing closer to use his whip handle. "Step in," this time with a jab behind the ear.

The prod set Dick off like a nerve being touched, the electric surge of his rage so powerful that Far Stream took an involuntary step back. He wheeled about and knocked Addie off his horse and sent him sprawling onto the siding, stunning him with the blow and the impact of the fall. He was bellowing now, trunk raised, displaying, warning. Far Stream started blaring as well, upset.

The other men stood frozen. Addie lay helpless, within reach of an enraged elephant with three-foot-long tusks.

Kill him, said Duncan, in a sullen mood himself lately.

Leave him, said Betsy at the opposite end of the line.

Dick took a step forward, flailing his trunk and trumpet-ing fiercely. He was nearly on top of Addie. All he had to do was thrust down his head or stamp his foot and the young trainer would be dead.

Movement off to the side. It was Betsy. She was charg-ing. Head lowered, she threw all her weight, four full tons, against Dick, knocking him down. When he tried to strug-gle back to his feet, she came at him again, again butting him down.

The blows stunned Dick and took the edge off his anger. While he was down Addie scrambled up and commanded Betsy to lower her trunk and raise him onto her back like she did in the show. Eph did the same, riding forward on Basil. They moved in on either side of Dick and pressed in close, keeping him still while he was thoroughly chained.

The subduing, short and intense, was done right there on the siding, a length of canvas erected to screen the proceedings from a public unused to such things. Dick, already half beaten by Betsy, squealed his surrender after only ten minutes. Within an hour he was chained inside the car, three shadowy forms down from Far Stream, his head hanging low. She could smell the musk of his spent anger and the pine sap in the ointment Eph had applied to his wounds.

"You brought it on yourself," Eph had scolded. "You think I like doing that? I don't. It's because you caused us trouble. Now, you stay settled and do as you're told and we'll have no call to do it again."

❧

The show continued on in its circuitous journey to the West Coast, doubling back through Kansas, Missouri, Iowa and Wisconsin before returning to a westward track through Nebraska, Wyoming and Utah. By the middle of August Far Stream had traveled the better part of ten thousand miles; she had been unloaded from her car and reloaded again eighty-five times; she had paraded through the streets of eighty-five towns, performed in more than two hundred shows and been examined up close by a quarter million people.

It was in Wyoming that the price of a ticket to the show was doubled to one dollar. The change was not appreciated by all. It was this that may have led, several stops later in Utah, to the call of "Hey Rube."

Far Stream did not see the initial scuffle at the start of the evening. It occurred at the entrance to the main tent when a group of young men tried to force their way in without paying. There was some shoving and cursing before they were kicked off the lot, but no open fighting. That came later, when the men returned in the dark, armed.

The evening performance was over and the lot was quiet, everyone enjoying an uninterrupted night of rest thanks to the two-day engagement. The attack began with the sound of ropes being cut, two men working on the main tent, two on the menagerie canvas.

One of the night watchmen spotted them. He was the one who cried out, "Hey Rube!" It was the circus call to arms, the alarm-cry that the show was being attacked.

The first to respond were the canvas men sleeping in the tents or under the stars. They leaped up and seized whatever was handy, mainly spare tent stakes, five feet long and as thick as ax handles, and rushed out to drive away the attackers, taking up the "Hey Rube!" cry as they went.

They were soon joined by others who had been sleeping in the Pullman cars in the rail yard, thankfully nearby, until there were forty or more hardened circus men attacking the attackers. They went at them with a ferocity that was stunning, swinging with stakes and whips and canes and bare fists, swinging despite the occasional gun shot, swinging hard to cave in heads and break bones.

Far Stream knew what was coming as soon as she was roused from sleep by the first cry of "Hey Rube." She had heard it before and it scared her. She heaved herself onto her feet and stood alongside the others in the light of the single night lantern, quiet, apprehensive, listening to the shouts and blows and running and confusion outside. It ebbed and flowed around them and was occasionally thrown up against the canvas. Then the pitch was changing, lowering in tone, becoming more deliberate. The show people had the situation in hand now and were methodically cornering and pummeling the attackers who had not yet run off.

A young man fled into the menagerie tent. He ran inside, breathing in ragged gasps, trying to reload a pistol with shaking hands. "Stay back," he said, his voice strangled, coming to a stop in front of Betsy and turning on his half dozen pursuers.

"You only got one shot in that pistol," hissed one of the roustabouts, coming to a halt. There was blood on the end of his tent stake.

The man with the pistol was no more than eighteen. Far Stream could smell the liquor he had been drinking and the fear oozing out. "Stay back," he repeated, waving the pistol around, backing away from them, backing up against Betsy.

The glancing blow from Betsy's trunk struck him in the small of the back and spun him around. The pistol, swung wildly, discharged, sending a slug creasing along Betsy's cheek and piercing a hole through her ear. She made no sound, gave no indication of pain, took no step backward at the roar of the blast. Instead she seized the young man by the wrist and squeezed until there was a crack and the pistol dropped to the ground. Then, as he struggled, she drew him in close.

Addie was on the scene now. He didn't run for a pitchfork. He simply said, without much urgency, "Stop it, Betsy. Let him go."

Betsy didn't listen. She forced the man under her forefoot and held him down.

"Let him go, Betsy."

She didn't listen. She took the man's arm in her trunk, tore it off his body and cast it aside.

Everyone took a step back. A shocked silence punctuated by screaming but still no movement for the pitchforks.

Addie's voice grew sharper. "All right, Betsy, that's enough now. Stop it. Stop it."

She didn't listen. The pinned man continued to struggle, his one remaining hand pushing with utter ineffectuality at her foot as he gasped out high-pitched animal noises.

Betsy lowered her head.

"Betsy..."

It was too late. With terrible deliberation she pressed her head down on the chest, down until there was no more screaming, down until the ribs were all broken, down until the torso was flat in the dirt.

And then she stopped. She raised her head and backed away, returning to what was left of her hay. Within minutes she was throwing it about, swaying, idly chewing as if nothing had happened.

It was the first time Far Stream had seen one of her kind kill a man. It had been effortless. Easy. After the excitement and the upset had subsided, she too began rummaging in her hay as the body was buried there in the tent and dirt scattered over. Eph and Addie then shifted her and the others forward to pack down the earth, obliterating the traces. When the men were gone and the tent was once again quiet, she lay down to sleep over the hidden remains.

And she dreamed.

CHAPTER 9

THEY WERE WANDERING along the green banks of a river, the far side a featureless ribbon of grey haze in the dawn. The grass was lush here, long and tender and sweet. Far Stream worked her way through the patch that seemed to go on forever, enjoying each mouthful, pausing occasionally to swish about with her trunk and add to the family's shared inner hum of pleasure. There was no hunger here, no fear or anxiety. Only contentment.

Mother was a short distance ahead, in a cluster with Man's World, Seven Were Taken and the baby, Flowers for Lightning. The little one was starting to eat now, augmenting his diet of milk with mouthfuls of grass. He took a few playful bounds just as Far Stream looked up, then reared about and bounded back and ran into the leg of his mother and toppled awkwardly over. Far Stream flicked her trunk at her sister Red Moon beside her and they shared the amusement.

The sun was well up now, the air humid and clear, the cicadas beginning their drowsy day buzzing. And then the wonderful fragrance of ripe mangoes, drifting on the west breeze from somewhere nearby. Far Stream and Red Moon, followed closely by Red Moon's child Darkness at Day, meandered in that direction and soon came to the source, two trees heavy with red fruit. They swept up everything that had already fallen, squeezing the soft plump ovals between their molars and savoring the juice, then they plucked at what was hanging above until they had both trees stripped bare.

Come here.

It was Grandmother. She was calling them back to the river. Far Stream filled her mouth one last time before turning to leave, lagging behind Red Moon and Darkness at Day as she smacked over the last tasty morsels. The way took her through a patch of green melons, too delectable to pass by. She paused to sample them and found them to be perfect. She stayed longer to eat a few more.

When she looked up, Red Moon was gone.

She hurried along in the direction her sister had taken and soon found herself back at the river. She could see Red Moon and Darkness at Day joining the others, all of them some distance downstream. Grandmother was advancing into the water. She was leading the family to the far side of the river, a very great distance, a very long swim. *Follow me*, she was saying. The others casually trailed behind her, spouting loudly as they waded in.

Far Stream broke into a scurrying shuffle to catch up. It wasn't so very far but try as she might she couldn't seem to get any closer. It took a tremendous effort to advance just a few steps. *Follow me*, said Grandmother, casting a look in her direction before pushing into deep water. She was swimming now, her trunk held high. Far Stream kept trying to move forward, increasingly anxious, struggling hard to get closer.

She could scarcely see Grandmother's head now, bobbing in the water as she swam toward the far bank, the others in a straggling line behind her. *Follow us*, they called back to Far Stream before disappearing. With a tremendous effort she managed to reach the edge of the river where they had entered, trodden down and rich with their smells. She was crying now, pleading with her family to wait. She strained forward as if fighting her way through deep mud, forward until the water was lapping at her legs, was touching her chest, was up to her shoulders.

She plunged down.

☙☙

Far Stream woke with a start, her cheeks wet, her heart pounding. She laid in the darkness, gradually becoming aware of the breathing around her, the loud snores of Betsy foremost, beneath that the distinct whistling of Bismarck and the wet sputters from the baby with a cold in her chest.

She heaved herself onto her feet.

Seasons had passed. She had grown bigger. She now weighed four thousand eight hundred pounds, nearly two and a half tons, and stood six feet five inches high at the shoulder. She was fourteen years old.

The Great Forepaugh Show, as it was now called, had also grown bigger. The tents were bigger, the parade was grander, the performance was more spectacular with two rings and a stage of simultaneous action, the menagerie was expanded to include many more creatures—and the elephant herd was immense. "Twenty-two Trained Elephants!" newspapers advertisements now boasted. "More than have ever been seen together in any Christian land!"

Bismarck was among them. He was an African with oversized ears and a sag in his back that Far Stream found foreign and an inner voice that she could not comprehend. He was a male and approaching the age where males start to cause trouble. But he had yet to do so. For the time being his temper remained mild—certainly better than Dick's.

Another addition arrived in February 1881 by train from San Francisco, stinking of the fermenting stable compost that had been shoveled around her for the long winter journey. It had been done to keep her from freezing, the railway company having not allowed a stove in the freight car. She was led inside the winter quarters building and fed a pail of whisky and water to warm her while Far Stream and the others looked longingly on. She was dark and somewhat scrawny. The men called her Rubber.

Ten more elephants arrived a few days later. They had been collected by the renowned German animal dealer Carl Hagenbeck and sent across the Atlantic to New York by steamer. The shipment included elephants Jennie, amiable and nearly full grown; a smallish male named Gold Dust who befriended Duncan; a new baby Chicago to replace the previous baby, now dead; yet another Romeo, a female this time, the third Romeo Far Stream had known; a female African named Mongo for pairing with Bismarck; and a male Asian named Rocks with a propensity for trying to squash his keepers flat against walls.

Next came Bolivar, a giant tusked Asian, the biggest elephant Adam Forepaugh had ever acquired, purchased at the auction of the Van Amburgh circus in December 1881 for $7,100. He would be the show's counter in the upcoming season to Barnum's Jumbo, not quite as tall but weighing a thousand pounds more. And unlike Jumbo, who was only good for exhibition, Bolivar could dance, stand on pedestals and do a variety of tricks.

He was also dangerous to be around, worse than Dick. He clipped Eph with a trunk swipe as soon as he was led into Forepaugh's winter quarters. "Okay," said Eph, annoyed and limping, "I'll keep away from you, then."

Tippoo Sahib, purchased by Addie on an animal-buying excursion to Europe, proved to be much the same. Tip, as he was called, injured his first keeper within a month of joining the Forepaugh herd in January 1882, pinning the man against a post and breaking his shoulder. "Most of our elephants get ornery once in a while," Eph told a reporter during a tour of Forepaugh winter quarters. "But Tip here, he's ornery most all the time. He's got a powerful bad temper, because he's new, never been broken, and it's a dangerous job to learn an old elephant new tricks. He'll allow nobody to approach him but Adam Forepaugh Jr. and myself. Mr. Forepaugh can do anything with that elephant.

Anything. But a stranger couldn't get within a foot of him without being killed."

Here was Patsy Meagher, one of the new keepers, short and stocky and quick with the bull hook. It was seven o'clock, time for the morning trip to the big trough outside for a drink. They went in groups of five, Far Stream with Betsy, Rubber, Duncan and Gold Dust. It was early spring and sunny but still too cold for a wallow in the mud that covered the yard—supposing Patsy allowed them to wallow, which he wouldn't.

Duncan as usual tried to play the hog at the trough, shoving Far Stream and Rubber away and standing sideways to block one whole side, his head bobbing about with amusement. Far Stream, nearly as big, gave him a butt with her head and shoved her way in with an annoyed *You are weightless.* "Watch it," Patsy cautioned her with a tap of his hook. Rubber ended up as usual with the least room, just enough to squeeze her outstretched trunk through for a drink.

The morning practice started at seven thirty. Eph began by putting Far Stream and the trained core of others through the military drill part of the program. "Forward march!" "Right face!" "About face!" "March!" "At ease!" Hesitation and lagging were not permitted. Eph and his helpers, bull hooks in hand at the ready, demanded and got quickness, crispness, precision.

Addie, now a man of twenty-two, arrived at eight o'clock and work commenced on the orchestra number. More was now expected, something like harmony to replace the previous uncoordinated banging and honking and tinkling of the band act. Far Stream played a xylophone, much more difficult to master than the drum stick she had previously wielded. It had taken weeks of repetition to learn to strike the right keys in the right sequence, *bing-bing-bing-bing-bom-bom-bing-bing-bom-bom.* For the longest time it had made no sense at all. Even now, with all the players performing as taught, the effect was little more than plodding noise. It was only when Basil turned the handle on the organ that xylophone, bass drum, accordion, bells and cymbals melded together, very crudely melded together, into Gilbert and Sullivan's "A Policeman's Lot is Not a Happy One."

The dance act had also been made more elaborate. It was now called a dancing quadrille, eight elephants sashaying, swinging and do-si-doing in a country square dance while Addie made the calls. Far Stream had become particularly adept and graceful in the dance act over the years and mastered the new number before any of the others. Not so her first partner, Gold Dust. Poor Gold Dust became utterly lost in the lessons, the blows causing him so much anxiety that nothing would lodge in his brain. Far Stream tried to help him, repeating as they danced, *Follow me, follow me*, trying to get him to mirror her movements as Betsy and Basil had done for her years before. It didn't help. Gold Dust was too flustered, too bewildered. The men eventually gave up on him when he became unruly and Rubber was substituted as Far Stream's dance partner. After a rocky start and a break for the door that earned her a beating, Rubber settled down and slowly learned the routine.

The pyramid of living flesh was once again the finale. It consisted of nine elephants now, Bolivar at the center astride a platform eight feet off the ground. Rubber and Jennie, the most malleable, allowed themselves to be persuaded onto similarly lofty pedestals on either side, fearfully whimpering for the first week as they inched their way upward. Far Stream's position was astride the next pedestal down, five feet high, between Jennie and Betsy.

⋘⋙

"Hey Patsy," called out Eph Parker, standing before Far Stream and eying her strangely. "Am I seeing things or is Topsy gaining weight? Look at her. I swear she's packing meat it on."

104

The 1882 season was well advanced, a time when the elephants started to show their fatigue and look a bit lanky. It was all the hard traveling that did it, the physical and mental strain of the thousands of miles by train. It had already claimed two members of the herd: Mongo, who had grown sick and died in April, and one of the baby elephants, who had simply faded away. The young ones often didn't make it through a full season.

The other keepers had gathered around now, appraising. "I think you're right, Eph," observed Patsy. "Just look at her hips."

Far Stream did indeed look and feel in prime condition. She looked so good that she was moved to the center of the Oriental parade spectacle called "Lalla Rookh's Entry to Delhi" when Betsy was temporarily relieved of the duty on account of a painful corn on her foot. Far Stream would carry Lalla Rookh on her back, the beautiful Mughal princess of romantic fiction, ensconced in an ornate howdah draped with red gauze. The alluring enchantress was personated by singer Louise Montague, formerly known as Laura Keyser, selected by Adam Forepaugh from among thousands of applications mailed in from across the country, so the newspapers reported. Forepaugh advertised her as his "$10,000 Beauty."

"Keep this confounded creature still," Miss Montague snapped as they were forming up for the parade through the streets of Galena, Illinois.

Far Stream shifted from side to side. It was the first time she had had a full-sized howdah strapped to her back. It dug into her in places and made her uneasy.

"I said *still*. It's going to tumble me out. And when was the last time it was given a bath. You there, boy!" She snapped her fingers at Eph. "I want this creature clean before I ride it tomorrow. I said *clean*."

"Yes, ma'am," said Eph with good humor. "Hey Patsy, hold Topsy steady."

Patsy skipped up close to comply, close to the shapely legs that the Indian princess costume displayed to such advantage.

"I don't know why this change was made in the first place," Miss Montague continued. "I was just getting used to the last brute. Good God, it's hot. Let's get moving. Stop that shifting, I said. Let's get this—Oh!"

A spray of dirt flew through the open front of the howdah. Far Stream was dusting.

A single mounted knight rode at the head of the parade, followed by Adam Forepaugh in his brougham and the first of three bands. Further back, past the Roman chariots and the animal cages, past Cleopatra in her royal barge, past the five-elephant team drawing the tableau of St. George and the Dragon, came the Jubilee Singers with their popular tune.

> *We want the white folks all to know,*
> *Wait for 4-Paw.*
> *Look out for the great big show,*
> *Wait for 4-Paw.*
> *The finest horses, biggest tents,*
> *Get in there for fifty cents,*
> *Save yourself, for it's immense,*
> *Wait for 4-Paw.*

Far Stream came next, surrounded by mounted attendants, Lalla Rookh ensconced on her back. Miss Montague had at last stopped holding on with both hands to the howdah. Another few minutes and she released her grip altogether and began making courtly gestures to her subjects gathered on either side of the street.

The stealthy jab when it came caught Far Stream in a tender spot near the base of her tail. She squealed and reared up, throwing Miss Montague from her perch. The beauty fell screeching to the ground and lay in an undignified heap while Eph rode up to bring Far Stream under control.

The result was two sprained wrists, bruises and a bump on the head, necessitating that Miss Montague be left behind to recover. She was replaced in the role of Lalla Rookh by Josie Sutherland, Forepaugh's new "$10,000 Beauty." Josie understood better that the tag was an advertising gimmick, certainly not something to threaten legal action over, and that the actual remuneration was $50 a week.

August in Ohio and a glorious hour in a river watched by thousands lining the banks. Far Stream savored the dip with spouting and lolling and playing, pushing Rubber underwater—*Look, there is something down there*—head-butting Duncan, spraying Jennie and Bismarck and the new little one called Picaninny, then following Basil into deep water so that Eph had to row out in a boat and yell at them to come back.

It left her feeling benevolent while on display that evening, under the lights that were so much brighter than in previous years. The show was now traveling with an Edison Electrical Lighting system, the harsh glare softened by enclosing the carbon points inside frosted globes. One of them hung suspended above Far Stream's head, illuminating the elephant tent—the elephants had their own tent now, one hundred and sixty feet long by eighty feet wide. Lamps continued to flicker around the periphery of the canvas, to highlight the contrast between oil and electric and because the electric often broke down.

Patsy was stationed nearest Far Stream this evening, protecting people from their foolishness, referring most questioners to the man selling booklets.

"What do they eat?"

"It's all explained in the booklet, mister. Just five cents. You can buy it right over there."

"Why's her tail got that kink in it?"

"The booklet will answer all questions, ma'am. Just five cents. Right over there."

A sour-looking farmer: "None of them look as big as

Jumbo."

"Well, you're wrong there, friend. Bolivar down there, the big one behind the netting, he weighs half a ton more. And what can Jumbo do, anyway? Stand around and be looked at, is what. He's not trained like these elephants, oh no. Why, we're thinking of teaching Topsy here to *read* over the winter."

"Come away, Johnny," said a concerned mother, restraining her boy from ducking under the rope for a closer inspection. "The elephant will seize you."

Patsy lit up, pleased at the opportunity to use one of his jokes. "No need to fear, lady," he announced gravely. "For as the Good Book tells us, wonders never seize."

"Oh, Patsy," groaned Eph, doing duty nearby guarding Dick.

The evening performance. Far Stream banging away on the xylophone, the elephant orchestra working its way through an almost unrecognizable rendition of the Gilbert and Sullivan hit.

"What the devil are they playing? Can any of you folks make that out?"

It was a drunk, weaving his way through the audience, stirring up trouble.

"I don't know what the devil they're trying to play but it sure isn't no tune I ever heard."

People were turning. Some were laughing. Others called out, "Sit down." Far Stream remained focused on her performance, oblivious to the disturbance.

"Well, I'm just saying, is all. Those elephants aren't such wonderful musicians. C'on folks, admit it. They're just making noise."

Show attendants were approaching, two from either side. The drunk clumsily dodged about, trying to stay out of their reach, then fell flat on his face, which started the crowd roaring with laughter.

"Throw that no-good out! Throw him out!"

The attendants each took a limb and hauled the man, protesting and wriggling, out of the tent to a hearty round of applause.

~ഇൗ~

September in Missouri.

"Morning, Topsy."

It was the undersized acrobat tumbler who had joined the show two months before, christened "Bull Cow" by the others. He also played the drunk during the elephant band act. He had the makings of a good clown.

"Look here, I brought you something."

Far Stream reached out for the offering, a stale loaf of bread. Bull Cow had recently begun dropping by most days with a treat.

"Ha, ha," Bull Cow laughed as he pulled the bread away and hid it from the probing end of her trunk.

"Don't be teasing her, now," Eph called out from the other side of the tent.

"Oh, I'm not teasing her," Bull Cow breezily called back.

He held the bread out again and again withdrew it when Far Stream reached out. A third repetition, her impatience growing, and he let her have it. She savored the bite for the fleeting moment it lasted and reached out for more.

"Hey now, don't be greedy," Bull Cow chuckled, playfully giving her trunk a slap. "That was a whole loaf. I'll bring you something tomorrow." He beckoned for her to again extend her trunk. "Yes," he cooed, "you're my sweetheart. You're my girl." He stepped closer and took the waving end of her trunk and raised it to his chin to nuzzle.

Bull Cow's teasing with the bread had annoyed her. His familiarity now was too much. She pulled her trunk away and flicked it at him, nearly knocking him down.

Shock on Bull Cow's face, then hurt and anger. "Why'd you do that?" he said. "I was being nice to you. I was being *nice*."

He stalked away.

Far Stream didn't watch him leave. He was a new man. He hadn't earned her respect. She didn't need him. Her eyes were instead on Eph. Had he seen her? Was she in trouble?

No, his back had been turned.

The whistle sounded shortly after to form up for the parade, then there were visitors crowding around, then the afternoon performance, then the quiet hour.

The quiet hour.

She carefully scanned the inside of the tent. She was the last one in the line of swaying forms, furthest from the entrance, chained to a stake, facing Gold Dust. The entrance was closed. The men were resting.

There was Patsy, curled up on some hay, sleeping, dead to the world. And there was Charlie, Big Dumbie and Albert.

Where was Eph? She craned around, looking. She couldn't see him. If he was outside, he might return unexpected.

No, there he was, laid out flat under a wagon, sleeping like the others, mouth wide open. They were all tired out. They wouldn't hear.

No sign of Addie. He was not usually around at this time. To be sure, she waited for another few minutes, watching, listening.

Nothing. Everything was quiet. No one would see.

She moved to the end of her chain and stretched out so that she could reach the back of the tent. The bottom of the canvas was secured to the ground with small stakes planted every five feet. She drew one of them out with her trunk.

The bottom of the tent was now hanging loose—loose enough that she could get at the wagon that was always parked in the screened-off storage area on the other side of the canvas. She cast a final glance at the men. They were still sleeping. It was all clear. She eased her trunk under the edge of the canvas and began running it over the sacks in the wagon.

I want one, begged Gold Dust and Romeo and the others who were watching like they did every day. Far Stream ignored them. She lifted one of the sacks off the pile and tore it open and shook out the contents, heaping hay over so the man would not see. She then tucked the empty burlap back in the wagon, reinserted the stake in its hole and pressed it back down.

When everything was back in order, she started gorging on the generous serving of oats—fifty pounds, all to herself. Teasing the others watching with envy gave her almost as much pleasure as the eating itself.

CHAPTER 10

CHICAGO. The city had been completely rebuilt since the great fire, the cleared debris used to fill in the lagoon that was now called Lake Park. It was here that the tents were erected for the ten-day engagement.

It had been dark and overcast when the elephants were led the short distance from the Illinois Central Railroad depot. Far Stream therefore had not seen the great expanse of water that bordered the lot and extended all the way to the horizon. But she knew it was there. She could smell the decay of the shoreline, hear the churning and hooting of ships.

"Stop your dawdling, Topsy."

Joe Beatty, one of the newer keepers, gave her a nudge to get her moving when she paused on her way to the main tent the next day to gaze out over the lake, sparkling now in the afternoon sun. She shook her head. She was not yet used to Joe and found his presumption annoying. She shuffled a few paces to catch up to Basil already passing inside the canvas.

The big top for 1885 encompassed two rings, a raised platform in the center, a hippodrome track for races encircling the whole. Far Stream moved along the track and entered the ring where an elevated sloping runway had been brought forward. She took her position beside Basil at the end of the runway and stood flicking the ground as the ringmaster introduced The Great Klein. Joe gave her another tap to remind her to stay still.

Eph Parker, wearing boxing gloves and stripped to the waist, was desperately fighting on the central platform. It was the second round and John L. Sullivan had already knocked him down three times. Eph circled slowly, fatigued, wary of John's mighty wallop. Then they were at it again, Eph feinting right, then darting left to deliver a flurry of blows.

"Right hook, Johnny," called the clown playing the part of John's trainer, hanging onto the ropes beside the giant bucket labeled in white letters, "SPIT." Some in the audience joined in with shouts of their own as they strained to take in the match along with what was happening in the other two rings. Loudest were cries of "Low blow! Low blow!" as John L. made free with hitting Eph under the belt.

Far Stream watched the match from her position at the end of the runway, her side pressed against Basil's. This was the mindless portion of her performance, the part where all she had to do was serve as an obstacle for The Great Klein to leap over. The mustachioed Prussian made his first jump, clearing her and Basil with ease. Jennie was now led forward, increasing the challenge to what the ringmaster termed "three ponderous pachyderms" as he wound up the tension.

John L. Sullivan swung hard. The blow caught Eph on the side of the head and sent him sprawling. Patsy, serving as referee, stepped between the two fighters and began a booming count as Eph struggled to get back on his feet, woozy from his fourth knockdown. He made it as far as his knees before collapsing completely, flinging his arms out in theatrical fashion. John raised his gloved trunk in victory and paraded around.

It was Adam Forepaugh's favorite new act, an economical, one-elephant routine that pleased audiences as much as the dancing quadrille and the nine-elephant pyramid, now enlarged to eleven. Far Stream had seen it developed from the beginning, from John L. Sullivan's return to the main building in Philadelphia the previous autumn, washed clean of the paint from his season as the white elephant "The Light of Asia," to become a regular performing member of the herd. The first few weeks of his training had been unpleasant—the sessions in which the men broke him of the habit of shaking the padded glove off his trunk, the endless repetitions in which he had been manhandled and beaten until he learned to sham-box with Eph, the blows to his legs to get him to drop in a feigned knockdown when Eph struck him in turn.

The Great Klein was ready. He stood poised at the top of the twenty-foot runway, facing the springboard and the three huge forms just past it, the mattress where he would land out of sight somewhere beyond.

"I shall proceed," he announced, looking about, theatrically anxious.

"We are ready," replied the men stationed around the mattress to assist with his landing.

"The Great Klein is about to make his attempt," intoned the ringmaster.

A deep breath, a pause, and Klein shot down the ramp and pounced hard on the springboard. It launched him high into the air, high enough to clear the three backs, knees tucked into his chest. He executed one somersault, two, then straightened to land upright on the mattress, the attendants steadying him so he wouldn't go sprawling. Great applause followed by heightened drama from the ringmaster: "Sir, do you dare attempt *four*?"

A recoiling look of horror from The Great Klein, accentuated with hand wringing and chest beating and pacing before he agreed. On the central platform, Little Sandy was launching into his act with his laughing donkey and the other Motley Monarchs of Mirth.

"He agrees, ladies and gentlemen. The Great Klein agrees! He will attempt to fly over *four* of the great beasts,

four of the noblest creatures of Biblical creation, a feat that
will surely put his life in great peril. Bring forth..."—a
sweeping arm to a drawn curtain—*"Bolivar*, the largest
elephant in the world!"

Bolivar was led forward and put into position, increasing to thirty feet the distance from springboard to mattress.
The Great Klein conveyed his profound trepidation, gestures and head shaking at the ringmaster for tricking him
with an animal of Bolivar's gargantuan size. Far Stream
remained scarcely aware of the proceedings. She was more
conscious of Bolivar, currently in one of his placid periods
but still potentially a danger. On the hippodrome track she
could see the three-wheeled velocipede being prepared for
John L. Sullivan's next act. In addition to learning to box,
he had been broken to the task of standing on the rear platform of the unwieldy contraption and working the pedals
with his two front feet.

A twang from the springboard. The Great Klein was air-
borne, a hint of breeze brushing past Far Stream's back, an
"ooh" from the audience and he came down with a grunt,
the steadying hand of the attendants saving him from hurt.
He gave his bows and made his exit and Eph marched forward, in his scarlet velvet tunic now after a quick toweling.
He would lead Far Stream and the others through their military evolutions. Addie would follow with the dance.

A foreign gentleman entered the elephant tent after the
show. He had a proposition, he announced, to lay before
Ephraim Parker.

"I will not waste your time with idle jaw-jaw, Mr.
Parker," he began when Eph came over, suspicious. "I
know you are a skilled trainer, and I know that you receive
here only thirty dollars a week. You are worth a great deal
more, sir. A great deal more. I represent a German concern
that is prepared to pay you that sum."

"To work with elephants?" Eph sounded dubious. In his
years with the circus he had encountered just about every

kind of sharpie, huckster and fly-by-night artist.

"To train them, sir. To train them and to perform with them all across Europe. We will acquire six or eight of the beasts for you to . . ."

"Who the hell are you? What do you want?"

It was Adam Forepaugh, striding up, angry. One of the keepers, seeing what was transpiring, had run out to fetch him.

"Ah, Mr. Forepaugh. I am presenting an offer to Mr. Parker to accompany me to Germany. His services would be . . ."

"Trying to poach my own people under my own canvas." Forepaugh's voice was full of quivering fury. "I don't know how they do things in Germany, scrub, but in this country a man playing that dirty game it apt to get thumped."

For the first time, Eph set aside his usual deference to his employer. He placed a hand on Forepaugh's shoulder and said: "Hold on." And to the foreign gentleman: "How much?"

The man shoved a card in Eph's hand and turned to hurry away, calling over his shoulder, "Five thousand dollars."

Eph was gone. Far Stream saw him go, dressed in his best suit, boots polished, carrying his bag. She had sensed the finality when he had paused and extended his hand. The realization that he was not coming back nevertheless took two days to sink in. When it did, it upset her. Eph had been the one constant in her life going back to her first days with the circus, back to when he had been an oversized boy and she had been small and named Baby Annie. He was the one human she could rely on, the one human she had allowed herself to trust fully. He had reprimanded her with sharp blows more times than she could remember but he had always been there to take care of her, to feed her, to give her water, to scrub her. To make her feel safe.

And now he was gone. It felt like a betrayal.

Addie soon noticed a deterioration in her performance. "You're loafing," he said as he laid into her with his whip handle after the show the following evening. He hadn't dared touch her in front of the audience but now, in the elephant tent after, he didn't hold back. She knew enough not to resist. Not against Addie. She absorbed his dozen blows and, through a clouding sense of confusion, made an effort to sharpen her movements in the next show. But it was hard. She felt less inclination to please.

It was toward the end of the Chicago engagement that she escaped.

✌✧

She drew the stake from the hard-packed earth in the tent where she was tethered.

Betsy looked over sleepily. *What are you doing?*

Far Stream didn't answer. She passed silently by her companions.

Where are you going?

And now Basil and Duncan: *Where are you going?*

She didn't answer. She made her way to the entrance.

None of the men saw her, not even the broken-down hands who served as night watchmen. She slipped out of the tent with an ease that surprised her and was in the black night, the moon a sliver behind shattered clouds that seemed to race overhead.

There were two figures off to the left. She went to the right, around the outside of the tent, then a quick shuffle behind the sideshow canvas and onto a side road beyond. It led her toward a warren of warehouses crisscrossed with railway tracks.

A man curled up on a scrap of grass under a tree, the last of the greenery extending back from the lakefront. Far Stream approached the sleeping form and stood over it for a moment, the end of her trunk caressing the dirty clothing. It was a tramp with a bindle; not Eph. He shrugged off her touch but did not awaken. She backed away and moved on.

Warehouses on both sides now, a long dark alley, the smell of lumber, coal and burlap, naphtha in drums behind brick walls and locked doors. On the breeze, in intermittent snatches, traces of cattle dung and boiled hides somewhere to the south.

A cross street, also deserted. She turned. Railway tracks, the laboring huff of an engine slowly approaching, then the lamp as it rounded a bend. She walked ahead of it along the tracks, the train getting closer, the lamp light catching her and casting a shadow forward that steadily grew darker. There was no piercing shriek of a whistle. The engineer apparently had not seen her blocking the tracks. She broke into a fast shuffle, hemmed in by a line of box cars, until she was able to turn away onto a street heading west.

There were men here, a huddle of murmuring forms under the warm glow of a street lamp, another squatting on the curb, quietly smoking, sounds of laughter filtering up from a cellar. She passed right by and no one seemed to notice, not even the smoking man staring glassily at a spot on the pavement directly under her feet. It was as if she were a ghost, a three-ton apparition.

She paused to examine one of the many fragrant piles of garbage lying along the side of the road. Crumpled newspapers. Oyster shells. Feathers. She probed deeper until she came to the orange skins and apple peels she had detected. She extracted them delicately and ate, casting occasional glances back down the street at the men who were unable to see her.

A turn round a corner and a little way further and she was among towering edifices of stone turning black with the soot and smoke that blanketed the city. The whole district was dark, the power supply turned off for the night to the electric lights that proliferated many of the buildings and the arc lamps outside on the sidewalks. She proceeded down the middle of the street, past great banks, past places of business, past a tall hotel, past the occasional figure hurrying blindly by. She had been here before, marching in the parade watched by thousands, music and clapping and cheering. Now it was deserted, quiet, a whole different world.

She came to a river. She followed it north.

It was a sewage-smelling stretch of brown water, sewage all the way as it turned east and widened, gently swaying masts and funnels with dim lights winking, the occasional rustle of activity, black hulks resting in mud. She was beyond the grand buildings now, in among flimsy tenements lining the embankment, then an open space of broken foundations showing where buildings had been.

A lone shack up ahead, light flickering from the window casting an orange square on the ground. She approached and lowered her head to look in through the cracked glass.

It was a small room, a table in the center with an oil lamp upon it. There was a man and a woman seated at the table. The man was black, like Eph. But he wasn't Eph. He was older, with grizzled hair and chin whiskers, dressed in the clothes of a workman, eating out of a bowl. He stared into the wick of the lamp as he ate, the woman leaning in close to catch the light as her hands darted with needle and thread.

The man raised his gaze to the window and stared straight at Far Stream, straight into her eyes without seeing. He continued to eat. Far Stream stared back at him for a while, until she became aware of the dim reflection in the cracked window of her own eye.

She moved away with a sinking feeling of sadness. She was alone. There was nothing for her out here in the city. There was nothing for her in this man-world away from the circus. She continued along the bank of the river, the shifting breeze now blowing off the lake guiding her onward to the depot where the trains lay and from there back to the lot.

The tents were still quiet. No one had missed her. She wandered about, circling the canvas that glowed softly in places, flicking about at the litter, touching the ropes and stakes that held up her world. She made three meandering rotations, then moved down to the edge of the great expanse of black water, the sun still submerged somewhere beyond it, wading in until the waves were lapping at her belly.

She doused herself with water, feeling no pleasure from what was usually a treat.

She waded in deeper.

She was swimming.

The water went on and on and on.

༺༼

She wasn't missed until sunrise. A flurry of activity followed, harsh words thrown at the night watchmen, an examination of prints in the soft earth that led one way and another and only added to the confusion. The morning was half gone, the entire area searched, when someone cast a glance at the lake and shouted: "Good God, what's she doing out there?"

She was emerging from the water, wading in through the shallows. Addie and Patsy, the first to reach her, found her exhausted and distant. "Where the hell have you been?" were Addie's first angry words. Patsy, looking at her with concern, was gentler, more understanding.

She was unable to perform in the afternoon performance or again in the evening, much to Addie's annoyance, scarcely touching the food that was set before her. The tents came down after that. It was time to move on. Aurora was the next stop, then South Bend, Goshen, Kalamazoo, Grand Rapids, Far Stream back in the line up, two shows a day, Patsy stopping by often to coax her to eat.

"Come on, Topsy. Don't be stubborn. Eat your hay like a good girl."

Far Stream listlessly took some, whisked it about and eventually put it in her mouth. It didn't taste like anything good.

"That's a good girl. You'll get to feeling better, I promise."

Patsy stepped closer to pat her on the side. Far Stream swept her trunk at him. He backed away.

CHAPTER 11

THE TRAIN WAS HEADING EAST from Honesdale, Pennsylvania to Monticello, New York, a relatively short run that would see them arrive well before dawn. Far Stream rode with the rest of the dancing quadrille in the eighth car from the engine, a half dozen men sleeping in bunks in a compartment at one end. Among them was Philo Word, yet another new trainer, and Nate Biscuits, Little Blondie and Otto, new keepers. The outside of the car was emblazoned with the name of the man who now leased her. The sign read, "Frank A. Robbins' Wild West Show, Hippodrome, Circus."

Basil stood beside her in the darkness, legs solidly braced, fast asleep. Further down the line were Rubber, Jennie and Duncan, all of them drowsing. Gold Dust stood on her other side, munching his hay, the chains of the martingale harness the men had placed on him softly chinking. Charlie and young Billy rode in the next car, alone.

Far Stream reached over and idly helped herself to what was left of Basil's hay, more out of habit than for any satisfaction there might still be in the thieving. Like some of the others, she had endured a period of upset after being leased to Robbins, upset followed by aggression that had been sharply quelled. Being sent away from the Forepaugh circus was largely to blame. It compounded the sense of loss and betrayal following Eph's departure, the feeling that everything familiar, everything that made her feel safe, was falling away. And then there had been the loss of Betsy, who had been left behind. Betsy was the closest thing Far Stream had to a mother. Without her, Far Stream never fully recovered her capacity to feel enjoyment. Without her, life was no longer the same.

A booming, echoing crescendo as the train crossed a bridge over a river, followed by an instant return to the flat clickety-clack cadence. They were leaving fields behind now, entering forest, acrid pines, peppery magnolias, oaks and elms, junipers and beeches, the stab of a skunk somewhere among them, each odor distinct through the smell of dung inside the car and soot blowing back from the engine. Far Stream drowsily sampled them all until her head was drooping and she was no longer aware.

≈≈

Thirty-five.

That had been the greatest extent of Adam Forepaugh's elephant herd, the high water mark reached during his competition with Phineas T. Barnum. It was a tremendous expense that Forepaugh concluded in early 1886 he could no longer afford. He accordingly began to make changes, selling off some of his animals and leasing out others to reduce the size of his herd.

The leasing out of the dancing quadrille, the show's premier act, surprised many observers. To Forepaugh, it just made good business sense. Frank Robbins, a former employee and protégé of sorts, was paying him well, and he still had other elephant attractions that were just as appealing: John L. Sullivan's boxing number and newcomer Picaninny's clown act being foremost—compact attractions from which he could earn money all the year round, on the road during the regular circus season and throughout the winter with weekly rentals to theaters.

The move had been traumatic for Far Stream. She was taken along with the rest of the quadrille first to the headquarters of the Robbins circus in Frenchtown, New Jersey,

122

there to be broken into accepting commands from their new masters, head trainer Philo Word and his half-dozen keepers. Jennie, Rubber, Basil and Billy accepted the change with little resistance. Far Stream, distrustful after Eph's departure, did not. She was chained by each leg and methodically beaten—no malice, just a steady succession of blows until she squealed her compliance. "Lay into her," Philo had barked when one of the new men showed distaste for the labor. And in a quieter tone, after the job was completed: "It's the only way. An elephant that doesn't fear you is an elephant that'll kill you, sooner or later."

Duncan resisted as well and received a similar beating. Charlie and Gold Dust showed violent tendencies that ran deeper and were dealt with even more severely. For Charlie, it took three days.

It was Gold Dust who caused the most trouble during the quadrille's first months with Robbins, breaking loose or wandering off on several occasions. He was sternly reprimanded each time, especially after bolting during a performance and running trumpeting about the tent, upsetting the audience before escaping outside. He eventually settled into the simmering resentment that necessitated the fitting of the martingale to restrict his movements and prevent him from lashing out.

Charlie, after a period of relative quiet, came roaring back to life in August, breaking loose from his chains and going on a rampage inside his rail car. By the time the men got him under control he had mauled two camels to death, a heavy loss for the show. He then turned on his keepers, plunging a tusk into the leg of one, knocking down a second without serious injury, smashing the collar bone and ribs of a third. It earned Charlie a session with hot irons until he submitted, followed by the fitting of a martingale harness like that worn by Gold Dust.

Far Stream for her part maintained an obedient silence. She performed to the level Philo Word required, she shuffled to and from the train in her place behind Basil, she did as commanded, she gave little cause for concern.

The year wound down. Electric lights came to the show the next season, the white glare to which Far Stream had grown accustomed with Forepaugh, and Frank Robbins prospered. He made the bold gamble of booking the circus into New York City's American Institute over the winter, clanging steam pipes and audiences in damp wool coats, an expensive and ultimately ill-advised venture.

It was now the summer of 1888.

❧

A piercing screech jarred Far Stream from her dozing. It was followed by a hard jolt that threw her so hard against Gold Dust that they both toppled over. Another moment of careening and shaking and the rail car had spent its momentum, its iron wheels dug deep in the dirt.

It was another derailment. Far Stream had experienced more than a dozen of them over the years, some relatively mild, others leaving her bruised. They usually occurred at night, when she was dozing. They were always upsetting.

The panicked shrieks and trumpeting gradually subsided. Far Stream struggled back to her feet. She probed the soreness on her side with her trunk, then reached out to touch Basil. Her older companion was shaken but all right. Gold Dust was not quite so lucky. Restricted in his martingale harness, he had twisted his neck and was hurting.

At the end of the car, Philo Word, Otto and the other keepers could be heard swearing as they extracted themselves from their bunks or picked themselves up off the floor. They joined the other circus people outside, calling back and forth, barking orders, running past on the siding. Then the glint of a lantern through the gaps in the plank wall.

The door was unlocked and opened. Philo, in a halo of flickering yellow, climbed in and held his lantern high, anxiously surveying the elephants inside.

124

"They look all right," he called out to the others. "Let's get them out and moved down to that clearing. Otto, lay down the step."

Philo began unfastening chains. He paused at Gold Dust. "You going to give me trouble?"

Gold Dust didn't. He moved awkwardly to the exit, his head at an angle, his neck very sore.

"How about you?" Philo asked Far Stream. She was also cooperative. She moved with difficulty down the slanted car and exited in turn. When they were all assembled in the nearby clearing, Philo said, "All right, it's just eight miles into town so we're going to walk them. Blondie, you get up front. I'll take the rear. The rest of you boys spread out and keep attentive."

They set out down the line of stalled cars, down past the steaming engine and into the night. The only light came from the moon, a frosted stain on the clouds. It was almost full. Far Stream could feel it pulling. The only sound was the chink of chains, the crunch of footsteps on gravel, the swish of trunks snatching bites of vegetation on the move. The men, settling down now, grew too tired to speak.

A few miles of this, a kind of walking meditation, and the upset faded and Far Stream began to feel peaceful. It was like being back in the old days with the wagons, walking the roads behind the first Romeo she had known, Eph on horseback beside her. She had a flash of memory of skirting a field in the moonlight, crossing a rain-swollen stream, stopping to rest under a tree while Eph smoked his pipe, talked to her and made her trust grow.

And then, as she relaxed further, her eyes almost closed now, she found herself drifting back into the forest, something she had begun to do increasingly now, even awake. She could sense Mother and Grandmother walking behind her, her sister Red Moon just ahead with Darkness at Day.

They were with her. She could hear them. She could feel them, very close

Home is this way, she murmured, awash in the sensations. *Home is this way.*

The notion seemed to excite young Billy. *Home is this way*, he repeated. *Home is this way.*

Soon others in line were taking up the refrain—*Home is this way, home is this way*—until they were all repeating it with growing excitement. Far Stream, roused from her reverie, forgot that it was she who had started the commotion. Eyes open, she joined in the chant, increasing her pace. *Home is this way, home is this way.*

"Hey, slow down," said Nate Biscuits, giving her a tug on the ear with his bull hook. The other men along the line were doing the same.

"Slow them down, damn it!" Philo called from the rear.

Louder commands, sharper tugs with the hook. Far Stream eased her pace.

They continued on in silence. The first hints of sunrise began to color the east. The forest receded, giving way to the next town.

❧

"See how they dance, ladies and gentlemen! See how they dance!"

Far Stream was performing in the center ring with the rest of the quadrille, now comprised of just seven members. She pranced and swayed and pirouetted and bowed under the harsh illumination of the Brush carbon-point lighting, scarcely aware of Philo Word with his stick, scarcely aware of the band competing to be heard over the sound of the rain on the stained canvas.

"See how they require no instruction!" The ringmaster, smiling broadly, took a discreet step away from the water trickling onto his shoulder. "See how they dance of their own accord, for the pleasure of it!"

The exhortations drew light applause. The audience was meager this evening, many kept away by the downpour that had turned the lot muddy. It was another blow to the Robbins concern at the end of an unprofitable season—a fatally unprofitable season, for the heavy debts incurred in New York City over the previous winter could not be repaid.

The tents came down for the last time after the evening performance. It was late October and cold and everyone was shivering, tired and dragging. Far Stream was once again kept back with Basil to help move the wagons, the squelching mud being too much for the horses. She preferred this sort of work—straight-forward, sensible labor. She put her head against the back of the first wagon and pushed it along until it was on firm road, then she turned back for another, requiring no more guidance from Otto than an indication of which wagon to go to. The rain had ended, the clouds parting to reveal a half moon.

Another hour and the work was finished, the churned-up lot bare save for a scattering of debris. Far Stream followed Basil back to the train to be chained inside the car with the others. It was two o'clock in the morning but there were still a few locals out to watch as she passed. "Yee-hah!" roared a drunk, waving his cap as if to start a stampede. It startled the horses and brought a storm of abuse from one of the drivers. Far Stream only veered a step to the left as she continued wearily onward. "Go on home," Otto told the man, too tired to feel anything more than sour annoyance.

It was two hundred miles back to Robbins' winter base in New Jersey, cold all the way. A long wait, a change into another rail car, also unheated, and Far Stream and the quadrille were again on the move, returning to Forepaugh headquarters in Germantown outside Philadelphia. When they arrived she was breathing heavily from congestion in her chest. It made her sluggish and dull as she shuffled into the menagerie building for the first time in three years.

The stalls lining the periphery of the practice arena were empty. The Forepaugh show was still on the road, not due to return for several more days. Far Stream spent the time in a funk, weak and dragging, causing some concern for the men employed to take care of her and the others. They gave her the hot vinegar treatment and fed her medicine that was bitter. It loosened her bowels and did not make her feel better.

Blasts from a steam whistle and the chug of an engine on the siding leading into the Forepaugh complex heralded the return of the circus. The double doors were thrown open and here was Patsy Meagher moving down the line, greeting each of the elephants returned by Robbins. "Hello there, Topsy old girl," he said when he got to Far Stream, extending his hand for her to examine. She remembered him well but managed only a listless caress. Patsy patted the end of her trunk, noted the discharge, and moved on.

Here was Picaninny being led past, dark skinned, perfectly proportioned, his manner as strangely fruity as ever. He acknowledged Far Stream with a *huh-huh-huh* sound resembling men's laughter and continued on. John L. Sullivan followed, decidedly bigger than when Far Stream had last seen him. He paused and extended his trunk in a friendly manner and she took it, happy to see him. He was getting older but there was still no hint of male violence within him. She did not mind him being this close.

Tip, gaunt and weary, his head hanging, was next. He had the appearance of having recently weathered a session of disciplining and did not look up as he passed. Far Stream did not greet him. Bismarck, the big African male with the impressive tusks, appeared to be in better condition but was also subdued.

A warm welcome from Dick. He was in a good mood despite his heavy burden of chains, the sort of mood where Far Stream could like him, his trunk jauntily slung over his right tusk. He was allowed to pause for a moment of touching—the men knew this was important—and Dick said to her happily, *I will eat all your food.*

She asked about Betsy. She was anxious to be reunited with Betsy. She learned from Dick that Betsy—the being known to her own as Hunger Valley—was dead.

The news swept aside the tendrils of good feeling that were returning, leaving only loneliness as Dick was chained beside her and presented with a serving of hay. She took a step back, staring down at the ground, ignoring Dick beside her, ignoring the others being led past. She stood there immobile for a long time, the voices of the men rising to a crescendo outside. It was only when the roars of rage started that she roused from her blackness.

She recognized one of the voices. It was Bolivar, bellowing louder than she had ever heard him bellow. The other voice, a piercing shriek, was new.

And then with a crash they were both inside the building, splintering one of the doors as they fought with each other, their movements hampered by their connected leg chains, joined together for the final transfer from the train to their stalls. Men with hooks and pitchforks cautiously followed behind them, keeping an awed distance from what totaled nearly ten tons of elephant fury.

There was Addie. He was holding a spear, motioning needlessly for the others to stay back. He was saying something about Bolivar. He called the other elephant "Chief."

A yank in opposite directions, the chain snapped and the two immense forms lurched apart. Regaining his balance, Bolivar turned and butted Chief in the chest with force enough to shake the whole building, staggering him but leaving him still on his feet. Another exchange, a flash of tusk, a seam opening in Bolivar's shoulder. Then he was backing away, trumpeting, snorting and lashing, backing away because Chief was in the grip of a madness that demanded respect.

"Don't let them get out," Addie ordered. "Patsy, you and the boys get around to the door there. By God, don't let them get out."

Bolivar had been agitated by Chief's outburst but he was not in his own time of madness. He was thus tractable as they drove him into the stout holding cell where he had spent many weeks. Getting Chief under control proved a much bigger problem. Any attempt to place chains on his legs was met with a ferocious, deafening response, trunk lashing and head tossing, kicking, lunging and screaming. One of the men failed to get out of the way. He was struck and thrown, his leg badly broken.

A pause in the noise and commotion. A ring of men, breathing hard, forks poised in a circle around Chief. "I don't think this is working, boss," one of them called out nervously to Addie.

Addie didn't think it was working either. He said, "Get the shotgun. It's in the office."

It took twelve shots fired point-blank into the meat of his legs and his haunches to subdue Chief long enough to get him thoroughly chained. Far Stream watched the process with alarm but was unsympathetic. Males when they were crazed were a curse on the world. She watched as Chief was dragged across the arena to the corner specially equipped with anchor bolts for the harder cases, trailing the smell of boiling violence and blood. She watched as the men secured him by the leather-bound rings permanently affixed to all four of his feet. She watched as the tension gradually ebbed from the building—and with rising excitement she began to see things.

The first thing to strike her was the unequal size of Chief's ears, the left side full, the right significantly smaller. This led her to note the deep lines around his eyes, double underneath, the patch of dark hair on his forehead, the bulge in his heavy jaw.

They were all familiar. When the initial shock of recognition had passed, she moved to the end of her chain and looked at the glowering newcomer and communicated eagerly, *I know you.*

Chief did not respond. He did not look up. He continued to examine his chains with his trunk, the iron rings anchored in the floor, feeling for a way to escape.

I know you, Far Stream repeated, excited now, looking hopefully at him. He was a link to her past. *I know you*, she repeated. *You are Three Times Falling. I know you.*

Chief finally looked up and cast her a glare. There was no recognition. His head went back down.

She tried again. *I am Far Stream. You are Three Times Falling.*

Patsy, noting her agitation, came over. "It's okay, Topsy, he's not going to hurt you. You settle down, now. Don't heave on your chain."

Far Stream swiped him back with her trunk and continued to lean out, trying to stir recognition. Three Times Falling was the first connection she had encountered to her family since the sea voyage that had taken her away from her home.

The blows were falling, Patsy's grim reprimand for aggression. She felt a surge of anger and lashed out again, again without contact, causing Patsy, short but powerfully built, to redouble his efforts. He knew how to handle a bull hook. She backed away.

I know you, Far Stream said again, this time pleading, willing her old companion from the ship to remember.

There was no answer. Three Times Falling kept his head down, his trunk keeping up its restless probing and swishing.

He had changed. He had grown big and scarred and twisted like Romeo and he didn't remember. Or could it be that he wasn't Three Times Falling at all? A long time had passed. Perhaps she was creating illusions to bolster her spirits. Perhaps she was becoming odd like Picaninny. It made her feel worse.

And then, from a different direction, a new voice came into her head. It spoke her real name.

It said, *Far Stream.*

She stopped swaying and stood very still.

Nothing. It must have been her dream world. She must have drifted away for a moment.

Far Stream.

She heard that. It was not a dream. She looked again at Three Times Falling to make certain the voice was not his. And then, turning about, she saw the figure, a newcomer who must have been led past her when the unloading of the train resumed following the disturbance. She was chained at the far end of the line in the corner, a female elephant much like herself, but older, with short tusks. She was gazing right at her with piercing pale eyes.

A moment of confusion, then a flood of recognition.

An inundation.

It was her sister Red Moon. They had not seen each other in seventeen years.

CHAPTER 12

FAR STREAM REMAINED in a state of excitement all through the rest of the day and on into the evening, straining at her chain so hard that Patsy became concerned she would injure her leg. He tried to calm her but had no success. He did not know what was causing her such agitation.

The next morning, when she was unchained for her turn at the trough, she broke free and ran to Red Moon, her sister, ignoring the shouts of her keepers, ignoring the raised bull hooks—bull hooks that were lowered at the sight of Far Stream in a loud, demonstrative reunion, so glad to see her sister that tears ran down her cheeks.

After reassuring himself that no mischief was intended, Patsy allowed Far Stream to be taken to the trough together with Red Moon, there for a session of splashing and playing that so clearly joyous that it made the men laugh. And then, in a move that cemented Far Stream's allegiance to Patsy forever, he had her shifted down to the end of the line, right next to Red Moon. It was where she wanted to be.

Over the next days, Far Stream and Red Moon shared their stories. They shared the anguish they had felt upon being separated from each other all those years before after leaving the ship. For Red Moon, separation from Far Stream had been followed shortly thereafter by separation from Earth Moves, Lone Tree Mountain, Three Times Falling and their other companions on the long journey. She never saw any of them again—all except Three Times Falling, who had reappeared two years before. He knew her and spoke to her when he was in his right mind but not when he was in his madness. When he was that way he was a curse on the world.

They learned that they had lived lives much like the other: painful learning, pent-up frustration, a succession of trainers and keepers, a blur of travel, walking, train rides in darkness, an endless succession of places and faces. Far Stream showed her sister the beings she had known from Romeo to Betsy; train derailments; a barn fire; a long run in the snow. Red Moon showed her similar beings; similar circus experiences; a year spent in a zoo, a time of extreme sickness when she had seen a bright light.

And then they moved further back into the past, back to their home and their family and the memories that for Far Stream especially had become hazy. There had been times when she wondered if it had ever really existed. Now, together with his sister, their minds open and sharing, she knew.

They shared memories of Grandmother and Mother, of Man's World and Seven Were Taken and Into the Mountains, quietly grazing in wisps of fog early in the morning. They shared playing with their cousins and Red Moon's beautiful little son, Darkness at Day. They shared Lightning, the blind one who had died groaning, and the baby Flowers for Lightning whose birth happily followed, delivered to them in the new place where the air had been fragrant. They shared the paths and the clearings, the streams and the pools, the trees and the fruit and the lush vegetation, the mist-shrouded hills, the deep valleys and the Shining Sun Cliffs. They shared their family history, the stories that Far Stream had been too young to learn when they had lived in the forest but that Red Moon remembered, the stories that lived on in the names. They shared it all with a clarity that was aching and it reassured Far Stream that that distant time was not a mere dream. The confirmation of its reality made her feel happy. The heavy sense of loss, renewed, made her feel sad.

Training for the coming season began after a few days of rest. New acts had to be learned, existing ones modified to keep the show fresh. For Far Stream, used to the many permutations of marching and dancing, the learning came quickly, her improved mental state lending poise and polish to her movements that even Addie commended and he was not easily pleased. Red Moon had more difficulty with some of the routines. The intricate steps of the dancing quadrille especially confused her. She struggled long and hard to learn them, mirroring her sister. She wanted to dance side by side with Far Stream.

✧

The madness that seized Three Times Falling at the end of the previous season had been the last straw for Adam Forepaugh. He had had enough of troublesome mature male elephants with their terrible mood swings. They weren't worth the aggravation of keeping, the expense of confinement and the lawsuits that invariably followed the injuries and deaths that they caused.

Bolivar was the first to go. Forepaugh donated him to the Philadelphia Zoo on Christmas Day, 1888. There was publicity to be had from the donation and Forepaugh reaped a good harvest, front-page news stories hailing his fine sense of charity and love for his hometown, his magnificent gift sure to delight Philadelphians for years to come as Bolivar enjoyed his retirement. "Now mister, let me tell you something," Forepaugh was quoted as saying to the zoo's superintendent. "That's the finest beast I ever owned, and he's all right so long as he can't do any harm. But mind you, don't ever let him get away."

Bolivar never did get away. Deemed too dangerous to be allowed any freedom, he was left permanently chained by three legs inside the Philadelphia Zoo elephant house, his restraints increased at the start of each summer when his generally irritable nature flared into unbounded rage. He was not let out into the yard; he was not allowed into the pool; he was not permitted to move more than a single step forward and back. He stood on the same spot, rarely lying down, incessantly swaying, for twenty years. By the time he died in 1908, his scuffing feet had worn a groove in the stone floor.

Tip was sent away next. He killed his last keeper, eighteen-year-old William McCamant, on September 25, 1888, the lawsuit from McCamant's parents following at the end of the year. Adam Forepaugh decided to get rid of Tip after that. He donated him, again with much publicity, to New York's Central Park Zoo on January 1, 1889. "He is the most vicious elephant I have ever seen," zookeeper Bill Snyder would say five years later, after being nearly killed by Tip twice, once by trampling, once with tusks. "I knew he was wicked when Adam Forepaugh made him a present to the park. No elephant that has killed or hurt his keeper is to be trusted."

Tip was kept in close restrains in Central Park until the day of his execution in May 1894. Poison was the chosen method. Prussic acid was used first, hidden in a carrot, then an apple. Tip, tasting the bitter powder, spit them both out. Tasteless cyanide was then tried, a huge killing dose rolled in balls of bran mash. That did the trick.

There would be no retirement to a zoo for Three Times Falling, known in the Forepaugh Circus as Chief. No zoo would take him. He was too bad.

≈≈

The men called it a "donkey." It arrived bolted onto a flatbed rail car shunted onto the siding outside the menagerie barn. After removing the bolts and running out a thick cable, the men started up the donkey and let it pull itself off the car, sliding onto solid ground on the oil-spattered skids that were its two feet.

Far Stream heard the men talking and working, the donkey coughing to life and settling into its steady breathing, its *ch-ch-ch-ch*. The noise stirred the memory of a similar sound heard years before, one tied to the terror of being hoisted from the hold of a ship. But then it died and with it the faded glimpse of an image. Red Moon beside her interested her more than the sound of the donkey and what the men were doing outside. She ate the twists of hay offered to her by her sister and made twists to offer Red Moon in return. They had begun to do this often, feeding each other. It gave them pleasure. The others found it quite strange.

On the opposite side, Dick periodically reached over, keeping up his tireless efforts to filch. His mood had remained surprisingly playful since his return to winter quarters. Far Stream swatted his trunk away, just short of annoyance, and returned to her sister.

The great double doors of the barn were opened. The donkey's thick rope was dragged in, a loop in the end.

"All right," said Addie. "Bring him out."

Three Times Falling was led out of the enclosure in the winter quarters building where he had been kept isolated from the others. There was a hemp rope around his neck. It was as thick as a man's forearm, the end dragging in the dirt.

"Hoo-yah," said Patsy, giving the giant a poke behind the ear to keep him moving, ready to leap back at the first sign of trouble. "Hoo-yah."

Far Stream turned to the sound. It was the same order Patsy used with her when shifting wagons on show lots. But he was quieter now.

Three Times Falling passed in front of her and the others. He did not look up. Blood remained encrusted on his legs and body, his wounds from the subduing the previous month having not properly healed, no one daring to tend them. He moved slowly, heavily laden with chains, a limp his only show of discomfort. Patsy led him to the thick iron posts embedded deep in the ground near the open barn doors. He was positioned between the posts and each of his legs was chained down, the restraints pulled tight until he was unable to move. He threw his head about somewhat during the process but otherwise did not resist. The tempest of his earlier madness had subsided, leaving him exhausted and empty. He stood stiff and alert for a time, then began to relax, picking at the hay pushed within reach of his trunk.

A half dozen men took the loose end of the rope hanging around his neck and pulled it to an anchor post behind him. Addie and Patsy then took up the looped end of the second rope that had been dragged in from the donkey outside. They cautiously approached the giant, one on either side so the loop was wide open.

"You're not going to give us trouble now, are you," Addie said softly. "You're going to stand there nice and still. That's good. That's . . ."

Three Times Falling shifted uneasily as the hemp rope brushed his trunk. Addie and Patsy stepped back.

"It's all right," Addie continued, soothing. "You just stand still now. Nice and still."

They got the loop over his great bumpy head and hanging loose around his neck. They made no attempt to tighten it. The donkey would take care of that.

Addie raised his hand to the man outside. "Okay, start her up."

The donkey coughed again to life, *ch-ch-ch-ch-ch-ch-ch*. A pause, Addie and Patsy watching Three Times Falling for any indication that he was about to turn mean. Nothing. He remained quiet, head down, pushing hay around, occasionally throwing it onto his back.

Without shifting his gaze, Addie raised his hand again to the man at the controls of the donkey and made a circular motion. The voice of the engine lowered as its gears engaged and its wheel started turning. The rope around Three Times Falling's neck began to slowly crawl out the door.

The slack was taken up. The rope rose off the ground. Feeling its weight, Three Times Falling jerked his head back to shake it off, break it. The movement tightened the noose in the rope running forward. The men on the second rope behind took up the slack.

Addie called out, "Slower..."

The donkey was throttled down. The rope was completely off the ground now, dipping slightly in the center. Another backward jerk by Three Times Falling. The men behind took up the rest of the slack in the rear rope and tied it securely down like a ship's cable.

"Slower..."

Both ropes were taut now and creaking, Three Times Falling transfixed between, his eyes bulging, his body stiffening as air was cut off along with the flow of blood to his brain. He stood that way for two long minutes, seeming to swell even bigger, the men looking on with varying degrees of wonder, the younger ones with mouths open, the older ones grim.

The end when it came was a gentle crumpling, a wilting subsidence. It was not at all like the thrashing and raging that had been anticipated and feared. Three Times Falling, the monster giant, the formidable killer, settled quietly to the ground with no struggle or fuss.

"Don't let it go slack, now," said Addie. "Keep up that tension."

Far Stream and Red Moon were watching with the others. They knew what had happened. They knew what the donkey with its *ch-ch-ch* and its hissing had done.

"Let's give it another minute."

The inner glow was still lingering there when the donkey winch fell silent and the ropes were allowed to go slack. Three Times Falling was taking a long time to leave. Far Stream watched the sparks and flashes dance over his body, rising, falling, flaring, fading. She watched, riveted by the sight that caused the herd wonder, leaning toward her sister so that their bodies touched and were one.

And then they were emerging, a thousand points of luminescent color rising up and coming together, a bundle of life breaking free from the dead weight of body and ascending into the air. It rose toward the roof and hovered there for a moment, the essence of Three Times Falling that was so real and so beautiful but which the men could not see. It hung there as all the elephants watched it, some making moaning sounds, some trumpeting, some quiet. It hung there and for a fleeting moment Far Stream felt herself bathed in its warmth.

~ళ్ళ~

FOREPAUGH AND THE WILD WEST!
1,400 men and horses! 1,000 wild beasts!
Acres and acres of cloud-towering canvas!
Seating for an entire county! Schools dismissed!
Stores closed! Mills shut down! All business suspended!
A holiday for town and country! The largest, the richest,
the best and most popular tented exhibition in the world,
now joined by the realistic, renowned Wild West exhibition,
will exhibit at
BRAINERD, THURSDAY, AUGUST 8

The Forepaugh show for the 1889 season opened with a Wild West extravaganza. It featured vignettes of Indians attacking a stagecoach and driven off by fierce gunplay; scouts captured by Indians and tortured with fire; a horse thief run down, apprehended and hanged; cowboys riding bucking broncos; Pawnee Bill and Lillie May giving an exhibition of trick shooting; and, for the stirring finale, a reenactment of Custer's Last Stand in the Battle of the Little Big Horn.

For Far Stream, the action-packed opening was heard as gunshots and whoops and martial music filtering through the canvas of the elephant tent. Her part in the show came later, after Picaninny's clown number and John L. Sullivan's boxing—John did the act now with Patsy—and Addie's presentation of his latest equine sensations, the tight-rope-walking horse Blondin and the trapeze-swinging pony Eclipse.

She cast hay about and flapped her ears as she waited for Joe to unchain her. She had been irritable lately. Strange sensations had taken hold of her body, sensations she had felt before but never so strongly, sensations that had left her frustrated, agitated.

Here was Joe. She had come close to squashing him the day before while he was paring her nails. Now, as he bent to unfasten the chain from her foreleg, the urge to stomp him flared up again. She let it simmer and merely whisked at him with her trunk, staggering him backward.

"Stop your capers," he roared, coming at her with his bull hook. The gloom hanging over the show had made him irritable too.

It had begun with the death of the two canvas men back east, knocked down and run over while loading a wagon. Then there was the old timer in the cook tent who had his legs cut off when he fell under the train. And then, within a week, a similar slip when the handholds on the side of the rail car were slick after a downpour. On that occasion the unfortunate show hand had been cut completely in two.

Far Stream danced in the quadrille in the evening performance for the one hundredth and eighty-seventh time that season. She danced as "Ophelia" with Red Moon facing her as "Hamlet." The others were Romeo and Juliet, Othello and Desdemona, Antony and Cleopatra. Addie, in his thirties now, still wearing the familiar gold-braid cap of his youth, had begun introducing them with Shakespearean names to keep the act fresh. They made their bows at the signal from Addie and launched into the number with the solemn grace audiences always found so appealing, a display that was wonderful and ludicrous at the same time, as apt to elicit appreciative clapping as knee-slapping laughter.

When they were finished, the Marvelous Eugenes took over the center ring with their trapeze act to close the regular part of the program. The hugely popular hippodrome races then followed: serious horse races, an "Arabian race" featuring camels, a comic event with ponies ridden by monkeys, man against horse, Roman chariots, a foot race between two Indians, Ogallala versus Brule Sioux. Far Stream appeared in the fourth event, the elephant contest. In her state of heightened agitation she easily won.

Back to the train and another jolting ride through the night. A parade in the rain in the next town in the morning, then back to the lot, Far Stream's feet sinking deep in the soft earth. "No elephants tonight," was the order after a farcical afternoon performance, the weight of the stumbling, squelching quadrille turning the center ring into a quagmire. An evening of ease, listening to the show unfold without her in the neighboring big tent. But still the agitation, the frustration, the casting about.

Apple, said Red Moon, holding out a twist of hay to resume their long-running game. They always started with things that were fresh and familiar. Far Stream ate listlessly, experiencing the sweetness with little pleasure, and after a long pause offered a twist in return, saying *Orange*. They continued on through bananas, pears, grapes and biscuits, Red Moon's communicated sensations sharp and exquisite, Far Stream's dull and tasteless and hardly worth the effort of sampling.

Don't look at him, Red Moon admonished again.

They continued on to the rarer treats they remembered, Far Stream making a slightly improved effort despite her awareness of his eyes. *Mango*, Red Moon said when they arrived at the more challenging past, communicating along with the hay a fair approximation of that long-ago taste. Far Stream made an effort to enjoy it, to immerse herself pleasurably in the forest like she could do when the agitation was not so heavy upon her. Then she could stand it no longer. The spell was broken.

She looked over at Dick.

Red Moon tried to dissuade her. *Don't do that. Don't listen to him.*

Dick's eyes were on her. He had been watching her intently like this for the past several days. He made the signal again that she found so alarming and yet so enticing. *Stay away*, she tried to tell him. What came out was, *Come here.*

The message visibly excited Dick. He began to extend. He looked about the tent like he did when he was intent on mischief. It was oddly quiet due to the change in the program, the handful of keepers absent, enjoying the gift of a few precious hours.

Dick took hold of his stake and drew it from the soft earth. He had known the trick for some time but had always been extremely judicious in its use. Pausing to cast his eye once more over the tent, he moved silently down the line to Far Stream, slowing when he grew near in order to first gauge her humor. He extended his trunk to her. She drew it into her mouth and sucked it. He did the same. Red Moon, careful now with Dick roaming, moved away to the end of her chain. On the other side, John L. Sullivan turned his back and became submissive in the presence of the bigger and more powerful male.

Far Stream's heart was beating hard now, so hard that it seemed to be shaking her whole body. Dick moved around behind her, his head close to her rump, his probing trunk taking in the scent that told him she was ready, the prospect drawing his excitement out to its dramatic full length. He was caressing her back now, her sides, her ears, her head, stoking the excitement rising within her, rising to a flood until she made a low, deep rumble that did not sound like her at all.

Hurry up, said Red Moon, exasperated at the inevitability of the proceedings. John risked turning his head for a peek.

A lurch and a stagger and Dick had her mounted, his immense weight bearing down on her pelvis, his forelegs splayed across her back, his trunk still caressing, his penis twisting and searching with the articulation of a huge anaconda. It brushed against her, she took a startled step forward, he staggered and stayed on. Then it was back and entering inside her, four and a half feet inside her, and he was straightening his legs and thrusting and the consummation was complete.

CHAPTER 13

FAR STREAM WADED EAGERLY into the Ohio River, watched by the citizens of Huntington, West Virginia crowding the bank and the railway bridge overhead. It was a fine morning for the treat of a splash and a frolic—a pure blue sky, a hot July sun, the roads dusty and parching during the parade to stir up the town and get all the folks lined up to buy tickets.

In a fit of exuberance she pushed past Red Moon and Rubber for deeper water and threw herself in with a splash that prompted delighted cheers from the spectators. Another few steps and the ripples were lapping her sides. She allowed her legs to go limp and her head to sink under, down until she was resting on her haunches in the silt at the bottom, breathing through her trunk held aloft. It was quiet and peaceful down here. She felt wonderfully light.

And then she was up again, rearing up sputtering and choking and spitting out water. John L. Sullivan, in even higher spirits, had plowed into her just as she was filling her lungs. A moment to recover and she went at him, playfully at him, spraying and shoving as Patsy Meagher and the others looked on from shore with big smiles. There was something irresistible about elephants sporting in water.

"All right, come on back!"

It was Patsy calling them out of the water, their time for bathing now over. It required several repetitions roared at

145

top volume before Far Stream took notice. She was too caught up in the fun. She took a few steps toward the bank before falling into a mock struggle with Modoc, then flopped under again, rose up and sent a jet of water in the direction of the people clustered on the bridge overhead.

"Do it again!" squealed the young boys.

Patsy bellowed, "Come here!"

She snorted and started to move grudgingly toward the bank. Patsy allowed only so much leeway before the hard look clouded his face and he tightened his grip on his bull hook. He was the boss now, promoted following Adam Forepaugh Sr.'s death during the winter and Addie's departure from the elephant tent to assume a managerial role. Far Stream didn't miss Addie and his hat with the gold braid.

She made it halfway to shore before receiving a dousing from Basil that called for retaliation. John L., Modoc and Rubber joined in to make a colossal mock battle, stirring up the water and bringing renewed cheers from the onlookers.

"Come here! I said come here! *Come here!*"

Far Stream relented and began to slowly move out, out and then over, meandering toward her sister. Red Moon had spent the thirty-minute swim time off to the side, swishing her trunk back and forth in the shallows, looking thoroughly wretched.

"Come on, Dick! Get over here *now!*"

Dick as usual was the worst laggard. He took a step, he stopped to fill his trunk with water and douse his back, he took another step, a small one, he stopped again, another leisurely dousing. Joe Beatty waded in, pant legs rolled up, to hurry him on. It only took the sight of the bull hook for Dick, in one of his malleable periods, to lower his head and shuffle forward to take his place in the line, leaving a trail of streaming water, his hide glistening black.

Young William "Whitey" Alf, recently hired and still green, made for Far Stream and Red Moon, slow to leave the shallows.

"Come on! Let's go!"

Whitey was new. Far Stream and Red Moon ignored his first order. He raised his arm to strike with his bull hook. They moved.

Early afternoon, heat rising inside the elephant tent, Far Stream drowsing with the others, Red Moon miserable beside her, unable to doze. The problem that had been plaguing Red Moon intermittently for some time had flared up again, this time worse than ever. Eventually she started to grunt in distress and looked pleadingly at her sister.

Far Stream left her hay and moved closer, taking Red Moon's stubby right tusk in her mouth and grinding on it with her molars. She had stumbled on the technique a few days before, after trying everything else she could think of, caressing and thumping and pulling and butting. Red Moon let out a grateful sigh as the vibrations passed into her jaw and deadened the pain.

Two o'clock. Time for the Fall of Nineveh. Far Stream was draped with gaudy fabrics and led by Whitey in blackface into the main tent, there to lend atmosphere to the Biblical spectacle that was the latest Forepaugh attraction. All that was required of her was to stand in the background alongside the others and a few dusty camels, cages of lions, hyenas and bears. At the fore, sprawled languidly on a divan, was Sardanapalus himself, the last Assyrian king, wallowing in Bacchanalian revels with his court and his harem.

Enter the dancing girls, voluptuous, undulating, cavorting, fulfilling the promise in the souvenir program of a "Grand Saturnalia." They moved in a wave across the center ring, sweeping seductively past the acrobats, gladiators and snake charmers, past the slave auction with its nubile offerings, a shocking amount of bare flesh—shocking but instructive considering the stern moral lesson in store. Whitey, his eyes wide beside Far Stream, became as usual transfixed.

Now here is Jonah, in Biblical robes and long beard to

147

pantomime God's dire warning. The people are too drunk with wine and sensuality to listen. They scoff. Jonah shakes his fist to the accompaniment of thunder and flashes of lightning and he turns his back on the city. Another tableau of wantonness and feasting and gossamer-clad frolics and it is too late for repentance. The trumpets are sounding. Invading armies are marching. The enemy is coming to wreck the vengeance Jonah foretold.

Sardanapalus is defiant as the enemy enters the city. He orders a funeral pyre erected and everything cast upon it— his wives, his concubines, his slaves and his riches. He then mounts the pile and sets it alight with a torch to perish along with all his possessions, writhing and wailing amid a convincing display of smoke and flames and explosions that billow the canvas. Far Stream stands still.

Back to the elephant tent. The draperies are removed. Then a return to the main tent for the dance number and marching, Patsy leading, the display drawing the usual appreciative clapping and laughter. Then back again to the elephant tent for another costume change in preparation for the show's grand finale, the race.

"Down."

It was Joe Beatty and Lou Hand with her blanket, six yards of fringed scarlet. Far Stream eased herself onto her knees while they positioned the fabric over her back, then rose and swished her trunk at Red Moon, who was once again hurting. The tip brushed Joe's head in passing, earning her an admonishment and a sharp blow.

"What's gotten into you lately?"

The men moved on to Modoc, slightly irritable this evening, then to John L. Sullivan, drowsily obedient and docile as always. Modoc got the royal blue blanket. John got the canary yellow and let out a yawn.

The men were getting dressed themselves now, Lou pulling on the scarlet smock that matched Far Stream's blanket, Joe donning the blue.

"Where the hell have you been?" Joe snapped when Whitey ran into the tent at the last moment. Joe was the most senior of the three and made it his business to keep the others in line.

"I'm here, ain't I?"

Whitey started to pull on the yellow smock he wore when riding John. He was young and careless and big talking and had a knack for rubbing older hands like Joe the wrong way. When he was finished he grinned and said again, "I'm here, ain't I?"

"Yeah, you're here," Joe replied, annoyed.

A moment of quiet before the return to the big tent, Far Stream resisting the impulse to throw hay on her back because it was not allowed when she had on her race finery. She looked about at the others, John with his head down, scarcely awake, Modoc dully swaying, Red Moon with her eyes closed, lost in her pain.

A sneeze from behind where the others were tethered. There was old Basil, the sneezer, looking startled, a spray of wet in front. There was Dick, momentarily roused from a doze, the end of his trunk resting on the ground, and Rubber and Picaninny and newcomer George.

Duncan was gone. He had become unruly and been donated to the Washington DC Zoological Gardens. Gold Dust, deemed equally unmanageable, had followed. It was part of the ongoing shift in the show that had begun with the disposal of Bolivar, Tip and Chief, a shift that came with the realization that mature male elephants were too dangerous to keep when they began to show signs of musth madness. It was a shift that would see virtually all male elephants gradually eliminated from circuses in favor of females. Females were less apt to kill.

The lilting band number signaling the end of the regular program and the start of the hippodrome races. Howls of laughter for the miniature ponies ridden by monkeys. More sedate clapping for the English gentlemen's horse race, five entries, three times round the track.

A tap on her jaw. Far Stream lowered her trunk for Lou and lifted him up on her shoulders. He sat with his legs behind her ears. Beside her, Whitey settled on John and Joe on Modoc. They filed out of the elephant tent, the tang of a grassy field trodden by a thousand feet strong in the air.

"Two bits says I win tonight," said Whitey as they waited in the twilight outside the flap opening onto the track inside the main tent. He was smiling broadly like he always did when his youthful brashness came out.

"Keep your money," said Joe.

"Okay, big talker. I'll take it," said Lou.

A roar of laughter inside at the conclusion of what was humorously billed the Irish race, circus employees pushing wheelbarrows. The contestants exited past to return the barrows to the menagerie and elephant tents as the muffled introduction began for the fourth event, the India race, "three ponderous pachyderms... over ten tons of thundering flesh... a spectacle nowhere else seen."

The flap was thrown back and Far Stream advanced into the Edison lighting.

"All right, gentlemen. Move 'em up here!"

Far Stream stepped forward at Lou's nudging to the chalked line. It would be once around the track that encompassed the three rings. She had done it many times before. She understood what was expected. She had even come to derive a certain satisfaction from the competition. But not tonight. Her sister's pain and her own helplessness to relieve it were distracting her mind.

The starter raised his arm and held aloft a large white handkerchief, held it and held it as the clowns leaned forward and forward, their grandly mimed betting with plate-sized dollars concluded. Then the handkerchief dropped and Far Stream was being pounding behind her ears, Lou's hard heels, and she was lurching forward, accelerating to a hurrying shuffle.

John L. Sullivan, rousing from his somnolence, took the lead, Modoc and Far Stream running even one length behind. "Go on, go on, go on, go on," Lou urged her, kicking hard and plying the flat of his bull hook. Far Stream lowered her head and tried to increase her speed. She started to gain on John as they went into the first turn, Modoc now a fraction behind her. The audience was on its feet, shouting with real energy, "Come on, Red!" "Come on, Yellow!" "Come on, Blue!"

Out of the turn now, seventy yards of straight going to the finish, John still leading, Far Stream a half length back, Modoc at her tail. And then stars were flashing all across the arena, lightheadedness sweeping over Far Stream, her legs no longer part of her body.

She staggered and almost went down. Lou was no longer perched on her shoulders. He was flying through the air to the accompaniment of a collective "Ooh" from the crowd as Modoc passed her on the outside on the way to the finish, John now well out in front, too far to catch.

Riderless, Far Stream slowed to a walk and veered off the track into the center ring, scattering the clowns who were no longer smiling under their paint. She stopped, legs wobbly, stomach queasy. She closed her eyes and gradually the flashing stars faded. The wild spinning of the canvas began to slow.

Patsy, watching from a dark corner, hurried over. "Steady, girl," he said. "Steady now. Steady." And to the clowns: "Go see about Lou."

The race was over. John had won it. There was Lou now. He was on his feet, testing his limbs, the clowns clustered around him brushing himself off.

"He's all right, folks! He's all right!"

The ring announcer's booming announcement, taken up with pantomimed relief by the clowns, elicited a flood of clapping and cheering, redoubled when Lou came limping back to Far Stream, waving and trying to smile.

"Damn," he muttered. "What the hell happened?"

"Lou, you must have sailed thirty feet."

"Come on, come on," hissed the ringmaster through a clenched smile, striding over. "Let's break it up. If you can walk, get her moving. Finish it out."

Far Stream continued the rest of the way around the hippodrome track to complete the circuit, Lou gamely limping alongside, cradling his arm, the crowd cheering loudly at the sporting display. John and Whitey were waiting at the finish to greet them along with Modoc and Joe.

Joe took Lou's good hand with real concern. "Are you all right, Lou?"

Whitey, grinning widely, followed, whispering as he did so, "That'll be twenty-five cents."

The show was over. The circus was being packed up in lamplight. Far Stream and the others were led to the trough for one last drink before returning to the train. She staked her spot at the water and pushed against Modoc and George to make space for Red Moon. They drank and sprayed together, then Far Stream began to grind on her sister's scored tusk.

"Look at that," said Joe, noticing. "Hey Patsy, look at that. Topsy's doing it again."

Time to return to the train. The order was given.

"All right, mile up."

Far Stream, her head still slightly woozy, was slow to comply. She wanted longer at the trough with Red Moon.

"Damn it," snapped Whitey. "What the hell's your trouble?" He raised his arm, about to deliver a blow.

It never landed. In one smooth motion Far Stream seized him in her trunk and swept him off his feet and plunged him head down into the water. She was in no mood to tolerate a reprimand from the new man just now.

Patsy reacted in an instant, racing over and roaring at her to release him, Joe and Lou not far behind. Far Stream turned her head, flinching, as they beat her but she did not release Whitey—Whitey with his arms and legs flailing as he was about to drown in water no more than thigh deep.

And then the vise grip relaxed and it was all over. Far Stream moved away from the trough and took her place in line with Red Moon and the others and began to flick at the ground as if nothing had happened.

Whitey reared up with a great sobbing gasp. He tumbled out of the trough and lay on the ground, a quivering heap, vomiting water.

CHAPTER 14

THE TRAIN WAS RUMBLING through forested hills at two o'clock in the morning, the next town forty miles ahead, the last twenty-five back. The poorly maintained rail line made the way bumpy; like riding on bare ties, complained Patsy Meagher; like a ship tossed about in a storm, according to Joe. The cars shuddered and jerked and jolted along, giving everyone a good shaking, workers and performers alike, knocking backs and hips and shoulders against the hard sides of bunks and generally making it equally uncomfortable to sit up, stand or lie down.

In the elephant car, Red Moon had at last quieted down after an hour of Far Stream grinding on her tusk, a welcome silence after her long session of groaning. In the lull, Far Stream hung her head and allowed herself to relax, bracing her legs against the car's swaying. She probed the bruises where the men had beaten her for her near-drowning of Whitey, working on her forelegs. They were still sore.

Relaxing further, she let her trunk drop. It swung a fraction of an inch above the car floor, the boards worn smooth by her scuffing feet over the thousands of miles. With the twisting and jerking that the car had been doing, the dirt in the gaps between the boards had worked its way out. Wafts of air now blew in through open cracks. Every time Far Stream's trunk passed over, she caught a whiff of the grease in the wheels.

Rattle-rattle-rattle.

At the far end of the car, Picaninny, the little clown elephant now grown quite big, was shaking his chain.

Picaninny had always been strange; not vicious or violent, just strange. There were the childish squeaks he continued to make on into adolescence, the odd head movements, up and down, side to side, up and down, an endless repetition. And there was the habit he had developed of fumbling with his chain, rattle-rattle-rattle until one of the others silenced him with a swat or a keeper came by and dealt him a sharp blow.

Rattle-rattle-rattle.

Then the sound of boards straining as Picaninny pressed his head against the side of the car: Creak . . . creak . . . creak.

Rattle-rattle-rattle.

Creak . . . creak . . . creak.

Stop it, Basil communicated sourly from three places down.

Rattle-rattle-rattle.

Creak . . . creak . . . creak.

Rattle-rattle-rattle.

Stop it. Be quiet.

John L. Sullivan, whose place was beside Picaninny, was as usual off wandering among the many pleasurable memories stored in his mind. At the moment he was revisiting a pail of corn meal and oat mash liberally sprinkled with salt, a treat he had eaten last week, or perhaps it was last month or last year. Time was not something John kept much track of. Whenever it was, the memory remained vivid. It pulsed and percolated in his head, then overflowed and seeped down the car. Far Stream, dreamily relaxed now, began tasting it too.

Rattle-rattle-rattle.

Creak . . . creak . . . creak.

Stop it. Be quiet.

Rattle-rattle-rattle.

Creak . . . creak . . . creak.

Basil scooped up a mass of dung and flung it down the car with an annoyed snort. It shot past Modoc and hit John. John sleepily opened his eyes and raised his trunk to examine the mass stuck to his side. It didn't interest him. He returned to his pleasant hot mash reminiscing. Picaninny, chastened by Basil's irritation, let go of his chain and contented himself for the moment with bobbing his head.

Far Stream's eyes were closed now, the clatter of the wheels beneath her receding, the heartbeat of the train moving through the night at twenty-five miles an hour, as familiar as the sound of her breathing. A little further and only the ebb and flow of the echoes remained, the soft muting indicating a buffer of trees on both sides. A sharp burst of intensity brought her head up a fraction. They were passing through a rock cut, train clatter bouncing back. Another lull, her head again drooping. Then a sudden drumming and booming—a bridge.

She looked up. The door of the car was open, trees bathed in filtered sunlight slowly passing outside, the sky an overarching tent of gray canvas. She gazed into the depths, feeling freedom beckoning from deep in the trees. She took a step forward but was stopped by the chain that a shiny black crow was pecking at with real purpose. It paused to gaze up into her eyes and then returned to its pecking, pecking, pecking, as if it really intended to wear through the iron. And then it was flapping up in her face, thrusting its head into her mouth and she was grinding on its beak, trying to be gentle for she did not want to hurt it.

A jolt threw her off balance and brought her back to her senses. She stumbled into Basil beside her, and Basil into Modoc and Modoc into John and John into Picaninny who hit the wall at the end. A flurry of snorts and huffs and grumbles as everyone regained their footing, grumpily trunk-swatting each other as they sorted themselves out.

A groan on the opposite side. Red Moon was hurting

again. Far Stream extended her trunk to probe inside the mouth of her sister, feeling the brick-sized molar that refused to make way for the new one erupting underneath. Its stubborn resistance was what was causing Red Moon such pain. Far Stream took her sister's tusk, deeply scored now, and again started grinding—grinding and grinding until Red Moon at last settled down.

Rattle-rattle-rattle.

Creak . . . creak . . . creak.

Be quiet.

Rattle-rattle-rattle.

Creak . . . creak . . . creak.

Stop it. Be quiet.

A lurch and a screech. Far Stream was thrown against Basil again. Another outburst of noisy irritation, Basil's trunk striking Far Stream in the ear, Far Stream striking her back, the car again slowly settling.

Rattle-rattle-rattle.

Creak . . . creak . . . creak.

Be quiet. Stop it. Be quiet.

The car took another lurch. Then another, more violent. Then a shaking jolting thumping crashing and Far Stream was thrown hard against Basil and back against Red Moon and the world was turning upside down and she was smashing against bodies and against the side then the roof as the car left the rails and rolled down an embankment, one complete rotation, and came to rest on its side.

Inside, a gargantuan jumble lost in darkness, dust and hay and confusion, a struggling, screaming, kicking mass of bodies piled upon bodies leaning against bodies, everyone tangled in chains.

Far Stream, straining and roaring as hard as the rest, was pinned on her side, Red Moon beneath her, Basil heavily on top, an unseen chain twisted around her thigh, digging in deep.

Minutes passed. The worst of the uproar subsided.

Down at the end of the car Picaninny managed to regain his footing, taking some of the strain off John. His movements rocked the car and set the others to shrieking and struggling again, the boards of the side of the car, now the floor, giving way now under their weight.

More shrieking and the sounds of struggling were coming from the second elephant car just behind, the one carrying Dick, Rubber and George and bunks for the menagerie hands. Dick's voice was loudest. He seemed to be in a panic. Then the sound of splintering wood as he began battering the car.

There were men outside. They were running, calling, climbing onto the upturned side of the car, fumbling at the door which was now above Far Stream's head.

A voice above: "Get a pry bar! This latch is all bent!"

A voice on the side: "You're head's bleeding, Patsy. You all right?"

And from down the track: "We need some light here! Bring a light!"

Far Stream remained completely, thoroughly trapped, her attempts to get up only causing pain for herself and Basil on top and Red Moon below. She gradually quieted down and lay still, regaining some control of her senses. Basil thankfully did the same, settling on top of Far Stream with a resigned sigh, holding her foreleg back to ease the strain on the chain that was twisted. She knew what had happened. So did Far Stream and Red Moon. They had been in many train derailments before, although never this bad.

The door was being forced open, a long harsh scraping. A head appeared above silhouetted against the moonlight. A lantern was handed up.

Here was Joe holding the lantern gazing down at the tumble of bodies. "We'll have to knock a hole in the roof," he said, leaning through the opening and looking down the length of the car. "Right down there where Lou's standing.

chances. He passed by to line up with the others. With the extra space now opened, Modoc could be brought to her feet. She was led out of the car and on down the siding, groaning from some injury as she went.

A second hole had in the meantime been ripped open at the opposite end of the car near where Far Stream lay pinned. "They're in an awful tangle," said Patsy, peering in with Joe when the hole was finished.

He reached in with his bull hook and poked Basil, who was the nearest.

"Up, Basil. Up."

Basil struggled to rise. The chain dug in. Far Stream roared and Red Moon bellowed and Joe said, "Stop. Stop. The chain's all twisted."

A closer examination by the light of a lantern, shadows dancing on the inside walls of the car.

"Lord, they're sure in a tangle," said Patsy. "I guess we'll have to take the chains off."

"Can't get at it," said Joe, eying the links disappearing beneath Basil on the outside of the heap. "We'll have to get Basil to shift." And to the others outside: "Get me a hammer and chisel."

The call went out. "Hammer and chisel! We need a hammer and chisel!"

The tools were produced. Joe cautiously stepped into the car. "Now you just stay nice and quiet," he said. Patsy, a gash on his head, stepped in behind with a lantern, holding it high.

Sharp ringing blows at Basil's forefoot, the chisel biting its way through the iron. A thud as the chain dropped to the boards, followed by a groan of relief from Basil as she was released from some of the strain. With her one leg free, she was able to move enough for Joe to get at Far Stream's restraints. Another few minutes of clanging, another thud and they were on their feet.

Basil, reliable Basil, led the way out of the overturned

car, the whole of it creaking and swaying under her weight. She let out a deep sigh when she reached the siding and safety, her agitation falling away. She passed by, following Whitey down the line.

Far Stream went next. She stepped stiffly through the ragged opening—her leg was hurting—and onto firm ground, the undergrowth hacked away and trampled down back to the trees.

She looked around. The front half of the train was still on the rails, the engine steaming and puffing smoke into the night sky. Three cars lay overturned in the middle, on their sides at the bottom of a shallow embankment, the two elephant cars and a third packed with led stock. The bunk compartment end of the rearmost elephant car was scorched and still smoking. The remaining cars further back were off the rails but upright.

"Mile up, now."

Far Stream allowed herself to be guided by Lou up the tracks. She limped as she went. Her leg had received a bad wrench.

"Tut."

She halted in line behind Basil, waiting for Red Moon to follow. Up at the head of the line she could see the distinctive shape of Dick's head in the moonlight. Circus folk were standing about, watching, conversing in groups, talking to others still in the cars forward. One man was sitting on the bare ground, his bloody head in his hands. A second lay flat out, very still, his friends hovering over.

She looked back. Red Moon, the last out, was emerging from the hole in the roof of the car. She stopped, half in and half out, and looked up at the moon in the night sky above the orange glow of the lanterns. She opened her mouth and slowly moved her head back and forth. She was acting quite strange.

Her head came down and her eyes met Far Stream's.

Then she was charging. Red Moon was charging. She

was trumpeting with excitement and agitation and fury and she was charging past the men who were unable to stop her and she was sweeping past Far Stream and breaking for freedom up the tracks where there was nothing but forest.

Far Stream's trunk swept out. The sudden movement surprised her, as if she had not made it herself. Her trunk swept out seemingly on its own and knocked Lou sprawling and her legs were moving and she was chasing after her sister and she was breaking away too and the men were roaring, "Stop her! Stop her!" and the cry was being taken up along the line, "Stop her! Stop her!" but she kept going, thundering past Basil and John and Dick and the others, past wide-eyed keepers and tent men and roustabouts and performers who were all scrambling to get out of the way.

She kept on going past the steaming engine until the tracks ahead were clear with trees on both sides. She kept on going to the gap that led into the forest and then she was plunging through it after her sister, crashing through the undergrowth and snapping off branches, smashing through brambly thickets and trampling down saplings, the sound of her passage obliterating the cries fading in the distance:

"Topsy! Topsy! Come back!"

CHAPTER 15

SHE COULD FEEL THE BRUISING from the derailment and the tumble down the embankment, that and the wrenching her hind leg had taken that was making her limp now that she had slowed to a walk.

Where was Red Moon? There were no longer moonlit gray flashes of her up ahead. She had been swallowed up by the forest. Far Stream paused again to listen for a call, for sounds of the passage of a large body crashing through undergrowth and scraping past trees. She heard nothing but her own heartbeat. It continued loud in her head, the echo of the panic she had felt in the train wreck and again when the urge seized her to escape after her sister. She made a deep long-carrying rumble and listened but heard no reply.

She continued on, alarmed at being alone but now in control of her senses, beginning to take note of her surroundings. She was beneath a rustling canopy of maples and pines, a spongy layer of leaves, twigs and needles crunching under her feet. There was no path to follow, only a meandering course of least resistance around brambly thickets and rocky outcrops, the sounds and smells of the train faded to nothing behind her. There was no acrid smoke, no steamy oily chug from the engine, no iron wheel clatter, no shouting, no odors of tobacco or bacon. All the sounds and scents of men were entirely gone, replaced by woodland aromas and a quiet that was somehow unnerving, broken only by the whisper of the wind in the trees.

A trace from her sister. She had veered downhill, down toward what Far Stream determined must be water. She made another deep rumble and this time, with a surge of reassurance, she heard an answering call. She headed toward it down the sloping terrain, traversing in places where the going was steepest, down and along until she came to a brook trickling over a bed of stones and gathering in a pool.

Red Moon was there. She was drinking the water and emitting a hum of deep satisfaction. She looked up, eyes twinkling, as Far Stream joined her and they began to caress each other, glad to be reunited. *The hurt is gone*, Red Moon communicated with gleeful relief, titling her head back and opening her mouth to reveal the new molar. Far Stream probed it as she absorbed Red Moon's story, the initial wonder when the old molar dropped out as she stepped from the rail car, the flooding sense of release that followed, the spasm of confused sensations that sent her running away.

They stayed by the pool until just before dawn, their sides touching as they drank their fill and spouted and groomed, silencing the cricket in its nook by the muddying water. What they needed now was food, something more sustaining than the twigs and leaves all about. With no path to make the way easy they followed the course of the water, stepping over rocks, pushing past trees, slowly, carefully descending until the brook leveled and widened and they were in a valley and the sky was turning purple then violet then blue in the east.

There. A small open space bright with the first sunlight, a patch of good green. They stopped and began to pull up the grass, shaking each mouthful to get rid of the dirt that clung to the roots. It was slow work, filling their bellies this way, no heaps of hay conveniently served out before them as in the elephant tent. In an hour the patch was used up, uprooted and trampled. Finding nothing more nearby, Far

Stream led the way onward, following the flow of the water until the terrain steepened and they were forced to angle away from the brook and try a new way.

It took them to a clearing dotted with yellow and blue flowers. Leaving the trees and entering the secluded meadow, Red Moon broke away with a squeal of excitement and began running about and spinning in circles, ears flapping, tail and trunk extended, a picture of such happiness that Far Stream began doing the same. *This is home*, Red Moon said as they played and cavorted, entwining their trunks and sharing their bubbling high spirits. Far Stream felt it too. She said, *This is home.*

With a sudden mutual impulse they started tearing at the trees at the edge of the clearing, breaking off branches, stripping off bark, using their heads and the weight of their bodies to smash. It wasn't a desire for destruction that moved them. It was an urge to exercise their capabilities, to express their full power, to show what they were. The effort left them breathing hard, muscles glowing, feeling good.

They browsed on through the morning, their initial delight settling into rumbling contentment witnessed by deer that wandered into the clearing. The animals were skittish, freezing and staring for minutes on end. Far Stream and her sister found that by standing still they could get the deer to relax and start grazing—and that with a sudden head shake they could send them bounding away.

The sun was high now, bright and warm on their backs. Far Stream closed her eyes and let herself drift, listening to the buzzing of insects, the bird songs, branches swishing in the breeze.

A fly buzzed by her ear. She heard the beat of its wings. She felt it alight and move across her brow in short darting motions. It was a strange and wonderful thing, this heightening of her senses, as if a mist had been swept away from her brain. She was experiencing everything more intensely than ever before, even as she was drifting off into a doze.

A rustle underfoot. She opened her eyes and drowsily looked down. It was a groundhog emerging from its burrow close to the curled tip of her hanging trunk. She watched as it looked about and began scratching and grooming, oblivious to the mountain of flesh looming over.

Very slowly, she directed her trunk at it and gently blew. The groundhog stopped its grooming and looked about, still oblivious to the meaning of the colossal grey columns rising up from the grass and the giant mass that was filling the sky. Far Stream blew again, this time a little harder, flattening the groundhog's whiskers against the side of its head. The little creature noticed the hole now in the strange grey thing hanging down. It cautiously approached to investigate. When its nose was almost touching the quivering wet tip, its black eyes peering into the dark burrow that was the end of a very long nose, Far Stream gave a sharp snort. It sent the groundhog tumbling head over heels and scampering back down its hole.

Toward evening, hunger momentarily satisfied, they returned to the brook for a leisurely session of drinking and spouting, Far Stream once again examining Red Moon's new molar, reassuring herself that her sister's pain really was gone. The sky was growing dark now. Crickets were beginning to chirp. They made their way back to the clearing, moving carefully through the trees and over the rough places until they were back on the grass.

Then it was night. The onset of darkness made Far Stream uneasy, the yips and the howls, the unseen flapping of wings, the little scuffles and squeaks in the grass, all of it made uncomfortably close, uncomfortably loud by her heightened senses. She was not used to this, being exposed under the stars, being away from the protective cover of canvas and the train and everything that was familiar.

And then she started to feel queasy. She was accustomed to a diet of hay, not fresh green vegetation with an ample sprinkling of dirt. Everything she had eaten during the day was gurgling inside her, her intestines filling with gas, cramps in her bowels. From the noises coming from Red Moon it was clear her sister was enduring the same. Both of them remained on their feet through the darkness, sides lightly touching, unable to sleep.

Things began to look better again with the return of the sun. The cramping eased and Far Stream resumed her browsing at the side of her sister, denuding more of the small meadow. They took another trip to the water; they watched the animals, more skittish deer, a porcupine that waddled toward them and required a wide berth, a bear that stood on its hind legs and stared at them intently before harrumphing off. And then it was dark again and the enveloping vulnerability returned. Far Stream, feeling very tired, briefly lay down this time but was able to doze for only a few minutes. Fatigue mounting, she tried again near dawn. This time she sank deeper.

She awoke with a start from inside the car tumbling down the embankment, rending iron and splintering wood and clattering against stone that briefly echoed then faded.

Red Moon was gone. The clearing was gone. All around her was white.

It was only when she rose to her feet that she saw her sister a few paces away, a disembodied head floating on low-lying fog in the grey light of morning. The head dipped down and disappeared as Red Moon searched in the mist for whatever forage remained. Far Stream joined her, two heads rising and falling, but she found little. When the sun appeared over the surroundings hills and burned off the mist, they saw that this place, their new home, was already exhausted.

They would not be able to stay here. They would have to move on.

Their searching for a way forward took them back through the trees, the passage slow and difficult in places, skirting around obstacles, pushing through thickets, constantly investigating with their trunks as they went, for so much of the vegetation was new, unfamiliar.

The terrain began to slope upward, up and up until the ground became rocky and the tree cover thinned and they encountered a profusion of shoulder-high shrubs, still more of the unfamiliar, deep green leaves and clusters of pink flowers. Red Moon stopped to sample. She found them palatable and began stripping one shrub after another. They had been walking for three hours and she was hungry. Far Stream did the same. They spent some time at this, cooling themselves with their own water, before moving on, up and up the rest of the hillside, then down and down into the next valley where sparkling flashes glimpsed through the trees confirmed the presence of the lake they had smelled at the top.

The trees here were comfortably spaced, the canopy high, adequate room for their big bodies when they needed shade. The lake, a quarter mile across, was a perfectly smooth mirror of clear water. And near where they happened to meet it, a meadow—a spacious rolling carpet of grass with a wealth of succulent reeds by the shoreline, food enough to satisfy them for a long time.

They waded into the lake for a delightful hour of drinking, lolling and spouting, playfully pushing, for they were both very happy. Then they wandered about their new meadow, tasting the banquet that had been laid out before them, satisfying themselves fully that this was the place.

This is home, Red Moon exulted.

This is home, Far Stream agreed. And then she stopped and her head went down and she arched her back strangely and was violently sick.

She grew worse as the day worn on and it became evening. The vomiting continued until there was only dry heaving, her eyes streaming so heavily that the new land around her, her new home, was unseen. Then her other end loosened and a profound weakness engulfed her. She lost control of her legs. She sank to her knees. She was vaguely aware of Red Moon trying to offer her comfort, holding twists of grass to her mouth, dribbling in water, urging her to *Get up, get up*. Finally, with her sister no longer there, she gave in to the sickness and lay down on her side.

How long it lasted Far Stream did not know. She was sporadically aware of a hot sun beating on her, of struggling to breathe, of being cold in the darkness, of rain pattering down, of another night passing, perhaps two, perhaps three. Then the world disappeared completely and she plunged down into the earth, there to wander through her childhood forest, to dance in the circus, to ride on the train, then still further down to the twilight at the very edge of existence. There were beings there, beings she had loved dearly, others she had almost forgotten, all of them welcoming. She communed with them and allowed them to caress her. And then she was leaving, seeing the faces of men.

She gradually returned to her senses in the meadow, her body weighed down by a great weakness. She lay in the grass blinking and staring for a long time as the events of the previous days seeped back into her memory. She knew she had to get back on her feet. She tried to do so but failed. She lay back and rested. She tried again. She tried again.

It took many heaving attempts and all of her strength to stand up and then stay there, for the effort made her dizzy. When the meadow stopped spinning she looked about for her sister. Red Moon was not there. In her lingering confusion, Far Stream did not find the absence particularly upsetting. She tottered to the lake and drank. She wandered along the shoreline and ate a few mouthfuls.

In the early afternoon, her strength returning, her confusion lifting, a feeling of unease began to creep into her brain. Where was Red Moon? Where was her sister? She looked about the clearing again and through the trees but failed to see her. She listened for a call, a sound, a signal. She heard nothing. She made a low rumble that carried a long distant. She listened for an answer. She heard nothing in return.

The sky darkened. Thunder rumbled in the distance. A drop struck her back, then another, then a light patter of rain.

And then the heavens opened and on came the downpour. It swept across the secluded meadow in waves, lashing rain and violent buffeting wind, strong enough to rock Far Stream on her feet. She turned her back to the tempest, rain sluicing off her, cold infiltrating her body. Then, driven by a powerful gust, she took a step toward the trees.

Another gust, another step. The storm did not want her to stay here. It prodded her out of the clearing and into the forest, wind howling in the branches, trees swaying, cracking and creaking, less rain getting through.

The storm passed. It ebbed to a drizzle, the trees dripping, then the clouds parted and out came the sun. She looked back at the meadow, glistening wet through the trees, but she did not return there. She knew that she shouldn't. She turned away and pushed her way onward, heading she did not know where. Just onward. Toward something. To whatever was pulling her in.

The way led her down an incline to a stream. She paused for a drink here, then continued up a slope beyond. Up and up she went until she came to a ridge, then down and down the far side until she could see flashes of blue through the trees. It was another lake, smaller than the one she had left behind but just as mirror-like, the surface glittering gold.

She reached the lake and looked across the water. A cliff rose up from the opposite shore. There was something familiar about it.

The lake erupted. Red Moon rose to the surface with a great sputtering snort. Another snort, a head shake and she caught sight of Far Stream.

You are a slow one, she said. *I've been waiting for you.*

Far Stream ran into the water with a cry of joy and relief,

glad to be reunited with her sister. She happily bounded and thrashed and cavorted, the darkness that had been clouding her mind forgotten, the weakness weighing down her limbs from the sickness dispelled.

It soon became apparent, however, that Red Moon did not feel the same. There was something different about her. She was distant, preoccupied, not interested in playing. She kept pausing to look out across the water, willing Far Stream to follow her gaze.

Far Stream finally did so. She looked at the cliff on the far side of the lake. It rose out of the water to a height of three hundred feet, sunlight falling upon it, the rock face warm beige and ochre, the upside-down reflection in the lake making two. It was strangely familiar.

The Shining Sun Cliffs.

Red Moon left her and moved deeper into the water, leading the way to the opposite shore. Far Stream watched her sink into the lake and start swimming, disturbed by her strangeness, confused because the view of the cliff rising before them was not quite the same as the image in her mind. Then, not wanting to be again left behind, she followed, murky billows rising as her feet stirred up the silt. She waded in until her head was awash and her trunk extended, the ripples off it forming a "V" pointing forward. Swimming, swimming, and then her feet were touching the bottom and she was hauling herself out of the water, dripping, on the far shore.

Red Moon had moved on ahead. She could not have gone to the right. That way was blocked by a tumble of rocks at the base of the cliff, now rearing up directly overhead. Far Stream advanced into the trees to the left.

The going was rough, stabbing raking branches over boulders, then steep. She continued on, following a zigzag course upward, forcing her way through thorny growth that could not be skirted, stumbling over jagged rocks hidden under a rotting blanket of leaves, flapping her ears at the heat and the insects that buzzed around her, attacking in clouds.

Far Stream was high now, the terrain leveling, the forest cover still dense. She stopped and listened. Where was her sister? She tried one direction, came to shelving rock and tangle and could go no farther. She tried another way, more impenetrable tangle, this time perilously down-sloping, and again, slipping and scrabbling over pebbly gravel. She peered about but saw nothing, sampled the air but smelled nothing, listened hard but heard only the sigh of the wind.

It was blowing from the west. She turned to face it and proceeded, more cautiously now, pushing through undergrowth prickly and scraping. And then the trees fell away and she was at the top of the cliff and there was Red Moon at the edge, as still as the rocks all around her, gazing out across the whole world.

Far Stream took a step toward her and stopped, mindful of the sheer drop-off.

Look.

She looked out across the vista, miles of green forest under a dome of blue sky. It was like the view from the Shining Sun Cliffs that existed in her memory—and yet somehow different.

Look. They're waiting for us.

Far Stream looked. She saw trees. She saw sky. She did not see anyone waiting.

Let's go to them. They're waiting. They're waiting for us.

Far Stream took another step, then hesitated. She was afraid of falling. Red Moon was perched at the very edge now, somehow balancing there.

Let's go to them, Far Stream. Come. They're waiting.

Far Stream took another step. The gravel under her feet made the footing uncertain, giving her a feeling that she was being pulled to the edge.

Come. Let's go to them.

Why was Red Moon acting so strangely? Far Stream

took a step back.

Don't be afraid, Far Stream. Let's go to them.

Red Moon was drawing her to the edge.

Come. They're waiting.

Bare rock underfoot, loose skittering gravel, the drop perilously close now, three hundred feet down.

Let's go to them. They're waiting.

A moment poised before the fall, straining, resisting, then a lurching lunging scrambling with a shriek of cold terror and Far Stream was running away, crashing back through the trees.

No path to follow, no direction, only blind stampeding, oblivious to branches tearing and lashing. It took her downhill, a trail of destruction behind her, and traces of blood for she was bleeding, her feet, her legs, her sides. She ran until her breathing was ragged and her thundering heart filled her skull and the terrain was leveling and the ground was oozing and marshy and then splashing all around.

She had run into a lake.

CHAPTER 16

THE COOLNESS OF THE LAKE brought her back to her senses, her panic subsiding with the waves stirred up by the splash of her body. She did not move. She continued to stand in the water, bewildered, weariness creeping back into her muscles, the surface returning to a mirror smoothness that reflected her shape.

She could feel her feet now. They were cut and hurting from the crashing run down the hillside. She could feel the stinging of the scrapes on her sides. Still she did not move.

She looked out across the water. There was no sign of the cliff, no indication that this was the lake she had followed Red Moon across to reach it. No, this lake was different. She must have run down the opposite side of the hill and into yet another body of water.

She looked back at the shore. She could just make out her sister standing there. Red Moon must have followed her down the hillside. She was hanging back in the trees.

Far Stream looked away, out across the water. She closed her eyes and listened. Nothing.

She raised her trunk and sampled the breeze. There was a faint trace of wood smoke.

It was the scent of man, a scent that now conveyed comfort and warmth in this empty forest. She turned toward it, then turned back toward her sister. She turned toward it again. Again she turned back.

An uncomfortable image began to form in her mind, brought to her on the breeze in the smell of the smoke. It was of elephants lined up outside the barricade that had been used to trap her family, bathed in the smoke of the fires of the men; the same elephants that had been ridden into the enclosure to subdue Grandmother, Mother, Red Moon, herself. For the first time in her life Far Stream made the connection—that there was no void between those alien beings and herself as she remembered. She was really one of them. She had been for a long time.

She turned away. The image faded. She continued to stand in the water as the sun passed its zenith and began its descent toward the hills. She probed beneath the surface for vegetation but found nothing. She filled her trunk and spouted. Still she did not move.

And then she was turning back to the smoke because there was really no other way she could turn. She was turning back to sample the acrid tang, allowing herself to slip back under its power.

She took a step toward it.

Don't go there.

She glanced back at Red Moon, a reproachful look. She was angry at her sister.

Don't go there.

Far Stream ignored her and waded on through the shallows, following the shoreline. It brought her to a promontory just as the sun was dipping behind the trees. Red Moon reluctantly followed, lagging behind.

Don't go there.

Again Far Stream ignored her. She climbed out onto the spit of land, head down as she pushed through branches until they parted and she was looking across water at a hillside and halfway up it wisps of white gently rising.

Don't go there.

She stood gazing at the smoke for a long time, feeling its captivity, feeling its safety, feeling its pull.

Don't go there.

She continued onward, shaking her head to dislodge Red Moon's voice. She veered toward a gap she had spotted in the trees lining the shore, a clearing littered with pieces of wood, a rope hung from a bough, the battered prow of a canoe sunk in the shallows. She waded out of the water and began investigating the clearing, pausing to poke at the rope that was hanging, making it swing. Then she advanced through tall pines on a path worn through the bed of soft needles. Red Moon refused to follow further. She stayed back, hidden deep in the trees.

The path led Far Stream up a gentle incline, the smells of man growing stronger—wood smoke, dried meat, sweat on wool and leather, other traces. And then a bend in the path and up ahead a small cabin. It was a low, rough-built structure, tree stumps surrounding it cut long ago, the tops grey and rotting. She lingered for a time, sniffing, observing. Then, with night coming on, she allowed herself to be drawn in the rest of the way.

The mud-chinked log walls did not reach her chin. The roof, the peak at eye level, was deep with needles and mossy and overgrown with creepers. There were no windows. She ran her trunk along the base of the door and up the edges, sampling the aroma of cooked food, tobacco and unwashed body, snuffling in the familiar. And then she lurched backward, startled by a whack that rattled the door.

"Get away from there, you damn bear!" screeched a voice from inside.

She hesitated, glanced back to where Red Moon was hiding, then edged forward and resumed her snuffling.

Another whack. "Get, I said. Get away from my door!"

At her third approach the door was flung open and a gun barrel thrust out, a small wizened man behind it clad in patched rags. "Get," he bleated. And then he was scrambling backward, his gapped-tooth mouth as wide as his eyes, the blast from his ancient musket blowing a hole through his roof.

"The hell beast of Revelation," he wailed.

The noise frightened her. She fled the clearing and ran back down the path almost all the way to the lake.

Don't go there, Red Moon coaxed her again from the trees.

Far Stream turned away with an annoyed huff and re-traced her steps to the cabin. She stopped when she caught sight of the man, an old hermit, standing in his doorway and muttering, his musket reloaded.

"Get away," he called out, making threatening motions.

She saw the raised musket, knew what it meant but felt no malevolence behind it. She stayed where she was.

"Get away," the hermit repeated, taking squinting aim as he eased closer. "I said get away now."

She shifted nervously but stayed.

He was within thirty feet of her, then twenty, telling her with each cautious curious step, "Get." Far Stream shifted uncertainly as he came closer, apprehensive of his weapon.

The man tried again, "You best get now."

She replied with a soft huff, the barrel now ten feet from her head. Then, because she could think of nothing else, she nodded. This brought the musket down, an amazed look on the scruffy old face.

"Are you what's called an ely-phant?"

She reached out her trunk. He took a step back, body braced, musket up, then stretched forward and extended a wary hand to touch it.

"That's soft," he mused, straightening, moving closer. Then, peering into her eyes: "You *are* an ely-phant, ain't you? I seen your like in a picture."

He began to walk around her, touching her sides, mar-veling at her hugeness as she explored him with her trunk. He was pungently fragrant, a hunter, but did not seem threatening. His words, his presence, the touch of his gnarled fingers—they made her feel safe. She conveyed her feelings to Red Moon. She knew Red Moon could feel them. But still her sister remained hidden deep in the trees.

After a period of mutual exploration, Far Stream followed the hermit back to the door of his cabin and watched through the opening as he stoked up the fire and prepared his supper, venison stew flavored with wild onions. He chuckled as he bent over the pot, delighted now with her company, her great head in his doorway, her presence nearby when he moved outside to eat.

"If I was to shoot you," he said, carefully chewing with his few teeth, "I'd have enough meat for two years, supposing I could get you all jerked. Oh Lordy, wouldn't that be some job." He wheezed out a laugh. "But don't worry, I'm not going to shoot you, 'cause I know I ain't supposed to. You're some kind of special creature. I know that."

Far Stream was hungry but she was even more tired. As the old man continued to mutter and croak by the glow of the fire he lit in the clearing, she swept a space clear of rocks and branches and settled comfortably down.

"Now why did the Lord send a special creature like you to my door? Right to my door He sent you. He's telling me something. Oh, for certain He is. He's sending me a terrible big message, I guess."

Her head was nodding. She couldn't keep her eyes open. With a long whistling sigh she lay back flat and fell fast asleep.

❧

"Ezekiel!"

It was the hermit calling from his cabin just after dawn, looking wildly about for Far Stream. She had awoken in the night and, feeling hungry, had wandered off for food after a long drink in the lake.

The old man at last spotted her and hobbled over on morning-stiff legs.

"Ezekiel! I dreamed it. Praise the Lord, I understand now. Just you give me a tick and I'll be ready to follow."

He hurried back to the cabin, hands raised to heaven. "Thank you, Lord, for thinking of me, a low sinner. Thank you for sending Ezekiel down."

Blundering and banging and rummaging inside the cabin as Far Stream continued her browsing, then the man was back with his musket and fire-blackened pot, provisions, a skin of water, a bedroll.

"I'm ready, Ezekiel," he said. "I'm ready. Lead on."

Far Stream cast him a glance and returned to her grazing. She was glad of his company. The vegetation, however, was far from luxuriant here.

"I'm ready to follow, Ezekiel. I am ready to follow."

Far Stream continued her lethargic meandering through the trees, pulling at the sparse grass she was quickly depleting. She would soon have to move further down the hill, closer to the lake.

"All right," said the old man, sloughing off his load and sitting. "I need to be patient. See, I'm being patient. I'm patiently waiting on you. Lead on when you've a mind."

He watched and waited until mid morning, following Far Stream's every move as she worked her way down to the water, sweeping up sparse clumps of vegetable matter that suited her taste, pausing occasionally to look at Red Moon hidden among the trees where the old man could not see her. She was no longer angry. She wished her sister would come out.

Far Stream's wandering eventually took her onto a second path she had not seen the previous day, one that led off to the east. This brought the hermit lurching to his feet and scurrying over, his face radiant, expectant.

"So it's *this* way," he exulted. "Lead on, Ezekiel. Lead on."

Far Stream, seeing the old man rush toward the path, moved on ahead along it, the realization striking her that he would take her somewhere and that she wanted to go.

They proceeded up the path together and over the rise

and down into the next valley, each following the other, Red Moon trailing unseen behind, on and on, mile after mile, generally northeast. When the sun was high they came to a branching, the old man again eyeing Far Stream intently as he squatted to rest.

"Which way, Ezekiel?" he kept saying. "Which way?"

Seeing the old man drinking from his skin and feeling thirsty herself, she headed down the path toward the faint murmur indicating water not too far distant. "To Enterprise, is it?" said the old man, scampering ahead.

They spent the night on the bank of a river flowing strong out of the mountains, the old man lighting a fire, Far Stream staying close. She drank and ate what she could find and took a long bath, urging Red Moon to join her, the hermit laughing uproariously each time she spouted and falling over with glee when she sprayed him. In the morning, another long period of waiting as Far Stream continued her browsing and the old man his watching, grinning as he chomped open-mouthed on his breakfast. Then finally there came what he took as a sign and he was on his feet and they were both moving down the path that began to widen in the afternoon with the river, widen until it was a road and the old man was whispering, "I don't want to stop at the mill, Ezekiel. Don't lead me there."

They passed the mill, a boy out front staring, the hermit cringing then relaxing as Far Stream kept ambling on. There was a small town just ahead and she was curious. She wanted to see.

Railroad tracks, two cars on a siding, a dirt street lined with unpainted wood buildings, horses, wagons—a small peaceful town, the sort the Forepaugh Circus train passed through at night without stopping, the sort dimly glimpsed through the cracks between the boards of the car. Far Stream made her way in, the heaviness of the forest behind her, the old hermit beside her, and everything changed.

Shouting. Running. Women sweeping up children.

181

"It's the elephant! Fetch the circus man! It's the crazed elephant come in!"

Far Stream, used to blocking out human hubbub, made her way to a nearby trough for a drink and a wetting, ignoring the townspeople staring from windows and doorways, the bolder ones still in the street tensed and ready to sprint for their lives.

"Lead on, Ezekiel," said the hermit, pleased with the tumult, proud of his familiarity with his creature amidst the fear all around. He eased his meager hams onto the steps of a dry goods store and stretched back to rest on his elbows. "Hello there, ma'am," he said gaily to the woman hovering in the doorway behind him. "You wouldn't be able to spare a man a slice of bread and butter, some nice salty butter? Maybe a wee taste of cheese? I'll let you take a look at my ely-phant there."

A pause, then a slab of bread was tossed out the door, no cheese, no butter. The hermit, nonplussed, picked it up and brushed it off and began pulling off pieces to stuff in his mouth.

A bearded man crept forward, rifle in hand, inexplicably crouching.

"Put that down," snapped the hermit, masticating. "Ezekiel's entirely peaceful."

"Mister," breathed the bearded townsman, "that beast's a terror. You best . . . ."

And then the townsman was scuttling to safety for Far Stream was moving. "Where's that damned article from the circus?" he called from a place of safety.

From somewhere down the street: "He's still sleeping."

"Well, for God's sake somebody wake him."

"Lead on, Ezekiel," crowed the hermit, delighted as he rose to follow Far Stream. She shuffled across the street to a pile of hay just inside the open doors of a stable, familiar hay, a heap generous enough to satisfy her considerable hunger. She began to eat to the accompaniment of whinnying and kicking from a horse in a back stall. After a cautious advance, the bearded man, still crouching, crept past her, released the panicked animal and let it run into the street.

"Shut the door, shut the door."

The hermit, finishing his bread, wiped his mouth with the back of his hand and brandished his musket. "You leave my ely-phant be!"

The stable doors swung shut on Far Stream, a plank slid down outside to secure them.

"Grab that old fool. Get his gun."

The sound of a scuffle, the hermit screeching, "Ezekiel, save me!"

Far Stream placed her head against the door and with slight effort splintered the restraining plank and burst it open. The knot of men struggling with the hermit released him and scattered and he scrambled to his feet kicking, spitting and cursing. Far Stream ambled over and looked about at the people cowering in doorways and peeking out windows.

"Hey, old timer."

The hermit retrieved his musket that had fallen and swung around toward the voice. It was Whitey Alf, peeping out a nearby doorway, rough and bleary-eyed from having been roused from his bed. He had been left behind to help with the searching but had spent the time mostly in bed.

"Hey, old timer," he repeated, "we been looking for that elephant there. How about you set that rifle down and we..."

The barrel came up. "You stay away!"

Whitey's head snapped back. "Whoa now, there's no need for that. I don't want any trouble."

"Well, you stay away and you won't get none."

Whitey's head slowly reappeared and this time Far Stream saw him. She walked over, glad to see someone familiar. "Hello there, Topsy," he said. "You've led us on a rare old chase, girl."

"That's my Ezekiel!" cried the hermit, tagging behind as Far Stream crossed the street and made her greeting.

"This elephant ain't yours," said Whitey, irritation rising. "She belongs to the Forepaugh Circus concern. She got loose a week ago about thirty miles up the line there and we've been looking..."

"He come to me! He come right to my door!"

"Settle down, damn it. Now, you've done us a service bringing Topsy in and Mr. Forepaugh will surely pay you a reward. So just settle down."

The gun wavered—it was heavy—but wasn't lowered. "Young fella, that there's Ezekiel and he's leading me onward and you best get stepping and you can keep your reward money because I don't—*Hey!*"

The bearded townsman, sneaking up behind, snatched the musket from the hermit's hands as three others grabbed his arms and restrained him. Far Stream swung about and took a step to protect him but stopped when she felt Whitey's restraining tug on her ear. "Tut," he ordered her. He spoke quietly, uncertain of her temper.

"Tut."

She stayed.

"Down," Whitey tried next, testing.

Far Stream lowered her head. The people looking on from a safe distance made an appreciative murmur, commenting to each other, "Look at that. The beast does what he says." And that gave Whitey—who prided himself on having a quick mind—an idea.

"Say," he announced, "for five dollars I'll give you folks a show. This is a trained circus elephant here, worth tens of thousands of dollars. She can do all kinds of tricks."

Looks exchanged in the crowd, hands digging in pockets followed by a general shaking of heads.

"All right, four dollars then. I'll have Topsy here give you a real Forepaugh show for only four dollars and all of you can watch. Bring out the kiddies too and see a real show!"

Four dollars was still too much.

"Oh, come on now. A chance like this don't come around every day, folks. Three dollars then. And that's my final offer. Three dollars for the whole bunch of you, every last one of you and all your kiddies, to see a trained circus elephant do tricks. Come on now, folks. I've got a real honest-to-goodness Forepaugh trained elephant here!"

"That's my Ezekiel," grumbled the hermit, still restrained, but no one was listening. A hat was passed, coins were collected, the jingling mass counted out and presented to Whitey.

Far Stream did as Whitey instructed. Her movements were automatic. They did not require thinking. Whitey was only a keeper, not her trainer like Patsy, and so he was unable to have her do much. But it did not take much to satisfy this simple crowd, a raised foreleg and a shaking head enough to elicit an enthusiastic ovation. And then the capper, Far Stream lowering her head and raising Whitey— Whitey grinning from ear to ear and three dollars richer— onto her back. Even the hermit could not help but join in the clapping, grinning and repeating with pride now, "That's my Ezekiel."

"All right, now," Whitey concluded after being lowered back to the ground, "everybody who wants to touch her, get in a line."

The touching was restrained and respectful. Far Stream did not mind it. When it was over she allowed Whitey to lead her down the street to the depot and she stepped up into a boxcar and stood still while he secured her foreleg with a new chain. She felt neither happy nor sad, only weary acceptance.

"You're all scratched up, aren't you, girl," Whitey said as he examined her closely. He removed a large splinter that had been troubling her just under her armpit. She touched his hand.

The door slid shut. The townspeople who had followed them surrounded the car to peer in through the cracks, whispering and chirping as she waited and the day faded.

It was late in the evening when Red Moon at last came out of hiding and emerged from the forest. Subdued, she allowed herself to be led into the boxcar and took her place beside Far Stream. Together, they shared the hay that Whitey forked in.

You should have come. They were waiting.

Far Stream made a low rumble but did not answer.

The chug of an engine, the sharp blast of a whistle, a jolt as the car was backed into and attached to a train. Then with creaking and swaying it was straining forward, slowly forward, gathering momentum as it left the small town in the shade of a valley where she had almost found the Shining Sun Cliffs.

You should have come.

The place was fading away in the distance.

They were waiting.

The place was fading. It was fading away.

౪౫

Seasons passed. Far Stream grew still bigger—more slowly now, for she was maturing. She came to weigh eight thousand pounds—four tons—and stand eight feet one inch high at the shoulder.

She was thirty years old.

CHAPTER 17

"THE MOST VICIOUS?" mused Patsy Meagher to the note-scribbling reporter. "I guess it would be Dick there, the big one on the end. He's had a go at just about every man here when he's in one of his spells. Nearly got me a couple times, nearly got Joe Beatty there last year, nearly got Mr. Forepaugh too, Mr. Adam Forepaugh Jr., back in . . . Hey Joe, when did Dick go after Addie and smash up that car?"

"That was in '89, I think."

"Yeah, that sounds about right."

The reporter made a note and continued. "Adam Forepaugh Jr. is no longer with the show, I gather?"

"No, he left in '93 and started up a rival outfit, 'The Only Living Forepaugh Show' or some such thing, went bust after a couple of seasons. That's when I went over to the Great Wallace outfit for a while."

"So there are no longer any Forepaughs connected with the Forepaugh-Sells Combined Circus?"

"That's right. And now Sid here,"—Patsy stopped in front of a towering giant, the largest elephant in the herd—"Sid's no sweetheart either. He came over with the Sells bunch."

"That's a fine set of balls he's got," observed the reporter, adding hurriedly, "Those brass balls on his tusks, I mean."

"Makes it harder for him to spear us," said Patsy.

"What about the way they're handled, the way you break them when they act up? It upsets some people when they read about it. They think it's brutal."

Patsy chuckled. "Well, it *is* brutal. Of course it's brutal. How else are you going to control these big things? With hugs and kisses? You'd be squashed to jelly inside a month. No, you've got to make them obey you, and that means they've got to respect you. Simple as that."

They moved down the line of grey forms inside the menagerie tent. It was pitched on the outskirts of Sioux City, Iowa, the forty-seventh stop of the season, 3,526 miles traveled so far, 10,218 miles and 131 stops to go.

"Of course, we've never had to do that with John here," continued Patsy. "Have we, Johnny?" He put out his hand and John L. Sullivan gave him a friendly hello. "Old John is getting to be a good age but he's still gentle, never gives us a bit of trouble. That's unusual for a full-grown male."

The reporter was consulting the provided list of the thirteen members of the herd. "I see you have two elephants here named Babe."

"That's right. There's Sells Babe"—Patsy pointed—"and Forepaugh Babe. Made it kind of confusing after the two shows joined up."

"That was two years ago?"

"Three. It was in 1896, the year before I come back from Great Wallace."

The reporter returned to the list. "And I see you also have two Topsys."

"Same thing," replied Patsy. "That leggy African there is Sells Topsy. She looks good in a parade with those pretty ivories, her and African Mike, but she's not much for performing. Africans just don't take to the training."

"Those tusks look dangerous. Has she killed anyone yet?"

"No, but she sure could. She's temperamental, turned on Frank Bloomer just last month in Milwaukee, threw him down and broke his shoulder and we had to leave him behind. So we watch her close.

"And now this is our second Topsy, Forepaugh Topsy, or Crooked-Tail Topsy as we sometimes call her on account of that kink in her tail." Patsy stopped in front of Far Stream. "Actually, she's our first Topsy, been with the show for, oh, I don't know, for ages. She's kind of the boss around here now, keeps the others in line. She's a big help for moving the wagons and drawing stakes, too. Hey Topsy, come here. Say hello to Mr. Moffett."

Far Stream looked up from her hay. It now came in square bales. She took a lazy step forward and extended her trunk.

"She seems friendly," said the reporter, stretching out to cautiously stroke her.

"Oh, she's not bad. She can be touchy sometimes, gives us a bit of excitement every now and then. And I guess you could say she acts kind of strange by times. But she's not bad."

"Where's her baby?"

"I think Melville's working with him. You want to see him? Little Barney's awful cute."

Far Stream made a twist of hay from the pile she was eating. *Apple*, she said, offering it to Red Moon beside her to sample. She idly watched Patsy and the visitor stride from the tent. She knew where they were going because she recognized the name "Barney."

She made another twist, continuing the imagination game, and held it out for her sister. *Cucumber*, she communicated.

Little Barney wasn't her real offspring. Far Stream had only played the part of his mother in the parade. He had replaced the baby that had died the previous winter, the sweet-faced creature the men called Cuba, who had in turn replaced a fuzzy-headed little beauty named Sally. The little ones came and went in an endless succession. They rarely survived.

Another twist of straw made and offered.

Turnip.

She ate it.

Far Stream's own baby, the only baby she had ever had, was stillborn years before, in the months following the return from the forest. It had come in the middle of the night, lying there still as she tried to coax it onto its feet, lying there still as she stood over it, protecting, when the first man appeared the next morning and called out to the others until all the hands were gathered around.

The loss plunged Far Stream into a deep depression. She became unwilling to perform, erratic and irritable with her keepers, a dead weight to the show. She would have been sent away had it not been for her sister, that last tendril of her real family which she could never let go of. She stood side by side with Red Moon, lost in each other's thoughts, swaying, until she found her way out of the blackness and gradually returned to herself.

After that, Far Stream and Red Moon became closer than ever. After that, they became one.

Watermelon.

Far Stream put the twist of hay in her mouth and tasted the sweetness.

A bump from John beside her, shifting as he dug up dirt with his forefeet to throw on his back. Far Stream gave him a shove in return to remind him of her position. She still liked John after all these years. He remained a gentle soul, simple, guileless, seemingly immune to the amorousness and male-rage that could seize Dick, Sid and African Mike.

African Mike—incomprehensible African Mike. Far Stream did not have much to do with him or African Topsy or with any of the others from the Sells Brothers' circus. They were kept apart in the tent; they traveled in their own car and performed their own act. For Far Stream, family was Red Moon first, then the other members of the dancing quadrille: volatile Dick and placid John, mild-mannered Babe and Rubber who had been with the show now for years, and newer additions Victoria, yet another Romeo and Betts. And of course there was little Barney, who did an act with miniature ponies.

Dear old Basil—Strong One Passes—had long since disappeared. She had been led away after falling sick with wheezing consumption, leaving Far Stream the largest senior female, a grandmother of sorts to the others. It was not like life in the forest with her real family. But it was the life she had and this was a kind of a family and Far Stream settled into the position of matriarch such as it was. Even with no freedom, the men giving the orders, there was a certain satisfaction in being a dominant female, in receiving a measure of respect from the others, in being able to tell the younger ones to be quiet when they got annoying and to give John a shove when he crossed the line.

The circus had arrived in Sioux City, Iowa an hour before dawn. Far Stream as usual had assumed the lead of the Forepaugh herd in the walk from the train, Red Moon beside her, Little Barney tagging behind. Once on the lot, she and John had set to work shifting the wagons, these ones to the cook tent, those with the plank seating to the big top, those others with the animal displays to be lined up inside the menagerie tent. They worked with very little direction, Whitey Alf or one of the other keepers merely tapping the back of the wagon to be moved. Far Stream understood now why vicious old Romeo, the first Romeo she had known all those years ago, had so willingly pushed wagons for the same men he sometimes tried to kill. It had to do with using her strength, which was a part of her nature. To express that nature, even in pushing wagons, felt good.

A lull descended upon the lot at mid-morning. Far Stream closed her eyes to rest before the first visitors arrived but she was unable to doze. She was feeling listless for some reason. Part of it was fatigue, the show now well into the season, another plodding season of numbing repetition and endless travel interspersed with stabs of excitement. There had been African Topsy's attack on Frank Bloomer that Far Stream had witnessed, Whitey's hook behind her ear. "Stay," he had commanded her sharply. She stayed. She had also seen high diver Charles Pritchett miscalculate his dive in the neighboring ring, striking the bottom of his three-foot-deep pool and dashing his brains out. She had heard the fight outside the tent in Wellston, Ohio; the punch-up in Anderson, Indiana when a gang of rowdies tried to force their way in without tickets; the howling of the worker in Marshfield, Wisconsin when he crushed his finger in a heavy cage door. There had also been the groaning death of the polar bear in the menagerie tent and the panicked stampede of a six-horse team in the parade in Marshall, Minnesota, smashing a tableau car and injuring one of the riders. "Don't even think it," Whitey had said as the parade ground to a halt. She didn't. She stood quietly, sheltering little Barney who paraded alongside.

There. There was the reason for her listlessness. The air pressure was dropping. She could feel it now in her ears. A storm was coming this way.

A few more hours, the afternoon show, and the men began noticing too. For them it was a bank of clouds appearing low in the west, a slowly advancing mass of cumulous with angry dark knobs. "That just might amount to something," observed assistant elephant superintendent William Badger as they were getting the tent ready for visitors to the evening performance.

"I hope so," groused Whitey, shoveling dung. "It'll ease some of this heat."

People were filtering into the tent now, the first evening arrivals, then more and more until a sizable crowd was milling about and gawking, throwing questions at Badger, Whitey, Joe and the others.

"How old's that one, mister?" asked a boy sucking on hard candy in front of his parents.

"Well, son," said Whitey, "Dick there's pretty old, maybe a hundred. Count up the wrinkles on his trunk and you'll get the exact number."

"Is he dangerous?" the father wanted to know.

"Dangerous? He's killed half a dozen men, so I guess you could say so. You might want to keep your boy back."

"Why does that one have them balls on its teeth?" This from an intense farmer, anxious to get full value for the price of the ticket he held like a flag.

"Keeps him from spearing folks, which he'd do if he could, believe you me. Sid there's an awful one. Get hold of you and throw you down and a jerk of that big head of his and your insides would be spilling all over."

"He's done that, has he?"

"Oh now, mister, the things I could tell you. Why, a year or two back ... "

He stopped at a hard look and head shake from Patsy, walking past in his tunic. Patsy was older now and less given to fooling with the patrons. The farmer rushed on.

Further down the line, a knot of men with fresh town haircuts clustered around sharp-eyed Badger. He had already saved Rubber from a plug of tobacco and was now discouraging an offer of whiskey to Far Stream.

"Come on now," urged the man with the bottle. "Elephants like whiskey, I heard that. Come on, just this one little bottle. Just to see."

The evening performance began with the grand double consolidated procession, a promenade inside the big top by all the performers, the horses, the fancy wagons and led-stock—everything that the show possessed except the side-show exhibits, which cost extra to see.

Far Stream's place was near the end with the rest of the Forepaugh dancing quadrille, carrying on her shoulders a young aerial performer named Gracie, little Barney trailing behind hanging onto her tail. She took her turn around the vast tented space, three hundred feet long and half as wide, oblivious to the audience, the thousand pairs of eyes staring. Then it was back to the menagerie tent to wait her turn to perform.

Outside, the cloud bank was advancing as the sky grew darker. The breeze remained steady, a hint of electric, then the smell of wet dust as the first drops darkened the ground. At the Edison Projecting Kinetoscope tent, a recent sideshow addition, the front flaps were lowered and securely tied down.

Then with a whoosh the skies opened and on came the downpour. "I *knew* that was coming," said a score of patrons inside the main tent as they strained to take in all three rings of simultaneous action, the somersaulting LaRue Brothers on one side, acrobats extraordinaire the Great Livingstons on the other, the Daredevil Lassards with their pyramid of chairs in between. Then voices raised in protest from beneath a trickle of water getting through a seam in what was advertised as waterproof canvas. The affected spectators were apologetically relocated, grumbles from some when they weren't allowed into the prime reserved seats that were still vacant.

Far Stream received a soaking on her return to the big top from the menagerie tent to take her place in the next act. Patsy was walking just in front, hunched under an umbrella, protecting his velvet suit. She could hear his boots squishing as they entered the ring, smell the wet wool of his pant legs mixed with the must of the canvas. She took her place beside Rubber in the center ring in quadrille formation, facing Romeo and John, Red Moon at her shoulder, and Patsy launched into his spiel, introducing them by the Shakespearean names that were sometimes still used. This evening he pointed at Far Stream and called her Julius Caesar. She had been Rosalind at Council Bluffs, Ophelia at St. Paul, Hamlet at Fargo. It didn't matter.

The music. Patsy's hand raised. Far Stream made her bow to Rubber and began her memorized movements. "Family circle," Patsy was saying, clapping his hands with the music, some of the crowd joining in. "Forward and back now. Dosedo. Swing your partner. Allemande left. Half sashay now. Star promenade."

Far Stream was scarcely aware of the calls as she stepped and swayed and shuffled. It was circle to the left with the others, stand facing Rubber, one step forward, one step back, circle around Rubber, now toward John, back to Rubber, forward, back, circle, turn left, turn right, step, on and on through the succession of movements imprinted on her brain by long training, endless repetition.

The Sells elephants, presided over by William "Star" Chambers, were going through their own memorized ambulations in the next ring. In the third ring, baby Barney was engaged in frolics with a troupe of miniature ponies. All around the periphery the spectators clapped and laughed and called out and craned forward, overwhelmed by so much to see. Behind them and above them, the canvas was starting to billow out and snap back.

A pause in Far Stream's engrained routine. Patsy stepped off his pedestal. New positions for the next number. The noise outside was becoming unsettling, the sound of the wind and the drum of rain on the canvas. And then a surge of pressure in her ears, causing her to falter at Patsy's signal to begin. They were off now and she and John were both out of step. Patsy glided over to give them a tap, the light prod he used when he was working them in front of people. Far Stream felt the touch, tried to focus, then stopped altogether as the pressure increased.

Suddenly it was quiet. The wind died to nothing, the rain patter subsided and the canvas became still. Patsy joined the audience in looking up at the tent, the music unnaturally loud. Then the band too petered out, clarinets, trombones, bass drum, tuba, all falling away until the only sound was the electrical hum of the overhead lighting and the tread of John, who continued to shuffle through the tattered remnants of the dance.

The wind when it returned struck the side of the tent like the giant fist of a colossus. It blasted through the entrance and tore at the seams and lifted one end up and then sucked it back down. The leap followed by the powerful compression dislodged the supporting poles at that end from their moorings, sending more than a ton of timber and twenty thousand square feet of canvas cascading down. It fell on baby Barney and the miniature ponies and on the spectators, many of them now on their feet. Some stood mute and frozen, others were shrieking, others were pushing and kicking and trampling, trying to flee.

The lights went out.

In the center ring the canvas sagged low on one side, low enough to touch Far Stream's head. The trapeze apparatus struck her a glancing blow as it fell, adding to her fright and sending her off across the arena. In the darkness and confusion she ran into one of the others, she couldn't tell who, a grunt from the impact, then a stagger. She reeled about and dashed her head against the side of another. It was Dick, standing oddly sedate where he had left off his dancing.

"Stay!" Patsy was yelling. "Stay!" His command brought her back to her senses. She thought of little Barney and called for him to come.

She could see now, her eyes adjusting to the last light of evening fading grey through the canvas. Here was Dick beside her, and Rubber, rooted but thrashing, and Victoria and Betts, milling about on the verge of panic. People were streaming out the exit, jackets and uneaten popcorn and twenty-five-cent trinkets forgotten, attendants urging them to move quickly, stay calm.

Victoria and Betts were off, charging for the same exit. Shrieking, a parting of bodies and they were gone with miraculously no crushed bodies left in their wake. Far Stream took a step in the same direction but was stopped by a powerful jab from Patsy. He was right among them now, a one hundred fifty-pound man in the midst of twenty tons of elephant verging on panic and about to stampede. "Stay put," he roared like a demon, striking at any movement. And then to Badger when he appeared from somewhere: "Let's get them out the back before they kill somebody. Cut a hole."

Here was Barney. He had somehow scrambled out from beneath the canvas where the ponies were still writhing and had found Far Stream in all the confusion, bleating with fright.

The sound of tearing. A big flap was opened and promptly blown aside by the wind. Then a barked command from Patsy: "Go on!"

Far Stream saw the gap torn in the canvas. She saw the way out. *Follow me*, she called to the others, pushing through the hole, ripping it wider. It sent a shudder through the half-collapsed tent and another collective shriek from the people still streaming out the opposite exit. Barney followed close behind her, then Rubber, then John and the others.

Outside, the full fury of the freak blow was already abating, replaced by rain pelting down so hard it was bouncing a foot off the ground. Freed from the terrifying sense of entrapment, Far Stream calmed as she led the way onward, water cascading off her shiny black body onto Barney beside her, her feet squelching in ground turning to mud. She circled wide to skirt the people milling about the collapsed big top, wide around the periphery of the lot back to the menagerie tent which had somehow escaped damage, picking up Victoria and Betts loitering near the trees.

A scoop and a toss of the trunk and she sent a shower of mud onto her sides and her back. Then another. Then another. It was almost as good as a wallow. The others began doing the same. By the time they were back inside the menagerie tent, Badger and Patsy were both thoroughly plastered and Patsy was groaning, "Look what they did to my suit."

❦

She performed her usual chores in dismantling the show, pulling up the stakes that held down the thick cables, then pushing the wagons onto the road leading back to the train. In the mud covering the lot the horses were largely useless. Far Stream's power was needed. Without it, the Forepaugh-Sells Combined Circus would be literally stuck.

There was no show the next day, an unscheduled holiday for the dancing quadrille. Then it was back to work in Manning, Iowa, the menagerie tent filling in while the gargantuan task of repairing the big top was completed, Far Stream and the others temporarily displayed inside a jury-rigged wall of canvas.

The sideshow "Black Tent" where the Thomas Edison moving pictures were shown, ten cents admission, had also been damaged. To keep the lucrative concern going, a corner of the elephant enclosure was screened off and used. When it was first put together and the projector set up and tested, the front wall was left off and Far Stream was able to watch. She saw flickering monochrome images of people walking about a spacious promenade, gazing up at a high tower. She saw a train approaching, coming closer and closer, then speeding past with passengers waving out the windows. She saw a man and a woman clutching each other, kissing and grinning. She saw two cats flailing away at each other with boxing gloves on their paws, a man's head looming enormous between them. She saw a magician use a cloth to conjure up a washtub full of water, then change it into five geese, then change the geese into a boy. It was all very strange.

Later that night, standing in a circle under the stars with the others, Far Stream took the lead in telling the stories. She began with one she had heard many times from old Betsy, long dead now but still alive in their memories, the

198

one that had occurred in the year Betsy was born and had given her the name Hunger Valley. She told a story given to her years before by Basil, of a being named Loud who had quelled a great storm. She told a story she remembered learning from the giant Bolivar in one of his lucid moments, of a time long ago when there had been a great flood.

And then she returned to the story of Sinkhole, one from her own personal history, for they all liked to hear it.

❧❧

Sid killed Patsy Meagher that winter during a session of training. There were no warning signs, no hint of the onset of musth madness. Patsy simply made a mistake, calling "Right face" at the point in the military drill where the elephants had been taught to turn left. Sid, the only one to obey the mistaken command, turned right while the others left-faced. That earned him some sharp strokes from Patsy, who was apparently unaware that it had been his own error.

Sid didn't take the blows well. He seized Patsy with his trunk and smashed him into the ground and drove one of his tusks into his belly. The six-inch brass ball over the tip proved no protection. With nearly five tons behind it, the ball went through Patsy. It went through his intestines and his spine and into the dirt.

CHAPTER 18

THERE WAS FROST in the air when Far Stream was led out of the elephant barn at the sprawling Forepaugh-Sells winter headquarters, "Sellsville," in Columbus, Ohio. She shuffled past the horse barn that had burned down the previous month and into the private depot where the train was waiting—the same train as last year, scrubbed cleaned and repainted for a new season.

She was in the lead with docile, submissive Rubber. They were chained together, Far Stream crowding in close in her usual manner to make room for her sister Red Moon. John and Babe followed together behind them, then Romeo, Betts, Victoria and the others, then the Sells group further back. It felt good to be out in the open after a long winter cooped up; good to be out walking even though her hips were stiff and the scenery was only boxcars and sooty railway siding. She picked up a stone and bobbled it as she went, then flicked it at Red Moon for fun. It went sailing past Whitey's head.

"Hey, watch it," snapped Whitey, red-eyed, giving her a backhanded jab.

Whitey had changed over the winter, ever since receiving the bad news from home about his mother. The painfully deciphered letter which he still kept in his pocket had left him moody and withdrawn, his old playfulness gone. He had also been affected by Patsy's death, as had the oth-

200

ers. They were wary and distrustful now of their charges, apt to lash out at the smallest infraction, suspicious that viciousness could be catching and ready to see it in even innocent movements. The tension radiating off them was palpable to Far Stream and her companions. It made them uneasy and sometimes fractious in turn.

Bill Emery, the new elephant superintendent who had replaced Patsy, was overseeing the move to the cars, riding up front on horseback. William Badger, assistant elephant boss for another season, took up the rear. Between them strode Whitey, Fatty Daniels, Daft Jim, Bert and seventeen-year-old Mortimer "Stick" Kelly—all seasoned hands except for young Stick, who was still proving himself. Joe Beatty was gone. He had moved on.

Far Stream took her place with Red Moon in the second of the five elephant cars, beside John at the end furthest from the small window. There was the usual banter after the door was slid shut and latched, mostly from the younger ones to relieve the boredom of the long wait. A joking offer of hay, *This is for you*, and quickly pulled back, *No, it's for me*; toying with the chains; jostling each other; throwing around a dried piece of dung rummaged out of the straw. In earlier years Far Stream would have felt more inclined to join in. Now, she generally preferred to stay silent. If something annoyed her she might say *Stop it* or *Be quiet*, perhaps deliver a swat if the offender was within reach. Otherwise she was content to sway in the dimness as she communed with her sister. Together, they would roam far away.

Her eyes were closed now, the interior of the rail car receding. She followed Red Moon down a path through vivid greenness, breathing in warm, humid air. They stopped at an open place to graze together, to throw grass on their backs, to share private thoughts. When they tired of this they would move easily onward, to a pool of clear water perhaps, or to a lush meadow. These were for Far Stream moments of peace and contentment, with only a hint that something was missing, that there was something she was searching for that she could not find.

The jangle of chains passing by outside. An angry snort. Badger's tense voice, "Watch him. Watch him."

It was Dick. The men were leading him back to the special car for troublemakers, equipped with extra restraints. He would be sharing it with Sid on this journey. Sid had shown no signs of meanness since killing Patsy the previous December—he had even acquiesced to having his tusks cut down to stumps—but the men were taking no chances. It was instead Dick who had plunged into musth madness as the snow started melting, the distinctive discharge first darkening the sides of his head, his behavior growing erratic, then the lunging, trumpeting, wild-eyed, full-blown rages. He had been heavily chained and allowed a week to settle. Then, with the season approaching, the treatment was given. It brought Dick down from the worst of his outbursts but a glowering menace remained. He was being taken along in the hopes that the spell would pass and he would again become useful. If it didn't, other arrangements would have to be made.

It was a long ride in the train, twenty-four hours heading east before a stop for a leg-stretch and water, then back into the cars to continue the journey, on and on eastward until they were out of the hills and entering a city and approaching the ocean and ships hooting in a harbor unseen. A wait of two days here in a warehouse amid heaps of freight and circus wagons, then a middle-of-the-night procession through streets largely deserted, the glow of electric lamps reflecting off cobblestones wet with drizzle, to a cattle ferry moored on a wide river smelling of factories, rusting ships, sewage, a bank of buildings a mile off on the far side.

Far Stream baulked when they arrived at the ferry. The gangway leading to the deck was narrow and looked none too solid. She allowed herself to be unchained from Rubber, to be led forward, to be prodded partway onto the gangway.

Then she paused to consider. She would take her time to advance.

"Go on," said Whitey, jabbing.

The prod annoyed her. She planted her feet more firmly.

"Go on, damn it."

Another jab. She whipped her trunk at Whitey, making him jump back. Badger tried next, more jabbing that only made Far Stream more stubborn.

"Bring John up here," said Bill Emery, assessing the situation. "We'll shove her on."

Far Stream didn't like John's big head pushing against her rump. She shoved back and staggered against the railing and for a terrifying moment it felt like she was going to topple into the water between the pier and the ferry. When John resumed his persistent pushing, she relented and moved on.

A short crossing over water, no delays this time in unloading, resuming formation on another pier for another walk past more warehouses and onto city streets, elephants then camels then llamas, streets that went on for three miles until they came to an imposing structure topped with a soaring great tower. Around the corner, double doors opened by a pair of night watchmen, a ramp leading downward, a descent underground.

It was musty down here, damp concrete, stored lumber and mildew as she entered the flickering gloom of a large basement, passing between rows of iron pillars supporting the floor overhead. The Forepaugh-Sells Twentieth Century Colossus, as the show was being billed for 1900, would open the season upstairs in the main hall of Madison Square Garden, Far Stream and the others housed with the menagerie in the lower level underneath. An advance crew of workmen had prepared the space to receive them, walkways, stalls, cages, red, white and blue bunting, a pleasant enough place when the electrical lights were turned on. At the moment the lights were off, illumination coming from a handful of lanterns. It was three o'clock in the morning.

She was awakened just after dawn by the sound of construction in the hall overhead, hammers banging, wagons rumbling, loads dropped onto the floor, shouted orders, things dragged about. Then the city was coming to life, adding to the tumult the clanging of trolleys, the bellow of hawkers, the hum of people scurrying by on the sidewalk, the thunder of trains.

Bill Emery led Far Stream and the dancing quadrille up to the main hall in the afternoon for a session of practice. Dick did not go along. Still sullen and threatening, he was left where he was, chained in a corner in the basement behind a stout railing so that visitors when the show opened could see him but not get too close.

The main hall had been laid out in the usual manner, three central rings with a hippodrome track around the outside for races. There was a good deal more seating, however, rows and rows of it in tiers that rose to the rafters, and the ceiling was girders and tin sheeting rather than the usual canvas, daylight streaming in through a large expanse of glass in the center. Activity was everywhere: a trainer working with a half dozen Great Danes; a slender young woman casually balancing on a ball in her street clothes; workmen climbing ladders to string ropes and wires high in the air and netting below; two bands rehearsing at opposite ends of the arena while Far Stream took her place in the center ring and began her routine. As she marched and danced and solemnly cavorted, a one-legged man added the whirl of movement and sound by riding a bicycle down a one-hundred-foot staircase, bump-bump-bump-bump, all the way down to the ground.

The parade to kick off the New York engagement began at eight o'clock that evening, the whole lit with calcium lights affixed to the wagons, a contingent of policemen leading the way. Far Stream walked with the others a third of the way back, behind the Goddess of Liberty in her gilded carriage and the band playing patriotic and popular airs. They made their way up one street and down another for two hours, past hotels and clubs with guests leaning out windows, through tenements with laundry overhead and children running alongside, on past houses that grew progressively richer until a halt was ordered in front of a particularly fine dwelling, the Vanderbilt mansion, and Far Stream left-faced and bowed on command.

Then it was again forward, the advertising banners some of them wore resuming their chaffing. "Nerve Exhaustion?" proclaimed the message hanging from Babe. "You want a good Sarsaparilla. That's Ayers." Rubber's message read: "O'Neill's, Sixth Ave. and 20th St., Best Selection of Hats in New York." And on Far Stream: "Dr. Moffett's Teething Powder. Allays Irritation; Aids Digestion," with the addendum on little Barney trotting alongside, "Will Make Baby as Fat as a Pig."

Another restless night, the noise of the menagerie amplified in the basement. Far Stream, swaying, eyes closed, sought escape with her sister. They took a leisurely walk down to the river to bathe in the warm water, Far Stream rumbling with pleasure as the sensations grew strong.

A voice in her head called her back to the basement: *Strong One Passes*. It was Victoria a few spaces down, wanting Far Stream to divert them with a story.

Then young Romeo: *Three Times Falling*.

Then Betts: *Sinkhole*, one of her favorites.

Far Stream responded with a dismissive snort. She was tired from the long train journey and these new surroundings and was not in the mood to tell stories. She returned to the pool of water to spend more time with Red Moon, leaving the others to entertain themselves. Then she lay down and drifted into a light sleep.

The sixteen-day New York engagement began, two performances daily, general admission fifty cents, box seats a dollar, menagerie open one hour before show time.

Still no improvement from Dick.

❧❧

"The old man wants to know what's taking so long."

It was one o'clock in the morning, the show packing up to vacate Madison Square Garden, and Bill Emery was near the end of his tether.

"Dick won't move," he snapped. "We've been trying for two hours."

The bespectacled assistant peered at Dick in the corner, defiant and bleeding, then strode back down the line past Far Stream and disappeared upstairs.

He was back five minutes later. "The old man says move him."

"Damn it, we *can't* move him," said Bill. "Did he say how?"

"No, he just said move him."

"Well, we've tried coaxing him and beating him. Go see if the old man has any other ideas."

The assistant disappeared again. When he returned he was trailing behind General Manager Lewis Sells, who said, "So Dick's misbehaving."

"Yes, sir, he is. He doesn't want to come out of that corner. Nearly got a couple of the boys. And now"—Bill waved a hand at the other elephants, shifting, uneasy—"he's got the rest of them spooked. Maybe if the Central Park Zoo will take him."

"They say they don't want him."

"Even for free?"

"Even for free."

"Well," said Bill, "he's no good to us like this."

Lewis Sells heaved a weary sigh. "So, I guess that's it then."

"Yes, sir, I guess that's it."

Far Stream heard the men conversing. She knew they were talking about Dick. Dick's refusal to move and the harsh treatment to force him had filled the basement with trumpeting roars and pungency that had upset her and the others. She had urged her quadrille companion to relent when she saw the men growing angry. *Come with us*, she had said but he wouldn't listen. *Come with us*, the others had tried. It did no good.

The chains on Dick's legs were being hooked from a safe distance and drawn together, leaving him hobbled. Block and tackle were fastened to the iron pillars supporting the ceiling and a heavy rope dragged in and laid out. Dick watched it all with glowering menace, ready to strike at anyone who got within reach.

"Go on."

It was Whitey, ordering Far Stream forward. She didn't comply. Red Moon began backing away.

"Go on now." Whitey punctuated the command with his bull hook.

Far Stream didn't like it. It pushed her upset into anger. She whipped her trunk at Whitey, catching him in his chest and knocking him down. Red Moon further retreated.

"Stay!" Bill Emery and Badger roared, both running over.

Whitey, shaken but unhurt, picked himself up and said, "She don't want to go."

"She's going," said Bill firmly. "We'll lose the whole bunch at this rate. Make her go."

Whitey was already regaining his composure, regretting the trepidation he had revealed. "All right, I got her," he said, his face settling into hardness. He gave Far Stream a whack on the foreleg with the flat of his bull hook, another on her head, roaring, "Go on!"

She refused. Whitey hit her again, and again. She could feel her anger building.

"Go on! Go on!"

That was enough. Far Stream lunged at him with sudden fury, trumpeting a loud warning. *Stay away.*

Whitey backed away. He wasn't paid enough for any more. He said, "She really don't want to go."

Bill Emery, muttering "Damn it," made a move toward Far Stream. Then he stopped, noting her cold glare.

"You're going," he told her quietly. "One way or another, you're going."

When Bill was done with her, she went. She went whining and shaking her head, making it clear that she was not happy.

"Stop it," Bill barked, meeting each movement of her head with a sharp reprimand.

She settled down and allowed a harness to be thrown over her shoulders. John L. Sullivan, quietly munching, was similarly harnessed at her side.

"All right, let's get this on." Bill motioned men to the cable.

The cable was thrown over Dick's head as he stood tense, suspicious and glaring—over his head and looped under his chin and run through the tackle that would increase its force. Far Stream gazed at him as the men worked, remembering the younger elephant she had known as River's Conception, the one who enjoyed stealing food and hogging the trough, the one who had come to her in the night. He was older now, more dangerous, meant to wander alone in the forest where his true nature would not be a menace to others. By confining him, the men had turned him into a curse.

The cable was attached to Far Stream's harness and Bill ordered her forward, Badger with John beside her, forward until she met resistance. A hard pull from behind; Dick was fighting again. "Heave on, there," ordered Badger. John, calm and relaxed as ever, lowered his head and leaned into his harness until the cable was groaning. For him it was no different than pushing a wagon or hauling on a rope to raise the big tent.

"Heave on," Bill cried at Far Stream, punctuating the order when she was slow to comply. Another moment of hesitation and she mirrored John's posture, leaning forward against the rope as blackness washed through her mind and Red Moon became very small in the corner. She leaned forward like John until their combined weight of eight tons forced a creak from the cable and the other elephants were turning away because they did not want to see.

"Heave on, there."

A minute passed. Far Stream continued to lean forward.

"Heave on, there. Keep it tight. Heave on."

Another minute, the cable buried deep in Dick's neck.

Then: "There he goes."

The basement shuddered as Dick toppled over.

"Take up that slack," Bill barked, for with the fall the rope had gone loose. Far Stream, troubled by what she had heard, refused at first to step forward. Bill went at her again, this time on her hind legs, repeating "Go on" with each blow until she complied and leaned forward again in her harness, helping John finish the job.

It was over. A small gathering hovered around the great body, the keepers, show people who had come down to watch before heading off to the train, curious passersby who had caught wind of the proceedings and wandered in off the street. They laid their hands on Dick to feel the warmth that was fading. They stroked the smooth tusks and felt the rough hide. They squeezed the soft end of the trunk and hefted the tail, careful to step around the flood that had come from the bowels. They wobbled the exposed ear from which little pieces were missing, cut off with pocketknives and wrapped in handkerchiefs as souvenirs.

And then the elephants, the twelve remaining, were being lined up to leave, the last of the show to vacate the Garden. Far Stream remained sullen and withdrawn as Whitey, in equally bad humor, cautiously chained her foreleg to Rubber for the walk back to the train. As they moved up the ramp, up from the musty damp of the basement onto the dark street, she continued to hear Dick's final thought in her head, that bewildered, wondering question that had come from him in the last moments as he lay on his side.

But it wasn't Dick's voice she was now hearing. The murmur was circulating among the herd's younger members, passed from Betts to Romeo to Victoria and back because what Dick had said seemed to them very strange.

What is this place? they kept repeating. *What is this place?*

Far Stream shook her head, annoyed. *Be quiet.*

"Stop it," barked Whitey, applying his bull hook. "What's gotten into you? Why are you being so bad?"

⋖⋗

"Topsy! Hey, Topsy!"

Far Stream heard the voice in the distance. She ignored it. She was spending more time away now, deep down in her mind in her secret green world.

"Come on, Topsy! Wake up, girl!"

Far Stream reluctantly opened her eyes, returning to the menagerie tent. It was the middle of May, the Forepaugh-Sells show somewhere in Pennsylvania.

Assistant trainer William Badger was standing before her, eying her strangely. "Ain't you the sleeper," he said. "Now look here. This is baby Boston. What do you think?"

A baby elephant stood beside him, a young female, not much higher than the bottom of Far Stream's belly. She was a replacement for Barney, who had grown weak and been led away a few weeks before.

"Well, what do you think?" repeated Badger, watching her for a reaction. Bill Emery, Whitey and the other keepers looked on.

Far Stream eyed the little newcomer. The stirring of motherly instincts within her no longer felt good. It felt dangerous, threatening, disturbing. She would rather stay with Red Moon.

She extended her trunk and gently pushed the little one away.

Badger shook his head sadly. "So you're done with being a ma."

The baby elephant, Boston, was led on down the line. Babe took to it and was given the role of her mother. They would walk together in the parade.

∝ᄼᄾᄽ

"Side."

A new town, a new state, young Stick Kelly working around her, cleaning up with shovel and barrow before the arrival of the next batch of show patrons.

"Side."

She did not respond to the command. She was somewhere else.

"Side," repeated Stick, growing impatient, giving her an ineffectual shove so that he could clear away the pile beneath her.

The touch tore her away from where she preferred to be. She opened her eyes and looked at Stick, irritated by the disturbance. Stick did not seem to notice the sudden mounting of tension.

"Come on, Tops. I said 'Side.' "

She swung her head and struck him down with her trunk, then she seized him and flung him beyond the reach of her chain.

"What'd you do that for?" Stick screeched in a strangled voice, on his hands and knees after a moment of shock.

The others were hurrying over, Bill Emery in the lead, Daft Jim right behind him suppressing a nervous outburst of laughter.

"You okay, Stick?"

"I don't know . . . ." Stick got slowly to his feet, testing his limbs. "I guess so . . . She grabbed me. You see that? . . . Ouch." He was feeling the scrape on his forehead.

Bill examined him and concluded, "You're lucky you didn't get worse. Where's Whitey?"

Stick looked around. "I don't know."

"All right, go get forks. Hey Fatty, you too. Get over here with a fork." Bill then leveled a hard gaze on Far

Stream and said in his sternest voice, "Lay down."

She shifted uneasily, rising apprehension making her waver. But the irritation was still strong. She did not do as he said.

He struck her on the foreleg. "Lay down."

The anger flared. She lunged. Bill evaded her and resumed his commanding position, arm raised.

"Lay down, Topsy."

This time Bill brought his bull hook down on her trunk, bringing tears to her eyes. She lashed out again, and again she missed him, encountering the tinges of the pitchforks being thrust at her by Jim and Fatty and Stick and now Whitey who had run over from the corner where he had been napping. The pain confused her and she backed away to the end of her chain, shaking her head to avoid the blows and jabs that kept coming, on her trunk, on her ears, around her eyes, on her forelegs.

"Lay down!" Bill kept roaring at her, seeming to increase in size until he loomed over her like a giant.

"Lay down!"

She lay down.

They continued to work with her until they were satisfied that she was under control. Stick remained unconvinced, however. He said, "Boss, this has been going on for a while. I think we should cinch down her head."

Bill Emery looked to the other keepers. Heads nodded in agreement.

"All right," he said. "Let's get a martingale on her."

❧

The Forepaugh-Sells Circus began the following season of 1901 again at Madison Square Garden, then moved on to the states of New England, back through New York, Ohio, Michigan and Wisconsin, then Minnesota, Iowa, Missouri and down into the South.

The run through Texas and Louisiana was particularly unlucky. One of the rail cars caught fire on the way to

Waco, destroying the band wagon and trunks of wardrobe and roasting a musician caught in the blaze. A second fire claimed one of the animal cars near Lafayette, cremating an elephant, several camels and a load of tentage. A derailment followed three days later on the approach to New Orleans. It wrecked four of the animal cars including the elephant car in which Far Stream was riding, shaking her up badly but causing no deaths.

And in the town of Paris, Texas, after two sold-out performances with overflow seating on straw, there was this:

A VICIOUS ELEPHANT

THE BRUTE TOSSED AND STEPPED ON HER KEEPER

PARIS, TEXAS, Oct. 1.—Topsy, a female elephant with the Forepaugh & Sells Brothers' circus, seriously injured her keeper in Paris last night while being loaded onto the train for shipment to Sherman. She lifted the man in her trunk and dashed him to the ground and tramped on his head and his stomach before he could be rescued. The injured man is Mortimer Kelly of Troy, New York, eighteen years old. His injuries are probably fatal.

CHAPTER 19

THE STRANGER APPEARED again late in the morning, walking furtively through the entrance still closed to the public. He was around forty years old, rumpled and unshaven, but not destitute judging from how he could afford a half bottle for Whitey to hang around the menagerie tent in the hope of getting a job. He had been following the show for a week.

"Let me help you," he said, striding up eagerly to where Whitey was serving out hay.

"Hey, there," replied Whitey, his voice gravely, his eyes puffy and squinting. The increase in his already heavy drinking had done him no good. He handed over the pitchfork and said "Just keep your distance" and retreated to a secluded nook to lie down. Daft Jim and Bert, working nearby, glanced over, disapproving.

Far Stream watched out the corner of her eye as the stranger began doling out fork loads of hay from the wagon. She took a step back when he reached her, the double chains securing her trunk to her shoulder harness chinking between her forelegs. She did not like having this new man around her. Whitey was the one who usually fed her, Whitey or Badger or one of the others she knew. She did not like having this new man near her. She did not like his hat adorned with a gold braid.

The stranger finished with the hay and approached her, extending his hand. "Say hello," he said. "Come on, say hello."

"You might want to be careful there," Bert called over.

"It's okay," said the stranger. "I've done this before." And returning to Far Stream: "Say hello, now. Say hello."

Far Stream allowed herself to be coaxed forward and cautiously touched him. His index finger was stained brown and smelled of tobacco. Satisfied, he continued on down the line, calling the new elephant named Mighty forward, then John L. Sullivan, then Betts.

"You still here?"

It was Bill Emery. The stranger turned with an ingratiating smile, nervous.

"Yes sir, Mr. Emery. I'm still hoping for that job."

"Look, we just don't have anything for you, Jimmy."

"But I know these beasts, Mr. Emery. And it's Jesse, sir. Jesse Blount."

"Well, you're wasting your time here, Jesse. Like I said before, my advice to you is to get out to Ohio and try the Great Wallace outfit. That's your best chance, seeing as how you said you worked around elephants with them before."

Jesse had indeed said that. Bill didn't believe him.

Bill stalked off, barking, "Whitey, where are you at?" He left the stranger, Jesse Blount of Fort Wayne, Indiana, looking unhappy.

❧

It was the end of May 1902 and the Forepaugh-Sells Circus was in Brooklyn, under canvas on a fenced lot near Ridgewood Park where Sid had run the race two years before against an automobile, a horse and a camel.

Sid remained with the show, ballyhooed as its giant, carefully watched and occasionally fractious but more or less manageable since his killing of Patsy. He cut an impressive figure leading the elephants in the parade, four and a half tons now, his skull truly massive with its great humping forehead, brass balls on the end of tusks that had grown out two feet.

Far Stream, eight thousand four hundred pounds, ranked as the second biggest member of the herd. Her head lacked the massiveness of Sid's and she remained tuskless—a nondescript elephant to the casual observer, gentle curves down her back and her sides, a droop to her ears that seemed to denote sadness, shoulders not especially bulky, a nice ample bottom, toenails that Whitey kept neatly groomed. Her most distinctive feature now was her martingale harness. It consisted of red leather straps encompassing her chest and her forehead and ending in a ring around the base of her trunk—a ring connected by double chains to the underside of her chest strap which restricted her head movements and prevented her from fully extending her trunk. It had been uncomfortable and awkward at first and she had resented having to wear it. But gradually, inevitably, it had become a part of her body.

African Topsy had for some reason been spared having to wear a similar harness after her fatal mauling of Stick Kelly in Texas the previous October. The management briefly considered getting rid of her altogether but, as with Sid, no immediate action was taken. When she showed no further signs of aggression, things were left to go on as before.

The Brooklyn engagement had begun the previous day with a long parade through the city. Far Stream moved in tandem with her new chain partner, Mighty, Whitey on her back in an Oriental costume, his face pale behind a black beard hooked around his ears. The streets were as crowded as any she had trod in thirty years of parading, carts, horses, wagons, spectators and the occasional automobile making for a tight squeeze in places. She tried to close her mind to the hubbub but it was difficult here, especially when the elevated trains thundered by on the lines overhead. It was so loud when she passed under the Fulton Street track that she involuntarily lurched, pulling on Mighty's leg and making him stagger.

"Ooh," moaned Whitey, rubbing his temples after settling her down.

"You're going to lose your job at this rate," cautioned Daft Jim, riding alongside atop Mighty. "Big Bill's watching, you know."

"Mind your own business."

Two hours of slow marching and it was back to the lot. A rush to return costumes and get to the dining tent where the lunch flag was flying, the smell of fried steaks, boiled potatoes, stew and coffee and freshly baked bread tantalizing in the air. Whitey lingered in the menagerie tent for a while because he didn't feel much like eating, then he wandered off and the place was empty of men.

Far Stream, glad of the quiet, slipped away. She found Red Moon playful. They spouted and jostled each other in the warm water, the martingale harness no longer restraining. They threw insults back and forth, purely in fun. *You are weightless.* They roamed through forested hills and into deep valleys as outwardly she swayed, and swayed, and swayed.

This time she spent together with her sister was for Far Stream becoming more and more real—and the hours of idle wakefulness in the tent or on the train stranger and stranger. There was the skunk that came to her repeatedly in the Forepaugh-Sells menagerie barn over the winter. It came right up to her to sniff about in the hay, occasionally stopping to look up into her eyes. And it had spoken. Then there was the shiny black crow that kept returning, flying into the barn and alighting in front of her and pecking her trunk.

Today, as Far Stream roused from her reverie, it was the mangy dog with the injured hind leg. It hopped toward her and gazed at her intently and came into her head, unbidden. *Dogs can't speak*, she said to shut out the intruder. This no longer drew a questioning glance from Mighty. He was used to her ways. *Dogs can't speak*, she said, turning away

217

until the little mongrel limped off and the canvas overhead started to tremble.

"Stop that, John!" barked Badger, returning from lunch, picking his teeth.

John L. Sullivan sheepishly stepped away from the tent pole where he had been scratching himself.

Far Stream's harness attracted the usual attention when visitors flocked into the menagerie tent prior to the afternoon show. It gave her a look of danger that seemed to fascinate certain people. She took their offerings with solemn grace while ignoring the body behind it, savoring the tasty morsels she liked, casting aside the tricks that rarely fooled her. When a clod was held out to Mighty beside her, she reached over to snatch it and flung it away.

"Ha, ha," chortled people gathered around. "That's a smart one."

"That's the one called Topsy," chimed in an elephant aficionado. "She killed a man down in Texas last year."

"That wasn't her," mumbled Whitey, leaning nearby on a rake.

"All right, let's line them up," called out Bill Emery. It was two o'clock, time for the performance. Far Stream proceeded with the others to the main tent and went through her motions. She was thirty-five years old and no longer performed them so sharply, the crispness fading along with her desire to please, her joints no longer supple. Movements like sitting up and kneeling required more deliberation to deal with the creaking discomfort that was becoming worse every year. It was particularly bad when she had to rear up on her hind legs and all her weight bore down on her hips. A stabbing sensation now frequently forced her to drop down and try again as Bill looked on, disapproving. She knew he was disappointed in her.

❧

It was night when the stranger crawled in under the canvas, cradling a beer mug containing a few last swallows of whisky. Far Stream was on her feet, swaying and drifting. The keepers were curled up in the dark, fast asleep.

A muttered word, a grunt—something brought her back to the present. She watched as Jesse Blount rose to his feet, extracted a half-smoked cigar from his pocket and clumsily lit it, the match flaring bright in the gloom. Drunk and unsteady, he looked down the line of elephants, nodding as if he had made up his mind about something.

He approached Betts, the first in the Forepaugh group at the end. "Come here," he commanded, his voice husky. Betts sleepily took a step forward and extended her trunk and allowed Blount to pat it. So did Rubber and Victoria, dark shadows in the flickering dimness of the night lantern, turned low.

Babe was next. *Go away*, she said. The command was repeated. *Go away* she said as she reluctantly complied.

When Blount came to John he was getting bolder. "You want a sip of this?" he teased when John innocently extended his trunk. "That what you want?" He held the mug out to John, then pulled it back and, chuckling, took a drink for himself.

He became even more careless when he reached Far Stream and began coaxing her forward. She did not want to comply. She did not want to touch him. The deeply engrained impulse to respond to the command, however, was hard to resist.

She took a step forward and extended her trunk.

"Ha," Blount laughed, slapping the tip.

She flapped her ears to convey her annoyance as she stepped back. Blount didn't notice. He had moved on to Mighty, then Romeo, then Tiny, the new baby.

Then he came back.

He was eyeing Far Stream's martingale harness, particularly the leather cross-straps up her forehead that Whitey used as footholds to climb onto her back for the parade. "I could do that," he mused. "I could do that easy, just as well as anybody."

He was too close. Far Stream said, *Go away.*

He continued to eye her.

She flapped her ears again as a visual sign. *Go away.*

He stayed where he was.

She didn't like this new man. She didn't like his hat with the gold braid. She huffed, a clearer warning. *Go away.*

The sound roused one of the keepers. "Don't bother them elephants," came a voice from the darkness, followed by a grunt and the rustle of a body turning over, resettling.

"I know what I'm doing," muttered Blount to himself. And to Far Stream: "Come here."

She held back.

"Come on. Come here," he said, mild and wheedling, holding out the mug.

She allowed herself to be drawn a step forward. She could smell the liquor in the mug. She would tolerate him for a taste.

"Come on."

She reached toward the mug that Blount was waving to entice her. The restraining chain around her trunk prevented her from extending it far. Blount rewarded her with a swat and drained the mug himself. It was a game. He started chuckling.

"Come on," he tried again, wagging the now-empty mug, his lit cigar in the same hand. "Don't you want a drink?"

Far Stream was flapping her ears when again she reached out. She did not like being teased. She reached for the mug and this time Blount let her sniff it. Then, with a twist of his wrist, he flipped it over and touched the lit end of his cigar against the finger of flesh on the end of her trunk.

She squealed in pain and lurched backward.

"Quiet there," called out Whitey from his bed of hay under a wagon, rousing halfway from sleep.

Far Stream fell silent as something stirred deep inside

her. It was the hard seed of resentment she carried, the seed that pulsed and twitched on occasion, causing her to lash out at her keepers. It was breaking open. It was breaking out of its shell and swelling into a great mass and growing and growing to fill her completely. And then something was collapsing, like a mass of snow sliding off a roof, leaving it bare.

She stood very still, gazing at Blount with his cigar and his gold-braid hat with a feeling she had never experienced before. It was not annoyance. It was not irritation. It was not any of those hot, confused feelings. This as something different. It was searing cold rage.

She looked at him. He had become very small, bent over in front of her, laughing. She towered over him like the giant she was.

It was all so very clear. And he was so very close.

"What's going on over there?" called out Whitey, hearing Blount's laughter and coming further awake.

Far Stream shot out her trunk. There was just enough slack in the chain for her to take Blount by the wrist. It instantly stopped his laughter. A moment of wide-eyed surprise, then panic. He tried to yank himself free, silent but for grunts because his throat was constricted. He twisted and pulled and wrenched and struggled until blood began to run from the end of his fingers.

She had him by the arm now, still no shouts or screams, Blount's larynx frozen. Then her trunk was around his waist and she was squeezing, a profound sense of release. She squeezed until the air was forced from his lungs and his gasps were silenced and his eyes burst red and were bulging out of his head.

"Hey, what's going on over there?" Whitey was sitting up now, peering toward the muffled sound of the struggle.

She forced Blount onto the ground and held him down with her foot. He kicked and grunted beneath her but there was no escaping. She looked into his eyes and smelled the fear pulsing off him and saw his panic and none of it, none of it, made any difference.

Whitey was on his feet, in his underwear, walking over. "Johnny? Tops? What's going on?" And then he was running. "Stop it, Tops. Let him go. Stop it. Stop it."

She didn't stop. She lowered her head to Blount's chest. He struggled harder, kicking furrows into the dirt with the heels of his boots, straining with his arms to push her massive head off him. She was scarcely aware of his efforts. She outweighed him by more than a factor of forty. She weighed as much as Jesse Blount and his father and his grandfather and every other Blount in his lineage together going back one thousand years.

"Stop it, Tops. Let him go. Stop it. Stop it."

She pressed down. Blount didn't cry out with pain. He couldn't. He was out of air. Whitey screeched for help and ran for a pitchfork. The tent was coming alive. A lantern was turned up. Here was Badger.

"Stop it, Tops. Come on, girl. Stop it right now."

She continued pressing down, oblivious to the blows and the jabbing, pressing down until there was muffled cracking, the rib cage imploding. The men stepped back. Daft Jim, horrified and unable to restrain himself any longer, let out a whoop of laughter. No one thought to give him the usual cuff in the head.

Far Stream pressed Jesse Blount's torso flat to the ground. Then she stopped, for the cold rage suddenly left her. She felt no inclination to pluck off his limbs, to pull off his head, to throw pieces of him at the men who were staring. When she saw that he was finished she merely kicked him away. He skittered a few feet and came to rest in a heap, legs twisted, eyes popping, mouth gaping like a fish pulled from a lake and thrown onto the grass. He lay there for a minute, shuddering and twitching as the others grabbed him by a pant leg and dragged him clear of her reach. Then he went slack.

The corpse was left where it lay until Bill Emery could be summoned from the hotel where he was staying. Far Stream ignored it the whole time. She resumed her place between John and Mighty, swaying gently, eyes closed, holding the end of her trunk in her mouth while the men watched her and discussed what had happened. The subsidence of her rage left her feeling weary. She wanted Red Moon but couldn't find her. She moved closer to John and leaned against his side.

She allowed Bill to approach when he arrived, hurriedly dressed and unshaven, but she offered him no greeting, remaining aloof.

"Come on, Tops," Bill said, soothing. "Let me see what's the matter." She finally presented her trunk, the delicate tip still throbbing. Her eyes remained cold.

"He burned her all right," Bill confirmed, peering at the red welt the size of a nickel. He examined the cigar stub that had been recovered nearby. "Now why would he have done a fool thing like that?"

"He was drunk," said Daft Jim, casting an accusatory look at Whitey.

"I guess he was," said Bill, shaking his head is disgust. "I just wish he'd stepped in front of a train or something if he was so keen to get himself killed. God damn fool. Hey Badge, let's try some of that Pritchard's Ointment."

The salve helped to ease the pain of the burn. So did the pails of cool water. The sun came up and the inside of the tent grew warm and Far Stream gradually came to feel like before, mental fatigue the only lingering effect of the outburst. The men continued to watch her closely, looking for signs, but they saw nothing, only a bland, sleepy expression as she ate and tossed about hay. At seven o'clock they led her outside to the trough to test her humor. She went placidly, chained to Mighty, without even a toss of her head.

Lewis Sells arrived with an officer from the Brooklyn Police Department just as Far Stream was being returned to her place. Bill and Badger and each of the keepers related what they knew of the story, the cigar butt was produced, the burn was shown. "If a man came up to you and stuck the red-hot end of a lighted cigar on *your* nose," said Bill, "what would *you* do? You'd hit him is what. You'd hit him damn hard. And that was what Tops did."

"So this fellow Blount wasn't one of yours," said the policeman, nodding toward the shape under the sheet.

"He's been hanging around looking for a job," said Bill. "He wanted to work with the elephants. He said he had experience with the Wallace show but I had my doubts."

"Talked to me about working on the railroad," said Whitey. "Said he was a brakeman. I guess he caught the circus itch pretty bad."

Far Stream watched them watching her as she gingerly continued eating, tucking the burned finger on the end of her trunk out of the way. When she was finished she returned to her sister, who had crept back to her side after the intense feelings had abated. They wandered off together for a long meandering walk through the forest, pausing here and there to probe and explore. When they returned to the tent the lame dog was again standing before them. *Dogs can't talk*, Far Stream told him, feeling refreshed.

The morgue van arrived and carted off the body, the policeman left, general manager Lewis Sells stayed for a consultation with Bill Emery and Badger. Next came the reporters—from the *Times* and the *Tribune*, from the *Sun* and the *Eagle*, and from the New York *World* with a photographer too.

"She doesn't look too fierce," said the *World* man after he set up his camera. "Could you maybe get her to raise her trunk or her foot?"

Whitey, charged with watching Far Stream, said only, "Nope."

The morning passed, smells again from the cook tent, visitors coming and going, then the afternoon show. "You better be good," Whitey warned as he unchained Far Stream and led her out for the procession. She gave no cause for concern. She completed her movements under Bill's close direction. She did the same in the evening performance. Things were returning to normal.

It was the next day that everything changed.

＊＊＊

"Which one's Topsy? Which one's the man killer?"

That was what visitors to the menagerie tent wanted to know after reading about the killing of Jesse Blount in the papers. It had been front page news, more widely reported than any elephant-caused death in previous years—more widely reported than just about anything elephant-related since the passing of Jumbo in 1885, killed by a train. "The Elephant Seized Him," read the headline in the Brooklyn *Eagle*, the first out with the story. "Man Killed By Elephant," began the piece in the *Tribune*. The *Sun* went with "Elephant Kills Tormentor." In the *World* it was "Burned Elephant; Penalty Death."

"Which one's Topsy? Which one's the man killer?"

"Oh, there she is. That one there, the one with the harness."

And so people gathered around Far Stream, drawn by the leather-and-chain martingale they recognized from the illustrations that had accompanied some of the newspaper stories. They stared at her in fascination, at the trunk that had encircled Jesse Blount's body, at the forehead that had crushed him, at the feet that had kicked him, at the giant mouth that could be imagined performing some other terrible act. They said things like, "She killed another man down in Texas." And: "Look at her now, so peaceful." And: "Didn't she squash her trainer a while back too?" And: "Yes, there was that fellow she killed, name of Patsy, and there was at least one other. So that makes four she's murdered so far."

Far Stream was aware of the shift in the tone of the

voices. She could sense the increased wariness of the people and she could plainly see how most of them, particularly women with children, now stood further back. None of that bothered her. Her irritation when it flared was due to the increase in the taunting, not just from older boys but from a surprising variety of people: well-dressed businessmen, hard-eyed young ladies, the occasional grandfather and unsupervised child in short pants. They tossed things at her. They reached out to poke her with canes and umbrellas. They dared each other to offer her treats and then, growing bolder, to tease her by pulling them back. They kept at her and kept at her until she satisfied them with an annoyed trumpet or a head toss or until Whitey or one of the others drove them away.

"See, this is what I was afraid of," fumed Bill Emery. "They're calling Tops a man killer now and they're going to turn her into one with their plaguing."

Toward the end of the six-day Brooklyn engagement Lewis Sells returned to the menagerie tent with a Coney Island amusement park owner named Paul Boyton. They made for Far Stream and Boyton appraised her. Then they talked price. Sells started at four thousand dollars, Boyton much lower. They did not reach an agreement.

Paterson, New Jersey was the next town after Brooklyn. Then it was back into New York State for a one-day engagement in Newburgh. Far Stream continued to attract boisterous, obtrusive attention—in the parade, in the menagerie tent, in the show.

"Which one's Topsy? Which one's the man killer?"

Then came Kingston.

 презентация

The run up from Newburgh had been forty-odd miles, an hour and a half of jostling inside the rail car as the train followed the west bank of the Hudson River, heading due north. The iron screech and jolt signaling arrival came early in the morning, staggering Far Stream against Mighty and

226

rousing her from a doze. A long wait, the engine up ahead breathing heavy then fading, toots from boats on the river, then the sounds of the show coming to life, rail car doors being opened, men and horses passing outside, wagons hitched up and maneuvered and loaded, excited chatter from the crowd of spectators that had gathered to watch.

Here was Badger. Far Stream recognized the cadence of his loping gait. The clink of the latch, Badger's voice, polite but firm, "Now stay back, folks. Please stay back," the screech of the door as it was slid open letting in a flood of daylight that made them all blink.

Far Stream was fourth to exit. "Come on, Topsy," Badger called out when it was her turn. She shuffled to the door and lowered one cautious foot, then another, then she eased herself the rest of the way onto the ground, the car rocking as it was relieved of her weight.

"That's the one. That's the man killer right there. See that harness? See those chains?"

"She looks sleepy."

"That's the way they are. These killers will trick you."

And from Badger and now Whitey: "Come on, folks, please stay back."

Far Stream remained largely unaware, lost in the monotony of the process. She could smell soot from the engine and piles of damp lumber, yeastiness from a brewery and what seemed like burnt oil, then wet earth because it had started raining, sending the onlookers scurrying for cover.

"Okay, mile up."

They started moving, following the cars forward up the track. The rain stopped and the crowd reassembled, bigger than before. Others were lining the streets ahead, a total of nearly two thousand.

"Tut."

Badger brought the front half of the procession to a halt. Something was holding up the Sells herd further back. The Forepaugh group needed to wait. Far Stream probed the ground with her trunk as she loitered, ignoring the staring people just a few feet away.

One of them, a young clerk named Louis Dondero, was holding a stick. "Hey there," he called out, wanting to attract her attention. When she paid no notice, he took a step closer.

"Hey... Hey, look over here."

She found a scrap of apple peel. It wasn't worth eating. She threw it away.

"Hey... Hey, look over here... Hey."

" 'Hey' yourself," snapped Whitey.

The sun was out now, beating down on Far Stream's back. She closed her eyes and began to fan her ears to cool down, oblivious to Louis Dondero as he eased closer and reached out with his stick to tickle her behind the ear when Whitey wasn't looking.

The touch sent an electric surge through her brain. It jerked her eyes open. She turned to face the young man.

"Hey," said Dondero, pleased to get a response.

She saw the toothy grin. She saw the stick. She saw the stranger, very small.

Inside, the restraints fell away.

Whitey noticed something. "Tops..."

She let out a snort and seized Dondero around the waist. She tried to raise him over her head to smash him into the ground. The chains restricting her trunk wouldn't let her.

"Stop it, Tops. Let him go. Let him go." Whitey was at her, frantically jabbing his bull hook with all of his strength.

She didn't feel it. She didn't hear the shrieks of the spectators as they scattered. She was conscious only of an impulse to smash this man with his stick, to crush him, to destroy him. She drew him in close and forced him to the ground and she raised her foot. She would mash his skull.

Badger arrived at a sprint, and Daft Jim and Bert, joining Whitey in trying to beat Far Stream into submission, roaring at her, "Stop it! Stop it!" as Dondero struggled and wailed like a deer stuck in a bog.

The pain of the jabs punctured her anger. She faltered. And in that moment's pause the feeling drained away. She relaxed her grip and let out a long sigh and allowed Whitey and the others to grab Dondero by the ankles and drag him away. They soon had him back on his feet, stunned, his clothes torn and muddy, his body heavily bruised but no permanent damage.

"Oh Lord, Topsy," said Whitey, panting. "You've really done it now."

෧৶৽

The sensational news reports of the attack, some attributing as many as twelve killings to "Bad Elephant Topsy," brought Paul Boyton back to the menagerie tent with Lewis Sells the next day. This time their haggling wound its way more readily to common ground.

"She's got a bad name now, I grant you," Sells conceded. "But she doesn't deserve it. She's only killed one man, not ten or twelve or whatever they're saying."

"I don't doubt that for a moment," said Boyton. "But she's got a bad name just the same and it'll frighten the kiddies. So I'm afraid I can't offer you one dollar more."

Further back and forth and they finally shook hands, Sells muttering ruefully, "Two hundred dollars."

"I'm going to need a man who knows what he's doing," said Boyton.

Sells turned to Bill Emery. "Who can you spare?"

"He can have Whitey," Bill replied quickly. "Whitey gets along with her fine."

CHAPTER 20

"HOO-YAH!"

Far Stream pressed her head against the back of the wagon loaded with salvaged timber, sunk to its rear axles on the lot bordering Surf Avenue on Coney Island. She dug her feet into the soft earth and strained as the man in front whipped the horses and Whitey cried out again beside her, "Hoo-yah!"

Another heave and the wheels ploughed out of the depression, the wagon rolling again on firm ground. She settled into a shuffling rhythm, pushing now with only a fraction of her strength, flapping her ears to cool herself for it was a hot and humid morning for autumn. She went slowly, kicking at the scattered droppings from the ten horses, following the canal to where vast piles of lumber were waiting to go into the framing of new structures that were being built all around.

"Tut!"

She stopped and straightened and let out a long blow, drawing laughter from pedestrians watching through gaps in the fence. There was chafing on her forehead and under the straps of her martingale harness, the result of two months of pushing and pulling and shifting, helping to build the greatest amusement park in the world.

Her time in the possession of Paul Boyton had been brief, just a few weeks of appearances at Coney Island's

Sea Lion Park before Boyton leased his failing concern to Frederic Thompson and Elmer Dundy, a lock-stock-and-barrel arrangement that included Far Stream and Whitey. That had been in August 1902. It was now October and the twenty-two acre site of Sea Lion Park was a beehive of activity, being transformed into a grandiose project that Thompson and Dundy called Luna Park. It would have the best rides and attractions ever imagined, from "The River Styx" and "A Trip to the Moon" to "Shooting the White Horse Rapids" and "Twenty Thousand Leagues Under the Sea." There would be a circus, a water show with performing sea lions and seals, an exhibition of premature babies in a recently invented device called an incubator, and model villages from all over the world: Japanese, Filipino, Irish, Eskimo, German. There would be a sprawling plaza and a canal in the style of Venice, a "Naval Spectatorium" with sixty thousand square feet of water, recreations of Yellowstone Park, the Florida Everglades and the caves at Capri, and a flaming, smoking depiction of the eruption of Mt. Pelée, recently in the news for having destroyed Martinique.

And most impressive of all, there would be extravagant electrical illumination. Luna Park would be set ablaze by sixty thousand lights in the outdoor displays and nearly as many indoors. There would be lights along the streets and out on the water, lights on towers, lights on the rides and flooding from buildings—electricity pulsing everywhere, everywhere surging, turning night on Coney Island into bright day.

Lunch time.

"Hey, Whitey. Okay we come over?"

It was a group of workmen, many of them Italians. They often stopped by at noon to gaze at Far Stream as they ate and smoked for the allowed thirty minutes. Whitey satisfied his appetite with sips from a bottle.

"Hey, Whitey," said one of the workmen, "Mr. Thompson don't see, eh? No good he see."

231

Frederic Thompson was personally overseeing Luna Park's construction. It was not always easy to spot him coming because he dressed like a workman in overalls, heavy boots and bicycle cap.

Far Stream, chained in the shade eating hay, ignored their presence, her eyes half closed. She would not be called on by Whitey to perform tricks for the workmen before heading back to her labors. She had put a stop to that a few weeks before. She had come to realize that some of the circus commands had less meaning in these new surroundings and that there was nothing Whitey could do if she didn't comply. So she didn't. She pushed and pulled when he told her to do so but there was no more sitting up, marching or dancing—certainly not during the noon break, which was for herself and Red Moon.

Lunch was over. Some of the men offered Far Stream the last bite of their sandwiches, the core of an apple, giggling with pleasure as she accepted them delicately with the end of her trunk. "That some animal you got, Whitey," they said.

Back along the unfinished Venetian canal, stagnant and muddy, to move another load.

"Hoo-yah!"

A pile of lumber on a skid this time, then an immense coil of electrical wire, then another heavily loaded wagon with which the horses needed assistance.

"Hoo-yah!"

She kept at it through the afternoon, the sounds of Coney Island growing gradually louder around her, the rumble of rides, shrieks of laughter, barkers along Surf Avenue braying about attractions that cost only a few pennies, a nickel, a quarter.

The work was fatiguing but she didn't mind it. Using her muscles in a natural way was more satisfying than performing under the big top. But she nevertheless missed the circus. She missed the presence of John, Babe, Mighty,

Rubber and the others. Even though she had become increasingly withdrawn as she grew older, having the others near had been a comfort, overhearing and at times joining in their communion, touching them when she needed to feel the closeness, jostling them when she felt playful. There had also been the familiarity, the security, of her world under canvas. She had felt a lingering sense of vulnerability since leaving, a feeling that Whitey's increased drinking and erratic behavior only made worse. One day he would be slow and sleepy and hardly bother to raise his bull hook; the next day he would get angry at nothing and strike her. She resented the treatment but bore it, up to a point.

At the end of the day Whitey led her to the trough for a session of drinking and spouting, then into the stable that she shared with some of the horses. He chained her, left forefoot, right hind foot, served out her hay and sat down to smoke.

"Pardon me."

A man was standing at the entrance. He was in his fifties, very tall, a black man dressed in a worn suit that hung loose on his body.

Whitey looked up. "What do you want?"

"I heard about the elephant. Mind if I take a look?"

Whitey shrugged and sucked on his pipe. "All right. Just don't get too close."

Far Stream eyed the man as he approached her. His limping gait and stooped frame were unfamiliar. But his soft brown eyes, the line of his chin, the smile that was creasing his face—these things she knew.

"Hello there, Annie."

"Her name's Topsy," Whitey called over.

Eph Parker held out his hand for Far Stream to examine. "Not when I first knew her. When she came to the Adam Forepaugh show we called her Baby Annie." He smiled again and indicated the bottom of his rib cage. "She was only this high."

A confusing tumult of emotions: happiness, bitterness, joy, hope and pain. They swept through Far Stream at the same moment and then they were gone and only friendship remained.

She reached out to Eph and greeted him gladly. Looking into her eyes and seeing goodwill, he stepped closer. She gently curled her trunk around his waist and began exploring his body, feeling frailty where there had once been vitality and muscle, feeling the ravages of the illness with which he was wasting away.

The first touch had brought Whitey jumping to his feet, alarm fading to astonishment as he recognized the affection. "She seems to know you," he said, walking over.

Eph was laughing now at Far Stream's caresses, the look of recent suffering falling away. "I guess so. We were together for, oh my, for fourteen years, I make it. We called her Baby Annie but then she sprung up and Mr. Forepaugh changed her name to Topsy. Oh, pardon me." He extended his hand to Whitey. "I'm Ephraim Parker."

Whitey brightened and shook his hand. "I heard of you. You were gone when I joined up with Forepaugh but the boys talked about you plenty. I heard you were in Europe, a real big elephant trainer with your own show."

"I did have my own show, yes," replied Eph, speaking in the polished manner he had acquired following his elevation. "Had a good run, too. But . . . ." He shook his head. "That was some time back."

Eph spent a pleasant hour with Whitey, remembering the past as Whitey took nips from a bottle. Eph recalled the old days touring with the Adam Forepaugh Circus by wagon, walking with Romeo and Far Stream through the night. He spoke of George Forepaugh, the first elephant boss he had worked for, and of Adam Forepaugh Jr. back when Addie had been the world's youngest elephant trainer.

"I seen Addie a couple years back," said Whitey. "He come by after the show when we were in Philadelphia. He didn't look too good, kind of used up. He was skittish too around the elephants. That kind of surprised me because I heard he was tough."

"Well, you get cautious," said Eph. "The close calls can do that to you. But you heard right about Addie. He was tough back then. Downright mean sometimes, I guess you could call it. You know he's the one that give Topsy that kink in her tail."

Whitey didn't know that. Eph told him the story. Far Stream snorted and threw a wad of hay on her back after hearing the name "Addie" repeated again and again.

"Ha, ha. She's listening." Whitey was slurring now, lolling back on his seat of hay bales.

Eph, warmed by Whitey's interest, went on to reminisce about the good times he had had in Europe, a feted elephant trainer attracting big crowds and very well paid. He had lost everything since, along with his health. But he still had the memories and he enjoyed them—memories of success and high living, fancy hotels and restaurants and beautiful women.

"That sure sounds nice," said Whitey, dreaming. "How much were you getting paid? It must have been some pile of money."

"Well, that first season in Germany they paid me five thousand dollars. Then there were other . . ."

"Five thousand dollars!" The enormity of the sum sat Whitey upright. "I only get thirteen dollars a week!"

In the third week of October Far Stream began laying out a skid line of timbers in preparation for shifting the attraction known as A Trip to the Moon. It had been a great success for Thompson and Dundy at Steeplechase Park, amazing visitors with a voyage away from the Earth in a craft swaying on gimbals as painted cyclorama views were cranked past. A Trip to the Moon was a veritable license to print money, well worth the effort of transporting it half a mile along Surf Avenue for reinstallation on the Luna Park site.

Laying the skids took the better part of a week. Then it was time to move the attraction itself. It was the largest thing Far Stream had ever been called on to push, an entire building, thirty-five feet wide and fifty feet high.

The skids were greased. The team of horses started pulling in front as Far Stream pushed from the rear. It was immensely hard work but progress was steady, fifty feet and rest, fifty feet and rest, the distance along Surf Avenue slowly covered in three hours as throngs of onlookers watched. Then the skids veered off the firm road surface and onto the soft earth of the lot and progress ground to a halt.

"Hoo-yah!"

Far Stream dug her feet in deeper and pushed with her head as hard as she ever had pushed. The structure creaked and groaned and shifted, then stopped. The horses were tired and were no longer effectively pulling. She stopped and raised her head, her neck sore, her leg muscles weary.

"Hoo-yah!"

Whitey jabbed at her to get her back working. He had begun drinking first thing that morning. She gave an annoyed twitch of her trunk and lowered her head to try again.

"Hoo-yah! Hoo-yah!"

She closed her eyes and strained until the load lurched forward. Some momentum now, several paces forward, then a slight depression and A Trip to the Moon bogged down again.

"Hoo-yah!"

It was no use. She raised her head and stepped back. That made Whitey angry.

"Come on, God damn it," he roared, plying his hook.

She didn't like it. She pushed him away. Whitey came back.

"You are torturing that animal," scolded a middle-aged woman, waving a furled umbrella in his direction. She was standing with a cluster of people watching from Surf Avenue through the gap that had been opened in the fence.

"Mind your own business," Whitey yelled back. He took a firmer grip on his hook and set into Far Stream. "Come on, get back to it." Far Stream pushed him away again, this time more forcefully, sending him staggering backward.

"Stop torturing that animal," cried the woman, stepping forward, oblivious to the mud on her shoes. "Stop torturing that animal this minute."

"You don't know what you're talking about," said Whitey. "So get going. Get on home and do up a batch of jam or something."

That brought the color to the woman's face and her umbrella thumping down into the dirt like a pike. "If you don't stop this very instant, I will call a constable and have you arrested. You can't go jabbing at an animal like that. Not in front of all these people. These *witnesses*! Not in broad daylight!"

"Listen, you old whore," hissed Whitey. "What you know about elephants don't amount to the shit on my boots. Now you just mind your own goddamn business and you get moving. Just shove off. Get!"

The harsh words staggered the lady backward, wide-eyed and sputtering, like a physical blow. "You...you...you dirty, drunken, insolent..."

"What's going on here?"

It was a Coney Island policeman, drawn by the sight of the crowd and what seemed to be a disturbance.

"Ha!" cried the woman, triumphant. "Constable, this...this *lout* has been torturing that poor elephant with that foul hook."

Whitey by this point had returned to Far Stream to administer punishment for refusing his orders. He managed to deliver one ineffectual blow before she knocked him off his feet.

"Sir," said the policeman, "I'm going to ask you to leave off striking that creature."

"Go away," Whitey barked, picking himself up. "Mind your own business."

The policeman drew his baton. "You're heading into trouble now."

"Just go away! You don't know nothing about elephants."

Whitey was arrested and charged with disorderly conduct. He pleaded not guilty in the arraignment hearing in the Coney Island courthouse two days later. The judge ordered him held on bail of $300. Frederic Thompson paid the sum to secure his release.

"I really appreciate this, Mr. Thompson," said Whitey after, hanging his head, sheepish now that he was sober.

"Well, it's not all bad," replied Thompson. "You got Luna Park in the papers. That's what we call publicity, Alf."

❧

It was December. A Trip to the Moon was on its new foundations, seating for thirty and flapping wings for propulsion and cyclorama paintings of fanciful moonscapes ready for hanging on rollers. Most of the other major structures were up and receiving finishing touches as well, pavilions and arcades, rides and towers and castles. The Venetian canal was starting to look Venetian; roads were laid out and ready for paving, promenades for boarding; miles of electrical wiring were being buried and strung as Luna Park began to assume its final appearance.

There was less work now for Far Stream to do, fewer loads to haul and wagons to push. Whitey increasingly left her in the barn, sometimes for days. She spent much of the time far away with her sister, oblivious for long stretches to her surroundings, feeling warmth despite the onset of winter, feeling tropical sunshine despite the overcast skies. Visitors would occasionally stop by to see her and she would scarcely be aware of their presence. They would ask Whitey, "Why is she swaying?" and he would shrug and say, "It's just her way."

A stray dog had started keeping her company in her waking moments, a little mongrel no higher than the top of her foot. She allowed him to walk about under her and even lick her trunk, liberties that surprised her without offering offence. He never spoke to her but he did look into her eyes in an endearing manner, seemingly communicating that he needed her presence. She was mindful not to step on him when he curled up beneath her and she was sorry when she nearly knocked him out with a sneeze.

"All right, Tops. Let's go outside."

It was early afternoon and Whitey was drunk. Without steady work he was spinning out of control. The continuing visits from Eph Parker weren't helping either. The stories of past fame and riches had stoked feelings inside Whitey that were now burning, feelings of jealousy and resentment that were making things worse.

Far Stream ambled out of the barn and into the daylight and allowed Whitey to climb onto her back like he used to do for parading. He hadn't done that in some time.

"So, Thompson wants publicity," he muttered, unsteady on her shoulders. "All right, I can do that. I can put on a show. Come on, Tops. Let's go. Let's go."

She moved forward, glad to be working the stiffness from her legs. They passed along the main promenade that was now finished to where men were working on the great archway that was Luna Park's entrance.

"Hey, Whitey," they called out, looking up from their labors. "What are you doing?"

"You better get out of the way there, boys," Whitey roared, flailing his arms like a wild man and almost falling from his perch. And to Far Stream, "Go on, go on."

"Hey, Whitey...."

And then the workmen were scattering for it looked like Far Stream would run them right over.

She passed through the grand arch and was on Surf Avenue, the dog trotting along just behind her. Bustling sidewalks here, wagons and cars passing, a streetcar line down the center, then shouting as people took notice. She moved into the middle of the street at Whitey's direction and started shuffling westward, down past lunch counters, souvenir shops and freak shows, the Atlantic Ocean with its bathing suit rentals, closed for the winter, off to the right.

"Mad elephant!" cried a man, diving back through a door.

"It's a mad elephant all right," Whitey exulted. "You best run for it. You best run."

This was unlike any parade Far Stream had marched in. It was much more exciting. She raised her trunk and, her breath steaming in the cold, gave an exuberant trumpet, earning a pat on her neck.

"That's it. Good girl. Good girl. That's it."

Far Stream made it a half mile along Surf Avenue, a half mile of mayhem without injury or destruction, before Whitey fell off. It was a gradual slipping slide more than a head-breaking tumble, dropping him unhurt into the custody of the policemen following a safe distance behind. Far Stream stopped and turned back, watching as Whitey became belligerent and was put in handcuffs. "Handle that elephant yourself," he bellowed, kicking and squirming. "Let's see you try it. She'll squash you flat."

Confusion. Far Stream did not know what to do. She moved toward Whitey when he called to her, "Topsy, come on," then stopped when she saw how this upset the policemen. They were yelling at him, "You keep quiet. You don't say a word to that beast."

When Whitey calmed down, the handcuffs were removed. With Far Stream hovering nearby, unrestrained, it was the only sensible option. A procession followed to the Coney Island police station nearby, policemen leading Whitey leading Far Stream in front, hundreds of spectators following excitedly in their wake. At the station house Whitey was led up the stone steps, leaving Far Stream once

240

again confused in the street. "Come on, Tops," he called to her gaily before disappearing inside, earning a shove from a policeman. She tried to follow, cautiously mounting the steps and inserting her head through the door that was far too small to admit her.

Fearful shrieks inside. "Call her off! Call her off!"

Whitey reemerged, grinning and waving at the swarm of onlookers, a flustered sergeant behind him. After a heated exchange on the sidewalk, it was agreed that Whitey would take Far Stream back to Luna Park in company with Patrolman Conlin, then return immediately to the station house to be booked.

Another boisterous procession back down the street, back through the Luna Park archway, back to the relative peace and quiet of the barn. Whitey led Far Stream to her place but he did not chain her as usual. Instead he turned to the policeman and said, "So, maybe I don't feel like going back to the station."

"Stop your clowning," said Conlin. "Come on, we're going back."

"I don't know. I think maybe I feel like staying."

"You're going."

"Well, I don't know. Maybe I feel like having Tops put the run on you instead. You ever seen what one of these beauties can do to a man? I have. One word from me and she'd take..."

Conlin drew his revolver and took aim at Whitey's pale forehead. "You say one word to that animal and I'll blow a hole through your brain."

Whitey accompanied him back to the station. Far Stream was left alone in the barn.

❧

Frederic Thompson again posted bail. When he stopped by the barn the next day, however, there was no contrition or thanks from Whitey. Whitey was drunk.

"So how'd you like that for publicity," was his greeting.

He was unshaven and unwashed and far too familiar. "I'd say that's worth a pretty good raise."

Thompson puffed on the cigar clenched in his teeth as he appraised his employee. "So, I guess it's true what I've been hearing," he said. "You're sure no good to me like this."

Far Stream could feel Thompson's anger. Whitey, his senses dulled by liquor, missed it completely.

"What do you mean?"

"I mean you're drinking. Far too much to be of any use around here."

Whitey's smile faded. A scowl that had been hovering just beneath the surface replaced it.

"Hell yes I been drinking. I been drinking because you ain't paying me enough to control this elephant and I'm the only one who can. And I get you publicity too. And what you pay me, thirteen dollars, that ain't right."

"Thirteen dollars is more than you're worth like this."

"What do you mean?"

"You're stinking drunk is what I mean."

"No I'm not. And I can control Tops drunk or sober so it don't matter. And I don't feel like controlling her at all for thirteen dollars a week. I want twenty...I want twenty-five dollars a week."

"That's ridiculous. You're already getting more than I pay a top workman."

"Can one of them Italians handle this elephant? I don't think so. Twenty-five dollars, that's my price."

"No."

"What do you mean, 'No'?"

Thompson puffed at his cigar for a moment to settle himself before replying. "I came over here thinking maybe I could get you back on track, give you another chance even though you don't deserve it. But now I see I'd be wasting my time."

Whitey started waving a forefinger about as he struggled

242

through his many resentments to get at the right words. "I want . . . I want what's right."

"Get that finger out of my face."

The finger stayed.

"Twenty dollars is fair. There's nobody else. Twenty dollars or I turn her loose. I know what's . . ."

And then he was reeling backward because Thompson had hit him, a punch in the nose that forced a yelp out of Whitey that startled Far Stream into taking a step back.

"Get out," Thompson said, his voice hoarse with fury. "Get out. Nobody speaks to me like that. Get out."

Whitey gave him a hurt look, as if his feelings more than his nose had been injured. He slowly got to his feet, hand to his face where the blood was now streaming, and started moving toward Far Stream, a smear of her dung on his pants from where he had sprawled.

Thompson stepped in his way.

"Don't you go near that elephant. I said get out."

Whitey didn't look up. He said, "I just want my coat."

Whitey was gone. Far Stream was alone in the barn with Frederic Thompson. She recognized him as the head man about the place but she did not know him. He made her uneasy.

Thompson retrieved his cigar that he had dropped in the heat of the moment and puffed it back to life as he stood thinking before her. She could hear the tick of the watch in his pocket. She could smell the cigar smoke mixed with the lingering musk of his anger, then behind that, very faint, a hint of apprehension that was rising for he now moving closer, his eyes on hers.

"So, what's it going to be?" he said.

He eased closer, his whole body tensing. She didn't like his presence. She shifted uneasily and made a low huff.

"What's it going to be, Topsy? I know you can be friendly. Are you going to be friendly?"

He was too close now. She didn't like his cigar. He was making her upset. She flapped her ears and gave a clearer warning. Thompson hesitated, then took another step and she knew she could not allow him to come any further.

Her trumpeting charge sent him scrambling backward, the end of her trunk striking his wrist but not catching hold. She continued to demonstrate as he ran from the barn but already the feeling was fading, leaving her sour and listless.

A period of quiet and Thompson reappeared, eying her warily from the doorway, regaining his composure when he saw her return to her hay and her swaying.

"So that's it then," he said. "So you're going to be bad."

CHAPTER 21

THE BARN DOORS were wide open. Sunlight streamed in. She felt like wandering outside but the double chains kept her where she was. She could perhaps break them. But no, she had no compulsion to do so. She was feeling pleasant just standing here, warm and drowsy. She would just stand here and gaze at the world, at the frozen ground dusted with snow outside the door, at the gleaming fantasyland of Luna Park rising beyond it, spires and towers and other strange shapes that glowed brightly at night when the men tested the lighting.

Her sister must have wandered off. Far Stream wasn't much concerned. Red Moon had begun ranging further afield lately. She would soon return, perhaps with some new place she had discovered, a lush meadow where they could go off together, a secluded pool of warm bubbling water, a grove of trees heavy with succulent fruit where they could feast.

She shifted slightly, brushing against something soft underfoot.

A yelp and a scramble. She opened her eyes.

It was the dog, looking up at her, sheepish. She affectionately extended her trunk, reassuring him that she had not intentionally tried to squash him, that it was only a mistake. He licked the tip to forgive her, vigorously wagging his tail.

She looked about. The barn door was closed. There was no warm sunlight streaming in. It was another slate-grey morning judging from the small window, cold and crisp outside, the middle of winter. She resumed her swaying, slipping back into the languid rhythm that had been her life for the past month confined inside the barn, a month in which the lingering smells of Whitey had dwindled to nothing until only Eph Parker remained.

No sounds of work outside. The men were resting. There were only the seagulls and crows, cawing and squabbling over bits of frozen debris. She waited, the square of light on the floor creeping to the post marking the time when Eph arrived with her breakfast. She looked forward to his coming each morning, even though he was not the same man.

The light reached the post and kept inching past. Eph was late. She rummaged about on the floor around her, retrieving what bites she could find, for she was hungry. She then turned to the curled-up dog and nudged him off his bed and swept up the hay, one generous mouthful, still warm from his small body.

Eph came. He was walking even more stiffly, pain etched on his face. He set a pail of oat and barn mash, warm and steaming, before her and began cleaning up with the long-handled rake, then laid out fresh hay. It was all he did for her: feed her and clean up. It was all he had the strength to do since offering his services to Thompson and Dundy in exchange for Whitey's wages. He was quiet this morning. He didn't talk to her in the usual way as he worked.

The door opened, emitting a draft and a half dozen men in thick coats.

"How's she behaving this morning?" asked the only one Far Stream recognized, Frederic Thompson.

"Oh, she's fine, sir," replied Eph. "Nice and peaceful. But I sure don't feel right about this."

"Like I told you before, Eph, there's just no other way. We've tried the zoos, the shows. No one wants her."

246

"Yes, sir, I understand. It just seems like a shame is all. Is it still going to be a big show?"

"No, the animal cruelty people put the kibosh on that. Delicate sensibilities have to come first."

"We could have sold two thousand tickets," groused one of the others.

"Yes, well, it's too late to do anything about that," continued Thompson, a man of briskness. "Now, Mr. Brotheridge here"—the veterinary surgeon in the group gave a slight bow—"Mr. Brotheridge has something that should keep her quiet."

The man opened the clinking leather bag he was carrying. "I understand she'll like this," he said, removing a succession of bottles.

"She did when I knew her before," said Eph. "I expect she still does."

A half dozen bottles were produced from the bag: a smaller one, brown and square, and five larger ones Far Stream recognized as containing beer. She watched wistfully as Brotheridge opened one and poured a quarter of its contents onto the ground. He then topped it up from the brown flask and handed the bottle to Eph who in turn held it out to Far Stream, a rare treat. She wrapped her trunk around the bottle and upended it down her throat, scarcely noting the sharpness.

"I guess she does like it," observed the veterinary surgeon with a grin.

"How long do you suppose before she starts to feel it?" asked Thompson.

"It's hard to say with an animal of this size. She may not even feel it at all. With a man it would be just a few minutes. Oh look, she wants another."

Far Stream downed the remaining four bottles of beer in quick succession. There was no bite of added laudanum this time, just the delicious yeastiness and the fizz that she savored.

It put her in a good mood as the men watched, waiting for a reaction.

"Well," concluded Thompson when nothing was noted, "perhaps it will take effect more slowly." He turned to Eph. "So we're all set then."

Eph nodded slowly. "I guess so."

"You don't sound sure. I'm paying you to be sure."

"I'm sure, Mr. Thompson. It'll be fine."

"Good. So you'll bring her out at one o'clock sharp, as I told you."

Far Stream could sense something the matter with Eph. There was nervousness in him today. He looked at his pocket watch shortly after the men left, ten minutes passed and he looked at it again.

And then she stopped noticing. She was sinking into a feeling of profound relaxation. Her head was pleasantly swimming, the barn around her growing hazy and dreamy. Her eyes came to rest on the dog dozing before the stove where Eph was warming his hands. *Dog*, she said drowsily. He looked her way and then rose and came over, head down, tail wagging. She gave him a little push with her trunk, feeling young and playful. He crouched down on his front legs, hind quarters raised, instantly frisky, then started darting at her trunk which she waved about to tease him. *Crocodile*, she said, amused by his bared teeth.

Another thirty minutes drifted by, Eph continuing to take anxious looks at his watch. "All right," he pronounced at last, stiffly bending down to unfasten her chains.

She gave him a nudge and rolled him off his feet. He scrambled backward, arms and legs flailing, then relaxed when he heard her sounds and saw her amusement.

"Damn it, don't do that," he scolded. "These bones can't take it." And then his look softened. "I guess you're feeling that opium, aren't you?"

She stood still when Eph approached again to free her chains from the iron rings in the floor. The simple task, like so much else for him now, was an effort. "Good girl," he said, breathing hard when he was finished. He rewarded her with an apple. She had always been fond of apples. She held out her trunk for another. Eph checked his watch again. It was coming up to one o'clock.

"So, you ready to go outside?"

She understood "outside." She wanted to go outside. She moved toward the door without needing direction.

The dog left his spot by the stove.

❧

"Here it comes!"

The excited cry ran through the crowd of invited guests and fence climbers and out to the people crowding nearby rooftops overlooking the grounds.

"It's coming now! Oh, it's coming now, ha, ha!" And then the laughter was spreading, for it wasn't an elephant that was coming, but "Cupid" Langtry, the fattest man on Coney Island, draped in chains and snorting and squealing and putting on a great show as he lumbered along at the side of a clowning keeper. He walked out onto the platform built over the lagoon and continued mugging for a while longer, a makeshift noose around his neck, until everyone had had their fill. Then he sloughed off his restraints and bowed to the clapping and the reporters turned back to the Luna Park press agent.

"Six thousand six hundred volts," the man said. "The Edison Light Company has kindly set out Chief Electrician Sharkey—he's the tall gentleman over there—with Luna Park's own Electrician Black assisting. Edison superintendent Johansen is manning the switches at the power house."

"Where would that be?" asked one of the reporters.

"The Edison power house is just over there on West Third Street, just beyond that building. We are in contact by telephone with them. When the moment comes, Superintendent Johansen will shut down the power to all of Coney Island and temporarily divert it through those two wires you see over there."

"What would that amount to?"

"As I said before, it will deliver six thousand six hundred volts."

"So why don't you just shoot her?" This from the man from the *Sun*.

The press agent chuckled. "I asked the very same question. Apparently you need an elephant gun to do a proper job, and that's not the sort of thing you'll find in New York. England is the place to get them, presumably because of the excellent elephant hunting they have over there."

The reporters snickered at the joke and continued to scribble as the press agent went on to describe the disposal plans for the carcass: skin to Hubert Vogelsang on East Fifty-Ninth Street for tanning, internal organs to Princeton University for study, the two front feet retained by Thompson and Dundy to be turned into umbrella holders for their personal use. Then they were turning away, for a new cry was rising.

"All right, here it comes. Now it really is coming!"

⁂

It was dreary outside, an unfinished amusement park in midwinter, skeletal trees, dirty snow banked up in corners, building materials in scattered piles, grey overhead. To Far Stream it all looked watery, dreamy. She moved along the promenade bordering the iced-over inlet that would soon be the Venetian canal. She did not feel the cold.

They were heading for the center of the park. Up ahead was the long tracked ramp of the Shoot the Chutes ride, a spired tower beside it, a manmade lagoon at the base. There was something different today about the place, something apart from the buzzing in her head and the strange feeling of floating. Then she saw the people ahead, waiting, not the usual scattering of workers but a crowd of spectators, looking her way from the far side of the lagoon. There were others watching from beyond the fence, gathered on rooftops. She paused to gaze about—at the staring people, at the dog following just behind her, at the glimpse of ocean visible between the buildings off to the side.

A hint of unease crept into her brain. She wanted her sister. Where was Red Moon? Why was she staying away?

She made a low rumble. The only response was a command from Eph.

"Go on."

She skirted the edge of the lagoon, the spectators close now, well-dressed dignitaries in a front row, ordinary others behind on roughly built bleachers, some excited and talking, others silent and grim. She shuffled past them, her martingale chains clinking, noting the platform that had been erected out over the water connected to the bank by a short bridge.

Eph seemed to be leading her to it. She stopped, again feeling uneasy.

"Go on."

A nudge. She ignored it. Things were starting to intrude through the gauzy sensation of floating: the flimsiness of the bridge, the oddness of the platform out over the water, the loop at the end of the rope that hung there suspended, the steam winch at the base of the neighboring tower decorated with banners on each of its four sides. "Luna Park!" announced the two-foot-high letters. "Opens in May!"

Another nudge. "Go on now."

She ignored it. There were wires running out to the platform, wires suspended on poles planted in a line leading out of the park. And at the loose end of the wires, two men pulsing nervous excitement, each with his hand on a strange-looking device, a board like the top of a small table with a plate-sized copper disk nailed to it.

She looked about for Red Moon.

Are you there?

A jab this time, a light one, with the point of the bull hook. "Go on now, Topsy. Go on."

She turned to Eph and used her trunk to gently back him away.

"That elephant wasn't born yesterday!" someone in the audience called out.

Here was Frederic Thompson striding over. "What's the hold up?"

"I guess she don't want to go," said Eph.

"Well, try the apples."

She ate the fruit as it was offered, took a step forward at Eph's urging to get it. But she would not advance any farther. She had no intention of crossing the bridge to stand on the platform. Eph lay down a trail of grain but that didn't work either. She ate only what she could reach from where she was standing. She refused to follow it forward.

"I bet Whitey told her what was up," said one of the park employees.

A half hour passed, more coaxing and some firm words but no hard jabbing because Eph wouldn't do it. Finally Thompson sent a man off to Whitey's boarding house room nearby with an offer.

"He said no," the man reported upon his return.

Thompson frowned. "Any chance he'd come round if we sweetened the deal?"

"I don't think so. He's pretty mad. He said he wouldn't do it even for five hundred dollars."

"All right then, let's forget about the scaffold. Let's do it right here. Mr. Sharkey!"

The Edison chief electrician came over.

"Mr. Sharkey, she won't move as you can see so we'll have to do it right here where she stands. How long will it take to run your wires over?"

The wires were restrung. The camera operator dispatched by Thomas Edison Inc. repositioned his Kinetograph camera. Far Stream began to sway as she watched the men working around her, the floating feeling gradually subsiding, Luna Park becoming less dreamy, less watery, more grey.

Are you there? she tried again, needing her sister. When there was no answer she beckoned to the dog, wanting his company. He looked at her from where he sat but wouldn't come over. *Crocodile*, she said. He wouldn't come.

"All right, let's get the rope."

The thick hawser suspended from the tower was dragged over. Eph ordered Far Stream to lower her head. She obeyed and allowed the rope to be placed around her neck. It was left hanging loose.

Here was the man who had come with the beer earlier that morning. He stepped forward with a carrot, then another, then another, more than a dozen all together. She ate every one. They had something powdery inside them.

"That's four hundred and sixty grains," the man said to Thompson. "It'd kill a quarter of this crowd."

A tap from Eph on her right forefoot. "Lift." She did so. The copper plate was slid under and affixed. It felt awkward when she set her foot back down. She didn't like it.

A tap on her left hind foot. "Lift." The second copper plate was attached. She definitely did not like it. She set her hind foot down and kicked the plate off her forefoot.

"Stop it, Topsy," Eph scolded. "Now lift."

It took three attempts before she accepted the electrodes, lulled into acquiescence by a sack of apples upended before her.

"I'm sorry, girl," Eph said, backing away, his job done.

She started eating the fruit, sweet juice running down her throat, pausing occasionally to look about for her sister. She could feel Red Moon near her. Perhaps she was there behind that building. Perhaps she was over there, behind that tower.

She tried again. *Are you there?*

Then she noticed that her stomach was tingling. Another few moments and the tingling intensified into a burning. She kept eating the apples but the pleasure was gone.

Electrician Sharkey climbed up onto a pile of lumber. He said, "We're all set."

Her stomach was feeling worse now. There was a bloated bubbling-up sensation along with the deep burning.

Sharkey motioned to the man behind the movie camera that was aimed straight at her. The Kinetograph operator nodded and started to crank, two rotations per second. Sharkey then waved to his associate manning the telephone link to the power station. He shouted across to the open window, "All right, turn it on!"

The spectators standing nearest backed up. A pause. The lights in the signs visible along Surf Avenue flickered and died as the electricity was shut off in preparation for diverting through the two wires.

Far Stream picked up another apple and stopped. She was feeling very ill now, her stomach on fire. She let the apple drop and looked over at Eph. He was gazing at her with a look of deep sadness. In the many other eyes there was anticipation, tension and fear.

Dog, she said, wanting the little one's comfort.

She was going to be sick.

An explosion in her brain, a blinding flash, her trunk shot out, her body went rigid. A crackling sound, the smell of smoke and flesh burning and she was falling face down, tumbling face forward, tumbling into a hole in the earth that was becoming a bright tunnel that was becoming boundless white space that was becoming something different again, different again.

Her final thought was only heard by the dog. She whispered, dazed as the rope tightened, *What is this place?*

CHAPTER 22

IT WAS A CLEARING in a forest.

Far Stream looked about her. The place was familiar.

She took a tentative step. Then she knew.

It was the clearing. There was the encircling barricade all around her, the entrapping ring of rough timbers built by the men. But there were no men standing outside it now, looking in at her. They were all gone. Their fires had burned out and turned cold.

She moved to the place where Grandmother had been broken. The vegetation remained crushed and battered from her struggle, the ground underneath scraped bare and still deeply furrowed. She moved on to where Red Moon had been restrained, more devastation, and to where she herself had been tethered. The signs of her feeble fight here could scarcely be seen.

Then she remembered Sinkhole.

The breach was still there where the fading giant had used his head to smash through the wall. Far Stream's mother had gone this way, and her brother Fear Wind, and her aunts Seven Were Taken and Into the Mountains and baby Darkness at Day. She stopped just short of the gap and looked up the path leading on through the trees. The way was clear but she was afraid to pass through it. She turned back and returned, turned back and returned, wanting to escape the enclosure but afraid to step across the smashed timbers, afraid to move onto the path.

A sound up ahead. She stood still and listened. Eventually she saw a shape emerging, a form approaching, coming to her through the gap in the trees.

It was her sister.

Red Moon came close to her but did not enter the enclosure. She stood on the far side and reached out and they entwined their trunks across the space between them. The touching gave Far Stream a profound sense of relief, reassurance that she wasn't alone in this place.

They stood like this, sharing each other, until Far Stream was ready. When she was, Red Moon began to head back the way she had come. Far Stream moved to follow but then hesitated, her fear returning.

Come with me, Red Moon urged her. *Come with me*. She stopped to wait just ahead.

Far Stream stepped through the jagged hole in the barricade and followed her sister along the path leading onward, past landmarks long forgotten but now so familiar, through scents that restored the tapestry inside her mind.

The terrain was steadily rising now, and then they were out of the trees and atop a great rocky mass, approaching a high drop-off. Far Stream had been here twice in her distant childhood, accompanying her family on their migrations.

The Shining Sun Cliffs.

The view, from so high up, seemed to go on forever, an ocean of trees undulating across the landscape, glints of blue and turquoise far away in the distance. Yes, she had been here before, but never under this sky. She had never seen the Shining Sun Cliffs bathed in these colors. She had never seen them under clouds looking like this.

They stood together, gazing out across the vastness. Finally Red Moon stepped off the cliff and continued, on the new and very different path that led onward. Far Stream was alarmed by its appearance. Again she hesitated. Again Red Moon stopped to wait for her, urging, *Come with me*.

Far Stream wanted to come. She wanted to follow her sister but she was afraid. She struggled with herself and started to whimper. Red Moon returned and reached out her trunk and gave her a caress.

The touch dispelled the last of the fear. It fell away from Far Stream like the harness that no longer restrained her. She looked ahead, no longer questioning, fully trusting.

She took the first step.

⚘

She was born into the time after the great migration across the wide river. She spent the dawn of her new life on her side, quivering, bewildered and staring, a slate grey being with no scars on her body, with a tail that was unbroken, a soul that was perfect.

There were trees above her, the greenest of green trees gently swaying against the deepest blue sky. She began to see them more clearly as the confusion receded, the leaves and the birds and even the insects in flawless detail. Then she began to feel the warmth of the earth underneath her, and the softness of the grass growing upon it, long and lush and fragrant. There was no sound. Everything was tranquility, peace.

She was relaxed now, lying still, conscious of a sense of timelessness, conscious of feeling quite different. Then, very slowly, there came the realization that this was absolute contentment that was filling her being, absolute freedom from anxiety and discomfort, absolute and irrevocable release from anger, sadness and fear.

She was beginning to hear now, a soft hum at first, diffuse and faraway but somehow cozy, delightful. Then it was getting closer. Distinguishable sounds.

There was movement about her. She was being helped to her feet.

She staggered only once before mastering her new form. She was big. She was little. She was part of those who were now gathered around her, emitting happy trumpets, rumbles and chirps.

It was her family expressing their joy at her arrival. She was their Far Stream. She once again made them complete. They reached out to welcome her.

They said, *We've been waiting for you.*

A NOTE
FROM THE AUTHOR

BAD ELEPHANT FAR STREAM is a work of fiction. A real elephant, however, inspired the story. Her name was Topsy, an Asian elephant, trained to perform in the circus, origins unknown. She had a crooked tail, broken at a young age by hard treatment, reportedly by Adam Forepaugh Jr.; she performed in the Forepaugh Circus for many years as part of the dancing quadrille; she killed a man named Jesse Blount in 1902 and attacked another named Louis Dondero. And she was euthanized at Coney Island on January 4, 1903, the event immortalized in the Edison film "Electrocution of an Elephant." You can watch the flickering footage on YouTube.

I tried to incorporate as much as I could discover about the real Topsy into this story. Unfortunately, only tantalizing hints exist about her in the historical record prior to her widely publicized killing of Blount. In writing *Bad Elephant Far Stream* I therefore drew upon the experiences of other elephants as well—Topsy's contemporaries with other shows—to flesh out the story. Most of the episodes depicted here are therefore largely true. They actually happened—but not necessarily to Topsy.

In gathering information, I searched through scores of newspapers of the day, from the *Atlanta Constitution* and *Albany Evening Journal* to the *Washington Post* and *Wichita Daily Eagle*. I accessed these through Stauffer Library at

Queen's University in Kingston, Ontario (special thanks to the inter-library loan staff), and through a number of on-line newspaper archives, notably www.newspaperarchive.com; http://chroniclingamerica.loc.gov (the Library of Congress's collection); and the state listings at http://xooxleanswers. com/newspaperarchives4.aspx. Of these individual state on-line newspaper archives, the one for New York at www.fultonhistory.com deserves special mention. The site is strangely quirky—and massive.

A second major source was the Forepaugh Circus route books. These are detailed accounts for each year's happenings that were published at the end of each season: a list of employees, the line-up of acts, the route taken, a daily journal, miscellaneous articles and snippets—usually a total of more than 100 pages. By far the best collection of these route books is housed in the Parkinson Library at the Circus World Museum in Baraboo, Wisconsin. Circus World Museum Assistant Director Rob Richard kindly provided me with material from the Forepaugh route books for the years 1878, 1880, 1883, 1889, 1891, 1892, 1893, 1894, 1896, 1898, 1900 and 1902. I found the daily journal portion, a major part of each book, to be especially useful. It was here that I read of such events as Topsy's running in an elephant race as depicted in chapter 13 (she lost her footing and tumbled head over heels on at least two occasions, once in St. Louis, Missouri on May 24, 1893 and again in Marion, Kansas on August 30 of the same year, "turning a complete and artistic somersault"); the train derailment in chapter 14 (derailments and serious accidents occurred almost every season; the one in which the Forepaugh elephant car tumbled down an embankment occurred en route to Bluefield, Virginia on September 25, 1898); the tent blow-down in chapter 17 (Sioux City, Iowa, June 24, 1898); together with numerous other incidents and a wealth of descriptive detail.

Third, there is the elephant database at www.elephant.se, essential for tracking elephants with nineteenth-century circuses to the extent that information exists. Also noteworthy is second-generation elephant trainer William "Buckles" Woodcock's circus history website, http://bucklesw. blogspot.com. I should perhaps mention here that I diverged from the database's record on Adam Forepaugh's elephant Romeo, the one whose death is depicted in chapter 5. He was one of several circus elephants at the time named Romeo and thus they are easily confused. The account I found most convincing—that an elephant named "Canda" was brought from Ceylon in 1851 and renamed "Canada" and later "Romeo"—is that forwarded by Stewart Craven, at one time Romeo's trainer.

Another valuable source of information that went into the writing of this book was the Circus Historical Society's on-line library at www.circushistory.org/history.htm. This website contains listings of every stop in every town for many of the major circuses for most seasons. (Combine this with the listings at www.circusinamerica.org and you will have nearly a complete record.) It also has a virtual library of books and articles written by or concerning old-time circus impresarios, performers and trainers: Richard Conover's *The Great Forepaugh Show, 1864-1894*; Stuart Thayer's *American Circus Anthology*; Charles Day's book *Ink From a Circus Press Agent* and weekly column "The Circus in the Days of Old"; W.C. Thompson's *On the Road with a Circus*; Louis Cooke's weekly newspaper series "Reminiscences of a Showman"; Tony Parker's *On the Road With a Wagon Show* and a good deal more.

Even with such a valuable resource readily at hand on-line, some books still had to be tracked down the old-fashioned way through booksellers and inter-library loan. Of particular use among these were elephant trainer George Conklin's *The Ways of the Circus* (no date; circa 1920) and W.C. Coup's *Sawdust and Spangles: Stories and Secrets of the Circus* (1901). Another book deserving special mention is J. Emerson Tennent's *The Wild Elephant and the Method of Capturing and Taming It in Ceylon* (1867). The scene of the capture of Far Stream and her family in chapter 2 is based on Tennent's vivid eyewitness account of an elephant roundup near Kandy in 1847. Also noteworthy is *I Loved Rogues* (1978; revised edition of *Elephant Tramp*, 1955) by George Lewis and Byron Fish. This was an extremely illuminating volume for its wealth of detail on circus elephant behavior, particularly Lewis's account of an elephant named Sadie breaking down and crying during a session of training. "We brought her back and began to punish her for being so stupid," writes Lewis. "We stopped suddenly, and looked at each other, unable to speak. We were seeing something I've never experienced before or since. Sadie was crying like a human being. She lay there on her side, the tears streaming down her face and sobs racking her huge body. Bloomer and I stood dumbfounded for a few moments...." (p. 110). The scene in chapter 7 where Topsy cries is based on this.

A few other books of note: Charles Reade, *Jack of All Trades* (1858; an early shaper of the now outdated notion that elephants are vicious); Thomas Frost, *Circus Life and Circus Celebrities* (1881); A.D. Bartlett, *Wild Animals in Captivity* (1898); Carl Hagenbeck, *Beasts and Men: Being Carl Hagenbeck's Experiences for Half a Century Among Wild Animals* (1909); Cleveland Moffett, *Careers of Danger and Daring* (1913); J.H. Williams, *Elephant Bill* (1950); George Chindahl, *A History of the Circus in America* (1959); William Heathcote, *Sacred Elephant* (1989); Mark Shand, *Travels on My Elephant* (1991); Jeffrey Moussaieff Masson, *When Elephants Weep: The Emotional Lives of Animals* (1996); Ralph Helfer, *Modoc: The True Story of the Greatest Elephant That Ever Lived* (1997); Katy Payne, *Silent Thunder: In the Presence of Elephants* (1999); Shana Alexander, *The Astonishing Elephant* (2000; see especially chapter 7, "The Disappearance"); Caitlin O'Connell, *The Elephant's Secret Sense: The Hidden Life of the Wild Herds of Africa* (2007); Paul Chambers, *Jumbo: The Greatest Elephant in the World* (2008); and Lawrence Anthony, *The Elephant Whisperer: My Life With the Herd in the African Wild* (2009).

Of the many magazines I dipped into, one title proved more useful than all the others put together: the bi-monthly magazine *Bandwagon* published by the Circus Historical Society. Of particular note is the series of articles by Robert Sabia on "Frank A. Robbins: A Most Successful Failure," beginning in May-June 2000, which cover the time when Topsy was leased to this outfit. Also noteworthy in *Bandwagon*: Harry Parkhurst, "Memoirs of an Elephant Keeper," June 1943; Richard Ellsworth, "Journalists' Vacation Aboard Lew Sells' Private Car: With the Forepaugh Sells Circus in 1902," Mar.-April 1979; Bill Johnston, "African Elephants with American Circuses, 1804–1936," May-June 1992; and Bill Johnston, "Tough Circus Elephants," Jan.-Feb. 1993. I would be remiss not to mention as well George Ridenour's article on "Eph Thompson, Elephant Trainer" in *Ypsilanti Gleanings*, Spring 2010, upon whom I based the character Ephraim Parker; D.W. Watt's weekly circus articles, "Side Lights on the Circus Business," published in the *Janesville Daily Gazette* beginning on June 1, 1912; and Fred Kurt, "Size, Weight and Age Criteria in Asian Elephants," *First European Elephant Management School*, Nov. 2005.

To learn more about the historical elephant Topsy and the other characters—animal and human—who appear in this story, visit the author's website, www.samuelhawley.com, and click on "Topsy the Elephant."